Praise for Amanda Hocking

'Hocking hits all the commercial high notes . . . She knows how to keep readers turning the pages' *New York Times*

'A fast-paced romance . . . addictive' *Guardian*

'[*Wake*] will please fans and likely win new ones . . . the well-structured story and strong characters carry readers'
Publishers Weekly

'Drew me in and kept me hooked . . . cracking pace'
Sunday Express

'A well-told, simple fantasy story . . . You can have fun and get lost in a world' *Irish Independent*

'There is no denying that Amanda Hocking knows how to tell a good story and keep readers coming back for more'
Kirkus Reviews

'Enough surprises to keep even a paranormal-romance sceptic interested, and the writing is briskly paced and casual enough to make reading fast and fun' *We Love This Book*

'Pure imaginative brilliance! *Wake* is full of thrills, eerie suspense, and mystery . . . incredibly difficult to put down'
Book Faery

Available from Tor by Amanda Hocking

THE TRYLLE SERIES

Switched

Torn

Ascend

THE WATERSONG SERIES

Wake

Lullaby

Lullaby

AMANDA HOCKING

TOR

First published 2012 by St Martin's Press, New York

First published in Great Britain 2012 by Tor
an imprint of Pan Macmillan, a division of Macmillan Publishers Limited
Pan Macmillan, 20 New Wharf Road, London N1 9RR
Basingstoke and Oxford
Associated companies throughout the world
www.panmacmillan.com

ISBN 978-1-4472-0573-9

1 3 5 7 9 8 6 4 2

A CIP catalogue record for this book is available from
the British Library.

Printed and bound by CPI Group (UK) Ltd, Croydon, CR0 4YY

Lullaby

ONE

Aftermath

Harper woke up when the sun was just beginning to set, and squinted at the dim orange light streaming in through her curtains. For one moment—one brief, glorious moment—she'd forgotten about the night before, the night when her little sister had been attacked before turning into some kind of mermaid and disappearing in the ocean.

Then it all came back to her. Her head throbbed at the memory, and she squeezed her eyes shut.

After Gemma had swum away, leaving Harper alone on the dock at Bernie's Island, Daniel had checked on Alex to make sure that he was all right. When they'd arrived at the cabin, Alex had been lying unconscious on the floor. Harper hadn't seen what had happened, but it wasn't hard for her to imagine.

A horrible bird-creature stood over him. Its mouth was filled with razor-sharp teeth, and massive black wings stretched out behind it. Then it had shifted, changing form into a different kind of monster—the beautiful Penn.

It was almost impossible for Harper to wrap her mind around. When Alex had come to, he'd been certain the things he remembered were a bizarre dream brought on by head trauma. But Harper and Daniel had been forced to tell him that it was all true. The monsters were real, and Gemma was gone.

Then, after all of that, Harper knew she had to go home and attempt to explain to her father what had happened, even though she didn't understand it herself. Not that she could tell him the truth—there was no way any sane person would believe it unless he had witnessed it for himself.

So Harper told Brian that Gemma had run off with Penn and her friends. It was something close to the truth, but even that was still hard for him to comprehend. Harper stayed up all morning convincing her father that Gemma wasn't coming home, and that was one of the hardest things she'd ever had to do.

But she knew things were only going to get harder. Harper didn't even know what Penn and the other girls were, let alone how to stop them or how to get Gemma back.

Lying in bed all day wouldn't solve anything, though. Harper rolled over and grabbed her cell phone from the bedside table, meaning to check the time, and noticed she had two missed calls from a number she didn't know. Gemma had left her cell phone behind, so if she called, it would be from an unfamiliar number.

Harper's heart dropped to her stomach. She'd been so dead

tired that she'd slept right through her phone ringing. Harper hurried to check her voice mail.

"You have one new message," the automated voice told her, and Harper cursed herself under her breath. If she'd missed a call from her sister, she'd never be able to forgive herself.

"Hey, Harper, this is Daniel," his deep voice came through the phone.

"*Daniel,*" Harper whispered, and put her free hand on her forehead, listening to his message.

"I got your number from the surly girl at the library. I wanted to make sure that you got home all right and see how you're doing after . . . well, you know, what happened last night.

"I've been keeping an eye out for Gemma, like you asked me to. I took the boat out earlier, but I didn't see her. I'll keep looking, and I'll let you know if I find anything.

"So anyway, give me a call later." Daniel paused. "I hope you're doing okay."

When his message ended, she left her phone at her ear for a minute, even after the automated voice assured her that she had no other messages.

It was thoughtful of Daniel to call and check up on her, but Harper couldn't call him back. The strange dalliance she'd had with him had to be pushed out of her mind. If he found out anything about Gemma, Daniel would let her know, but that was the only time she should be talking to him. Whatever was happening to Gemma came first. Harper had to deal with that before she could think of anything else.

Harper had slept in her clothes from last night, and they stank like the ocean and sweat. She grabbed a change of clothes, then crept across the hall to the bathroom in case her father was home. There was nothing more she could say to him about Gemma's disappearance, but she knew Brian would want to keep rehashing it until it made sense.

She cleaned up quickly, then got dressed. She'd started to sneak back to her room when she glanced over at Gemma's. Something about the sight of the darkened room broke her heart. Pausing at the doorway, Harper couldn't help but wonder if Gemma would ever stay in this room again.

Harper swallowed the lump in her throat and shook her head, trying to shake off the feeling. Of course Gemma would stay here again. Harper wouldn't stop searching until Gemma was home.

When Harper turned back to her own room, she nearly yelped in surprise. Alex was sitting on her bed, staring down at the floor and looking forlorn.

"Alex?" Harper managed once the beating of her heart slowed. "What are you doing here?" She stepped into her room.

"Oh, sorry." He lifted his head and motioned toward the downstairs. "Your dad let me in. I came over to talk."

She glanced back behind her, half expecting Brian to be standing in the hall eavesdropping, and then she shut the bedroom door.

"How did my dad seem?" Harper asked.

"Okay, I guess." Alex shrugged, and she noticed a cut on his forehead, probably from whatever had knocked him out last night. "A little sad and confused. He asked me about Gemma, but I told him I don't know where she is."

She'd meant to call Alex so they could get their stories straight about what had happened to Gemma. The truth was that they didn't know where she was, and that was as good an answer as any.

"So, what the hell happened last night?" Alex asked her directly.

"I have no idea." Harper shook her head and sat down in the chair in front of her desk. "I don't even know what those . . . those *things* were."

"I can barely even remember what they look like anymore." His brow furrowed as he tried to think. "Last night's a weird blur of images that don't even make sense."

"That's probably because you hit your head," Harper said.

Alex seemed to think about it for a minute, then said, "No. I don't think so. I remember everything really clearly until we were in the cove and that song started."

Harper had actually forgotten about the song until Alex mentioned it. She couldn't remember the words, but the melody surfaced, like a half-forgotten dream.

There were a few minutes in the cove that Harper couldn't really remember, either. The events were a haze of confusion, though she recalled a longing and a pull toward the phantom song. Daniel had helped keep her from diving into the ocean the way Alex had, but that was about all she could remember until they were on the boat again.

"Did you swim to the island?" Harper asked, realizing that he must have.

"I think so." He shook his head again. "I can't really remember much. There was the song, then I was swimming, and then I was on the island. Those pretty girls were there, and . . . and Gemma. She kissed me . . ." He swallowed hard.

"Do you remember the creature?" Harper asked.

"The bird?" Alex asked, and she nodded. "Is that what it was? A really big bird?"

"It was more like a bird-monster," Harper tried to explain. "But then it changed and turned into Penn."

"So those pretty girls are some kind of shape-shifters?" Alex asked. "Because they turned into fish, right? Gemma and the girls turned into fish, then swam off?"

"Mermaids, I think," Harper corrected him.

"This is so insane," Alex said quietly, almost to himself, then he looked up at Harper, his dark brown eyes locking seriously on hers. "Stupid question time, but I have to ask. Gemma hasn't, like . . . always been a mermaid, has she? This isn't some family curse thing like on *Teen Wolf*?"

"No." Harper smiled despite herself and shook her head. "No. There's no history of mermaids or any other mythological beings in our family."

"Okay. Good," Alex said, then changed his mind and wagged his head back and forth. "Well, not really. If you knew what this was, it would be easier to deal with."

"It certainly would," she agreed.

"So you don't have any idea what Gemma or Penn or the girls might be?" Alex asked.

"No," Harper admitted regretfully.

"And you don't know where they went?"

"Nope."

"So. How are we gonna get her back?" Alex asked.

"Well . . ." Harper took a deep breath. "We figure out what they are and how to stop them, then we find them and we take Gemma back."

TWO

Metamorphoses

Marcy had been talking for a while, but Harper hadn't been listening. She sat at the desk, staring into space and trying to figure out what to do.

When Alex left the night before, they'd both agreed that they had to continue on with life like normal until they found Gemma. That meant going to work, even when Harper would rather be at home scouring the Internet for clues about what Gemma might have become.

She'd spent a lot of time on sites that claimed to be experts on Bigfoot and el chupacabra, but nobody had heard of a bizarre bird-monster that also turned into a fish-human hybrid and a beautiful teenage girl.

By the time she fell asleep very late last night, Harper had begun to believe that she'd made up the whole thing. It was some weird stress-induced hallucination. That was the only logical explanation for what she'd seen.

"But I was like, you can't make a fur coat out of basset hounds," Marcy was saying when Harper started tuning back in. "It's not like I'm Cruella De Vil, you know?"

"No, it's not," Harper replied absently.

Marcy scoffed and stared at her above her dark-framed glasses. "You haven't listened to a word I've said, have you, Harper?"

"You're not Cruella De Vil." Harper forced a thin smile at her.

Marcy rolled her eyes. "Lucky guess."

"How is that lucky?" Harper asked.

The bell of the library's front door rang as it swung open, and Harper pulled her eyes away from Marcy's annoyed gaze to see Alex come striding over to the desk. He grinned broadly, which was a massive change from the grim expression he'd worn last night.

"You heard from her?" Harper blurted out, interrupting Marcy midsentence after she'd begun talking about basset hounds again.

"No." Alex's smile faltered for a moment as he rested his arms on the desk in front of her. "But I do have good news."

"Yeah?" Harper leaned forward.

"I figured it out." His smile returned as brightly as before. "Sirens."

"Sirens?" Harper frowned in confusion. "Like police sirens?"

"Is this about Gemma?" Marcy asked, managing to sound concerned for once. "Did the police find her?"

"No," Alex said. "Where's your section on mythology?"

"Mythology?" Harper echoed, as he was already taking a step back from the desk.

"Yeah, like Greek mythology," Alex elaborated.

"Back in the corner, past the children's books," Harper said, motioning to the other side of the library.

"Great." He smiled wider, and before she could ask him anything more, he darted back to where she'd pointed.

"Alex," Harper said as she stood up, but he just kept going, disappearing between the shelves of books. "Marcy, can you cover the front desk? I have to go see what he's up to."

"Uh, yeah, sure," Marcy said, sounding just as confused as Harper felt. "If it's about Gemma, take as much time as you need. But I have no idea what mythology has to do with her running away."

"Yeah, me neither," Harper muttered, then followed Alex to the back of the library.

She found him already leafing through a copy of Ovid's *Metamorphoses,* in the middle of the mythology section. On her way after him, it had occurred to her what he meant by sirens, but the pieces didn't completely fit.

"You think they're sirens?" Harper asked skeptically.

"Yeah." Alex nodded without looking up from the book.

"I don't know, Alex. That doesn't make sense."

"Think about it." He lifted his head to look at her. "The song? That's what sirens are known for. Not to mention the whole mermaid thing."

"Right," Harper agreed. "But what about the bird-monster thing?"

"Still sirens." He flipped a page in the book, scanning it frantically. A moment later, he smiled again and held the book out to her. "See for yourself."

"What?" Harper asked, and Alex tapped a passage.

Aloud, she began to read, "*Why should it be that they have feathers now and feet of birds, though still a girl's fair face, the sweet-voiced sirens?*"

"See?" Alex said almost gleefully.

"Maybe you don't remember it, but Penn's face was not that fair when she turned into the bird thing," Harper pointed out.

"Obviously this isn't completely accurate," Alex said, refusing to be deterred. "Some books say there are only two sirens, while others say there are as many as four. Some describe them as mermaids, others as birds. None of them get it completely right, but maybe that's because they change form."

Harper narrowed her eyes, thinking. "What do you mean?"

"Maybe Ovid saw them as a bird." Alex pointed to the book in Harper's hands. "But others saw them as mermaids. The girls can change their shape, like you saw. The only constant is their song. And we know they have that."

Biting her lip, Harper stared down at the book in her hands. What Alex said made sense. Or it would have, if any of this made any sense.

"This is mythology, Alex," Harper said, shaking her head, and she handed the book back to him. "None of this is real."

He groaned. "Oh, come on, Harper. You saw the same things I did. This is real, and you know it."

"Fine." Harper crossed her arms over her chest. "Let's say

you're right. What we saw . . . they were sirens. Is Gemma one of them? How did she become one?"

"I don't know. So much of what I've read contradicts itself." Alex motioned to the shelf of books beside him. "I was researching on the Internet all night, but I was hoping that maybe actual books could offer some clarity."

"Well, how did the sirens become sirens in the first place?" Harper asked.

"From what I can tell, it had something to do with pissing off one of the gods."

Alex turned away from Harper to focus his attention on the books. His fingers trailed along the spines as he scanned for a title.

"What are you looking for?" Harper asked, moving closer to him to help him look.

"I read a passage from a book online. I think it's called . . . *Argonautica* or something."

"Here." Harper reached up past him, taking a worn copy from the top shelf.

She picked up an encyclopedia on Greek mythology, then started grabbing any book that might possibly have information on sirens, including one called *Mythology for Dummies*.

As she began gathering books, she handed them to Alex. Once he had a small stack, he sat down on the floor right between the two shelves and spread the books out around him.

"There are tables we can sit at," Harper said. "There's even an overstuffed couch."

"Here's good," Alex said, already flipping through one of the books.

Shrugging, Harper sat down across from him and folded her legs underneath her.

"So." She rested her arms on her knees and leaned forward. "Tell me what you already know."

"I don't know how much I 'know' per se, since there seems to be a lot of misinformation," Alex said.

"You think they became sirens because they angered the gods?" Harper asked, and he nodded. "But Gemma didn't anger any gods." Then she changed her mind and shook her head. "At least, I don't think she did."

"I don't think she did, either," Alex agreed. "So maybe she isn't one."

Harper thought back to the end of the other night, when she'd seen Gemma disappear into the ocean in the pale pink light of early morning. Even then, her tail had been unmistakable. Gemma had definitely had a mermaid form.

"No, she's one of them," Harper said definitively. "And it doesn't really matter to me why or how she became one. I just need to know how to get her back."

"That's the tricky part." Alex grimaced. "I haven't read about any way to undo their curse. Only how to kill them."

"Well, we don't want to kill Gemma, but I wouldn't mind killing those other bitches," Harper said, a little surprised by the vengeance in her own voice. "How do we do that?"

"I don't know exactly. Apparently, the sirens are fated to die if someone hears their song and escapes it," Alex said with a sheepish expression on his face.

"But you heard the song, and so did I, and we escaped it," Harper said. "And they didn't die."

"That's the only thing I've read so far," Alex said. "But according to what I read in Homer's *Odyssey*, the sirens should already be dead."

"Great," Harper muttered. "So basically what you're saying is that you don't know much more than I do?"

"Not really, I guess," he said. "But at least I figured out what they are."

"That's a start," Harper admitted grudgingly, and picked up a book off the floor.

With no better plan, Harper and Alex were left researching everything they could on sirens. As they went through the books, they spoke very little to each other. They were both too focused on figuring out how to rescue Gemma.

Harper wasn't sure exactly how long they'd been sitting there reading, but she'd had to change positions because her legs had gone numb. She sat with her back resting against the shelf behind her, the copy of *Argonautica* spread out across her knees.

Even Alex had moved, probably for the same reason. He lay on his belly with the book open before him. His fingers were buried in his dark hair, and his handsome features were hardened in concentration.

Harper glanced up from her book and caught sight of him. Something about the intensity of his expression moved her.

His devotion to Gemma nearly rivaled her own, and that made her feel a bit better. She wasn't in this alone.

"What are you doing?" Marcy asked, and Harper looked up to see her coworker standing at the end of the shelves with her arms crossed over her chest.

"Um . . ." Harper glanced back at Alex for help with answering the question, but he looked as lost for words as she was.

"Did you plan on doing any more work today?" Marcy asked. "Or were you going to hide out here all day?"

"Well . . ." Harper shifted so she was sitting up straighter. She knew she should be working, but she didn't really want to abandon her pursuit, either. That felt more important than scanning in overdue library books.

"If you didn't feel up to working because of Gemma running away or whatever, then you could've just said so," Marcy went on. "You didn't need to sneak off on false pretenses."

"No, we didn't," Harper said quickly.

Marcy narrowed her eyes, apparently hearing the conviction in Harper's words. "What are you doing?"

"We're, um . . ." Harper glanced back again at Alex, who hurried to provide a reason.

"We're, uh, we're reading . . . books," Alex responded lamely.

Harper gave him a severe look, like she thought he was an idiot, and Alex shook his head and shrugged.

"What are you reading?" Marcy asked. When neither of them answered, she bent down and picked up the nearest book, which happened to be called *Sirens: Handmaidens of the Sea*. "This is what you meant by sirens?"

"Uh, yeah," Alex said.

"Those really beautiful, creepy girls," Marcy said, putting the pieces together rather quickly. "You think they're sirens?"

"Well . . ." Harper swallowed and decided to answer honestly. "Kind of. Yeah."

"And they took Gemma or had something to do with her running off?" Marcy asked, her voice keeping the same monotone it always had, betraying neither a hint of skepticism nor belief.

"Yeah," Alex admitted. "We think so."

Marcy seemed to consider this for a moment, then she nodded as if it all made sense to her, and sat down on the floor.

"Have you figured out a way to get her back yet?" Marcy asked.

"Not yet," Harper said cautiously. "We're still looking."

Marcy held up the *Sirens* book. "Have you looked in this one, or do you want me to look?"

"You can, if you want," Harper said.

"Yeah, that'd be great, actually," Alex chimed in with more enthusiasm than Harper, who was still a bit reluctant to trust Marcy's acceptance. "There are a lot of books to cover."

"Cool," Marcy said, and opened the book.

As Marcy began to read, Harper exchanged a look with Alex, but he just shrugged and went back to reading his own book. Harper couldn't let it go that easily, though. She wanted to, but even after actually seeing the monsters, she'd found it hard to believe in them. And Marcy seemed to trust it with almost no evidence.

"So . . . that's it, then?" Harper asked.

"What?" Marcy lifted her eyes to look at Harper.

"You just . . ." Harper shook her head, unsure of how she wanted to phrase it. "You just believe in sirens?"

"I don't know." Marcy shrugged. "But you guys seem to, and I've never known either of you to be totally insane, so I figure there must be some truth to it. Besides that, I always knew something was off with those girls, and they fit the bill as sirens."

"Oh." Harper smiled wanly at her. "Well, thanks for the help."

"No problem." Marcy smiled back and readjusted her glasses. "My uncle saw the Loch Ness Monster once, too. So I'm a bit more open to things than you."

Bewildered, Harper shook her head. "Okay."

"Not that I don't appreciate the help," Alex said, as if something had just occurred to him, "but shouldn't one of you be at the desk in case someone else needs help?"

"There's a bell up there," Marcy said. "And this is more important, right?"

Harper normally took her job seriously, but Marcy was right. And Harper had an awful suspicion that if they wanted to help Gemma, they had better do it soon. Or it would be too late.

THREE

Revelations

Despite the fact that the three of them had spent the entire day scouring mythology books, they hadn't been able to find out much more about how to help Gemma. But when Harper came home from work, she was feeling better than she had since the night Gemma left.

It was reassuring to have Alex and Marcy working with her, even if Marcy wasn't all that helpful. Harper wasn't alone, and that made saving Gemma feel more possible.

That feeling of hopefulness evaporated the instant Harper walked through the front door and saw her father.

Brian stood in the middle of the living room. It looked like he'd walked into the room, then forgotten where he was going or why, so he just stopped. He hadn't shaved that morning, his eyes had bags beneath them, and his skin was ashen.

"Hi, Dad," Harper said as she closed the front door quietly behind her.

He looked up at her with a ghost of a smile on his lips. "Hi, sweetie."

"You didn't end up going to work today?" Harper asked him.

When she'd left for work in the morning he'd still been home, but Harper had been hoping he'd go in. He didn't have any paid time off left, and their whole family would be in really big trouble if he lost his job. Not only was he the breadwinner of the family, but his health insurance helped keep Harper's mother in assisted living.

"I thought she might come home," Brian said, his normally warm voice sounding gravelly from exhaustion and sadness.

"Have you eaten today?" Harper asked, walking past her father toward the kitchen. "I can make you something."

"I'm not hungry," Brian said.

"Come on, Dad. I'm making you something."

Harper went into the kitchen and opened the fridge. She pulled out lunch meat and mayo, and by the time she'd started making him a sandwich, Brian had wandered into the kitchen and sat down at the table.

"Have you heard from her?" he asked.

"No." She slathered the bread with mayo and refused to look back at him as she spoke. "You know I'd tell you if I had."

"I just don't understand why she'd run away," he said, with a now-familiar frustration taking over. "She had so much she wanted to do. And she was even dating Alex. Why would she leave? Even if she was mad at me."

"She wasn't mad at you," Harper reassured him. She put the

sandwich on a plate, then set it in front of her father, still without really looking at him. "You know this wasn't about you."

"But it doesn't make any sense!" Brian insisted. "I called her swimming coach today, and he said that her times have been amazing lately. She worked so hard for that. Why would she blow it to run away with some stupid girls?"

"She's sixteen, Dad." Harper went over to the sink to start rinsing off what few dishes had piled up, just so she'd have something to do. "Teenagers are unpredictable."

"But you guys weren't," Brian said, speaking louder to be heard over the running water. "Gemma may be strong-willed, but I've always known what I was getting with her. It's like the last week she's turned into something else."

Harper accidentally dropped a plate, and it clattered loudly in the sink.

"And the timing couldn't be worse," Brian went on. "There's that killer on the loose going after teenagers." He took a labored breath. "Something's happened to her, Harper."

"Those were all boys," Harper said, trying to cut off his train of thought. "And I saw Gemma leave. She told me she was running away. She's fine."

"She's not fine!" Brian shouted.

Harper leaned against the sink and closed her eyes. For a moment all she could do was breathe in deep to keep from freaking out. Her hands were trembling, and she wanted to cry. She had to convince her father that everything was all right, when in reality she had no idea if Gemma was okay or if they'd ever see her again.

"I went to the police today," Brian said, and his tone had leveled out again.

"Did you?" Harper asked cautiously. "What did they say?"

"They're looking for her," Brian said. "They don't prioritize runaway teens, and with everything that's been going on lately, they're going to do what they can."

"That's good." Harper had finished with the dishes, but she left the tap on, preferring the sound so it would drown out the silence and tension in the room.

"Harper, turn off the water," Brian said. "I need to tell you something."

She shut off the faucet but grabbed a rag to wipe down the counter, continuing her attempts to busy herself.

"Harper. Sit down. I need to talk to you."

"Just a sec, Dad," Harper said, scrubbing at a nonexistent spot on the counter.

"Harper," Brian said, with a firmness to his words that made Harper flinch.

She draped the rag over the sink, then went over to the table and sat down across from him. The whole time she kept her eyes lowered, afraid of how she might react if she looked at him directly.

Seeing her father so haggard like that, she was terrified she would spill everything to him. But she couldn't tell him about the sirens or what had really become of Gemma, and not just because he'd think she was insane.

In fact, that would be better than if he believed her. If he knew that Gemma was a siren, that she'd run off with actual monsters, he would lose his mind trying to protect her, and Harper couldn't bear the thought of that.

"I have bad news," Brian said gravely. He reached across the table, wanting to take Harper's hand, but she wouldn't give it to him. "When I was at the police station, I found out something."

She gulped, swallowing down the painful acid in her stomach that wanted to rise. She wasn't sure what else Brian could've possibly found out. And she wasn't sure that she could handle any more bad news.

"I don't know how to tell you this, but . . ." He paused, trying to form the words. "Bernie McAllister has been murdered."

And then in one horrible rush it all came back to her, pulling all the air from her lungs and twisting her stomach in knots.

Harper had managed to forget about it until now. But that wasn't quite right, either. She hadn't forgotten it. It would be impossible to forget about the death of someone who'd been so important to her.

Her mind had blocked it out, giving her a few more peaceful hours when she didn't have to think about it. But now it was back, the image of his body eviscerated in the trees outside of his cabin.

Bernie was one of the kindest people she'd ever known, a gentle old man with a soft British accent. He'd helped care for both Harper and Gemma after their mom had gotten hurt in the car accident.

Then the sirens had killed him, gutting him like a fish and leaving him to rot as they danced and sang and tore up his home looking for valuables. The worst part of it was that he gladly would've given them anything they wanted, and not because they were sirens who put a spell on him, but because Bernie wanted to help everyone.

"I'm so sorry, honey," Brian said, his own voice thick with tears. "I know how fond of him you were."

Harper put her hand to her mouth as silent tears slid down her cheeks. With the image of his body burning in her mind, she realized she had to form a response. Her father didn't know that she'd already found out Bernie was dead, and he couldn't know.

"How . . ." Harper croaked, barely able to force the word out around the lump in her throat.

"They're not sure yet," Brian said, but he lowered his eyes when he said it.

Harper had a feeling that the police had told him more than he was sharing with her, and for a split second she hated them for that. Brian didn't need to know the details of it. Everyone should be spared that gruesome image if they could be.

"They found his house ransacked," Brian went on. "They think it was some kind of robbery gone wrong."

Harper wondered if there was any truth to that. Had the sirens gone to steal from him, and he'd been a casualty? Or had his murder been their primary goal, and the robbery an afterthought?

"He had a doctor's appointment in town yesterday, and when he didn't show up, the doctor sent the police out on a well-being check," Brian said. "With a man of Bernie's age living alone, the doctor was being cautious. But nobody ever expected to find him murdered."

"Do they have any suspects yet?" Harper heard herself asking. Her hands were trembling, so she put them on her knees, squeezing them to keep the quaking at bay.

"Not yet," Brian admitted. "But they're looking." He paused. "They think it might have been the same person who's been killing those boys."

Harper nodded numbly, knowing for a fact that the same monsters who had killed Luke Benfield and the two other teenage boys had also killed Bernie.

"At least you just spent time with Bernie," her father said, trying to change the subject and put a brighter spin on everything somehow.

It had only been on Saturday, a few days before, that Harper and Brian had spent the afternoon on Bernie's Island, catching up with him and checking out his garden. She knew she should've found some comfort in that, a warm last memory with an old friend, but there was no comfort for her.

"I know this is a lot to take," Brian said. "Are you holding up okay?"

"Yeah," Harper said unconvincingly.

Fortunately, before her dad could press her more about how she was doing, her phone started ringing in her pocket. As she fumbled to get it out, her heart raced in hopes that it was Gemma, but then she saw the number. It was only Daniel again.

She stared at the screen and considered whether to answer it. Part of her really wanted to. If she was being honest with herself, it would feel really good to hear his voice, even if she wasn't in desperate need of a shoulder to cry on.

But the logical part of her won out, and she clicked ignore. He might know something about Gemma, but Harper wouldn't be able to hold it together in front of her father if Daniel told her something about her sister.

If Daniel had found something, he'd leave a voice mail, and Harper would check it the very second she was out of Brian's sight. And if Daniel hadn't found anything, not answering would save Harper from having a conversation with him. She couldn't have him distracting her right now.

"Who was that?" Brian asked, his voice brightening at the chance that it might be about Gemma.

"It was just, um, Marcy, from work." Harper stood up abruptly and shoved her phone in her pocket. "Sorry, Dad, I'm not feeling so well. I think I need to go lie down."

Brian started to say something, but Harper was already leaving, rushing upstairs. She didn't go to her room, though. She went to the bathroom, making it to the toilet just in time for her to throw up.

When she'd finished, she sat down on the cold tiles and rested her head against the wall. She pulled her phone back out. She clicked on the voice mail, just to be sure Daniel hadn't left any message, and he hadn't. Harper quickly scrolled through her contact list for Alex's number.

"Hello?" Alex answered.

"We need to find Gemma," Harper said.

"Yeah, I know."

"No." Harper shook her head, as if he could see her. "I mean, I don't give a shit what she is or what the girls are. I'm done researching. We need to find *her*."

Alex let out a sigh of relief. "I was thinking the same thing. We need to find her, and bring her back, by any means necessary."

FOUR

Withdrawals

Gemma woke up in a cold sweat despite the heat. The glass door to the balcony was open, allowing the wind to blow in, billowing out the curtains and filling the room with the sweet scent of the ocean.

The unfamiliarity of the room only added to her panic, and she sat up quickly, her heart racing. She was gasping, breathing in the salty air in heavy gulps, and that helped a bit. Her head still pounded, and the watersong rang in her ears.

That was the worst part. Everything about the last few days was horrible, but the watersong made it impossible to think or rest. It haunted her dreams, keeping her awake in the night, and made it so she couldn't even feel comfortable in her own skin.

She wanted to crawl right out of her body, but she couldn't. She was trapped in it, trapped with that incessant music and those awful girls in this colorless house.

That was the best way to describe the beach house—colorless.

Penn had picked it out, choosing the most luxurious property she could find on the ocean. Even Gemma had to admit that it was nice, very high-class and expansive, but it had to be the whitest place she'd ever seen.

The room she stayed in—the one that Penn had informed her would be "her" room—was entirely white. Not eggshell or ivory or off-white but pure, startling white. The walls, the curtains, the bedding. Even the artwork on the walls had a white frame, surrounding some kind of abstract painting in swirling shades of white and gray.

And the rest of the house was more of the same. What little color did manage to seep into the house was always pale gray or the occasional muted blue. It was almost unbearably pristine.

Gemma didn't know how anyone could live like this, but the home owner wasn't very helpful by way of answers. Not that Gemma had tried talking to him all that much. Penn and the other sirens had cast their spell on him, turning him into a mindless sycophant, and Gemma didn't really have any urge to interact with that.

Besides, her mind was preoccupied. Not only did she have that awful watersong gnawing at her constantly, she felt like hell. It was like the worst flu she'd ever had. Her entire body ached, from her bones to her skin. Nausea would sweep over her in awful waves, and it was all she could do to keep from throwing up.

"I take it you didn't sleep well," Thea said, seeming to magically appear in the doorway to Gemma's room. Her red hair hung loose around her face, blowing back in the breeze like she was the star of a music video.

"I slept fine," Gemma lied. She threw off her blankets, which were drenched in sweat, and climbed out of bed.

Thea snorted. "I can tell."

Gemma went over to her dresser—also white—and rummaged through the drawers for fresh clothes. She'd taken very few outfits with her when she left home, but Lexi had given her plenty of hand-me-downs.

The only thing she'd taken with her that really meant anything was a picture from home. It was of her, Harper, and their mom, taken shortly before the accident, when their mom still lived at home.

That picture—her one true possession—she kept in a drawer, buried beneath her new clothes. She'd left it in the frame, hoping that would protect it when she carried it in her book bag through the ocean, and it had, some, but the picture was all warped and wrinkled.

As she pulled out her clothes, she looked at it for a second, missing a family she knew she'd probably never see again, then hurried to cover it back up with clean panties and slammed the drawer shut.

"Did you want something?" Gemma asked. "Because I need to get changed."

"So change," Thea said, and didn't move from her spot in the doorway.

"Can I get a little privacy?" Gemma asked.

Thea rolled her eyes. "You need to get over it. We're all girls here."

"Isn't Sawyer running around?" Gemma asked.

"He's somewhere," Thea admitted, and looked away. She didn't leave the room, exactly, but turned her back to Gemma. "I think Penn gave him some kind of task before she left."

Gemma knew this was the best she could hope for, so she hurried to change into a clean dress and underwear.

"Penn left?" Gemma asked, not hiding the surprise in her voice.

"Yeah, Penn and Lexi went shopping," Thea explained. "New house, new clothes. That's their motto."

"Why didn't you go with them?" Gemma asked.

"I had to stay and babysit you and Sawyer." Thea glanced over her shoulder, and when she saw that Gemma was dressed, she turned back around.

"I don't need a babysitter," Gemma said.

"Yeah, you do," Thea said flatly. "You look like shit."

"Thanks," Gemma muttered.

She brushed past Thea and walked down the hall to the bathroom. Thea followed her, but Gemma hadn't expected any different.

When she looked in the mirror above the vanity, Gemma realized that Thea hadn't completely told the truth. While Gemma did look worse than she had the day before, and even worse than she had the day before that, she was still remarkably beautiful.

Her brown hair had golden highlights and soft waves, and even though she'd just woken up from a fitful sleep, it actually looked pretty good. She'd always been pretty, but since turning into a siren, she'd become radiantly gorgeous.

As a siren, she should've been a deep tan color that almost glowed. That glow was missing, and her skin had a weird ashen quality to it, yet even that managed to look lovely on her.

She grabbed a hair tie and pulled her hair back into a ponytail. Her hair was damp from sweat, and she didn't like how it felt hanging around her face.

"You must feel like hell," Thea commented.

Gemma could see Thea in the reflection of the mirror, standing behind her with her arms crossed over her chest. Gemma turned on the tap so she could splash cold water on her face.

"I feel fine," she said without looking at Thea.

"We can hear you moaning in your sleep," Thea told her.

There were only two things Gemma remembered clearly from her dreams: the watersong, and Alex.

She'd dreamt of the last day they'd spent together, kissing and talking and holding each other in his bed. But in her dreams, that day never ended, and she got to stay with him forever.

It had broken her heart to leave him, but she knew it was the best thing she could do for him. Whatever it was that she'd become, it would only bring him harm.

She'd made a promise to the sirens that if they spared him, if they left Alex and her sister Harper alone, then she'd go with them.

Gemma was determined to keep up her end of the pact. She'd do everything in her power to protect Alex and Harper. Even if that meant leaving them forever.

"I'm fine," Gemma insisted once she found her voice, then turned off the faucet.

"Today's, what? Wednesday?" Thea asked as Gemma dried her face with a towel. "So you've been a siren for . . . eight days now? Yeah. You need to eat something."

"I've been eating," Gemma said, but at the mention of food her stomach did a weird growling, and she pressed her hand over her belly as if she could silence it.

She'd been hungry before, but nothing had ever felt like this. This was *primal,* and it seemed to encompass her entire body.

When she'd been kissing Alex once before, she'd felt something similar, although slightly more intense. They'd been making out pretty hot and heavy, and then she'd "accidentally" bit him.

That had snapped her out of the strange hunger she'd felt with Alex, but she was unable to shake her current hunger. Fortunately, it was a lot milder, and she kept herself from biting Sawyer. But every day the watersong grew louder and her hunger grew stronger.

"Gemma, you know what I'm talking about," Thea said, looking at her seriously. "What you've been eating can't sustain—"

"I just need to eat more," Gemma interrupted her.

She didn't want to hear what Thea recommended she actually eat. Gemma already had an idea, but she wasn't ready to hear it aloud, for someone to put into actual words what she would have to do in order to survive as this new monster.

Thea sighed loudly but didn't argue with Gemma. "Suit yourself."

"I will." Gemma raised her chin defiantly, then walked past Thea out of the bathroom.

Thea trailed after her, into the hall and then down the winding marble staircase.

"You don't need to follow me all day," Gemma said, casting a look back over her shoulder at Thea. "I'm not going anywhere. I said I would do as you guys asked, and I will."

"I wasn't following you." Thea bristled, sounding annoyed. "I'm going out for a swim." She paused, her expression softening to something only moderately bitchy. "You can join me if you want."

Nothing in the world sounded more tempting than going out to the ocean for a swim. Gemma was hot and sticky with sweat, and the watersong was beckoning her. But ever since they'd arrived at the beach house on Monday, Gemma hadn't swum. She refused to do anything fun.

The sirens had killed people and nearly killed Alex and Harper, and now Gemma was a siren, too. She was the same evil that they were, and she shouldn't derive any pleasure from this life. That was her punishment for living and allowing herself to become one of them.

Gemma shook her head. "I'm just going to get something to eat."

They'd reached the bottom of the stairs, and Thea stopped, leaning on the banister, groaning. "You're making this so much harder than it needs to be."

"I'm doing the best I can," Gemma said honestly.

"If you would just eat and swim, you'd feel so much better," Thea said. "I know you're all hung up on the eating thing, but if you'd just spend, like, an hour in the ocean, you'd feel a million times better."

Gemma shook her head again. "Go swim. Don't worry about me."

"Whatever." Thea threw her hands up in the air. "I'm done."

Thea turned, heading out the back of the house to the beach. Gemma could see it through the windows, the crystal blue water splashing against the shore. She swallowed hard and looked away before she gave in to it.

She went to the kitchen to root around for something to eat, even though she knew none of the food would appeal to her.

The appliances were stainless steel and stood in sharp contrast to the stark white of the rest of the room. She'd just opened the fridge when the owner of the house, Sawyer, wandered into the kitchen.

"Oh," Sawyer said when he saw her, looking sufficiently disappointed. "I thought it might be Thea."

"She's out swimming," Gemma said. She grabbed an orange from the crisper, since it was the only thing that looked even mildly appetizing, then closed the fridge behind her. "You can probably join her if you want."

He glanced to the back of the house toward the ocean. A longing filled his face, but it quickly shifted to conflicted regret.

"Nah." Sawyer shook his head and ran his hand along the smooth gray-and-white granite of the island. "Penn told me to stay around the house, so I should do that."

That explained the conflict. Penn, Thea, and Lexi had enraptured him with their song, so he wanted to be with them constantly. But he also didn't want to disobey them. So if Penn told him to stay at the house, that overrode his urge to join Thea in the water.

Penn had even told her that when Sawyer was under direct orders from a siren, it wasn't just impossible for him to disobey. If anything tried to stop him, he'd destroy it if he had to. The enchantment made him so fixated on his cause that it could even give him a superherolike strength. The way a mother could tap in to her adrenaline to lift a car off her baby, a person under a siren's spell would do anything to do a siren's bidding.

Gemma had refused to sing and enchant him, which was why Sawyer had almost no interest in her. It had been hard to fight the urge, though. As soon as the other sirens began singing, bespelling Sawyer with their melody, Gemma had the strongest impulse to join in with them. Her very being tried to compel her to sing, and eventually she'd had to cover her ears and cower in the corner, hiding away from the sirens and their song.

Once Sawyer was under their spell, he'd gladly invited the sirens to stay in his house for as long as they wanted, with free access to his credit cards, his cars, everything he owned. And from what Gemma had seen, he seemed to own quite a bit.

Sawyer himself was stunningly handsome. When they'd come upon the house, Gemma had expected the owner to be some rich old man. So when she saw him, looking as if he could be a male siren, she was shocked.

He was young, too, probably in his mid-twenties. His skin was deeply tanned from so much time spent on the beach, and it stood out sharply against his clothes. He wore a thin white shirt with the top few buttons undone, revealing the smooth contours of his chest. His hair was dark blond, and his eyes were a shade of blue that rivaled Lexi's in beauty.

From what Gemma understood, it was only Sawyer's good looks that kept him alive. Penn was rather taken with him, at least as much as Penn could be taken with anybody.

"So . . ." Gemma said, attempting to make conversation with Sawyer since they both stood awkwardly in the kitchen together. "Do you own this house?"

Sawyer raised an eyebrow and looked at her like she was stupid. "Yeah."

"I mean, like, it's your house and not your parents' or something," Gemma said as she peeled her orange. "Because you seem awfully young to own a house like this."

"My grandfather died when I was nineteen and left me a third of his oil company," Sawyer explained. "And I built this house when I was twenty-two."

"You built this house?" Gemma asked, using a section of the orange to gesture around the room.

"Well, I didn't build it with my own two hands," Sawyer said, but he didn't need to.

His nails were perfectly manicured, and although he hadn't touched her, Gemma would guess that his hands were baby-soft. He didn't look like he'd done a day's work in his entire life.

"So what's the deal with all the white?" Gemma asked.

"It's pure and clean and fresh." Sawyer smiled as he talked about it. "I wanted a house that was filled with light."

"But don't you get bored?" Gemma asked. "Don't you ever want to look at something blue?"

Sawyer laughed a little and gestured at the windows behind him. "I have an entire ocean made of blue. I can see all the color I want."

"Fair enough."

She stared down at the peeled orange in her hands, almost willing herself to eat it. When she finally took a bite of a wedge, she instantly regretted it. Normally she loved the fruit, but now it tasted horrible, as if the juice were made of battery acid.

"Ugh." She grimaced and tossed the orange in the garbage, unable to eat any more.

"Was there something wrong with it?" Sawyer asked, watching her shake her head in disgust.

"No, I don't think so." She wiped her mouth with the back of her hand.

"Do you want me to get you something else?" Sawyer offered, making a move toward the fridge.

"No, that's okay. I don't think I'm hungry after all."

"Are you sure?" Sawyer asked. "Because I don't have anything else to do, and I can make a pretty mean omelet."

"That's okay," Gemma insisted, and started backing away from the kitchen. "I think I'm going to go lie down."

"Okay," Sawyer said, sounding disappointed.

He hadn't been that excited to see her, but he still seemed sad to see her go. Gemma might not have the same kind of hold on him that Penn and the other girls had, but she was still a siren. Without even trying, she could still enchant a man.

She hurried away, practically jogging back up the stairs. Taking a bite of the orange had made her feel even worse than she'd felt before. As soon as she got to her room, she slammed the door shut, then leaned against it.

Her whole body was shaking, and taking in deep breaths of the salty air didn't seem to help. She wiped the cold sweat from her brow, unsure how much longer she could do this. Eventually she'd have to feed.

FIVE

Searching

Both Harper and Brian had really let the housework slide since Gemma had left. Their minds had been on other things, so the house was in disarray. Newspapers were strewn about the living room, and empty beer bottles covered the table next to Brian's chair. In the small laundry room off the kitchen, a pile of dirty clothes was spilling out the door, but that had been building up since before Gemma left.

Eyeing their mess of a house, Harper chewed her lip. She didn't want to clean, and it wasn't out of laziness. It just felt sacrilegious somehow. Her sister was missing, and she had no right to resume her normal life as if something weren't horribly wrong.

The problem was that Harper didn't know where else to look, and real life didn't stop just because Gemma was gone. The garbage still needed to be taken out. The lawn still needed to be mowed. And her father still needed to go to work.

Harper was supposed to be working today herself, but she'd only been able to convince Brian to leave by agreeing to stay home. In case Gemma came back or called, he insisted that somebody be at the house at all times.

After Brian had finally left for work that morning, Harper had waited nervously near the front door. He'd already missed two days this week and then showed up late today. She was afraid he might not have a job waiting for him. When he didn't come back after an hour, she let out a sigh of relief and moved on.

The first half of the day she spent calling every missing children's organization she could find. None of them put Gemma high on their list, because of her age and because she'd left willingly.

Once Harper had exhausted all the organizations, she sat by the phone at the kitchen table trying to think of other people to call or anywhere else to look. But she was coming up empty.

Harper and Gemma had lived their whole lives in Capri, and they didn't have close ties with anybody outside it. Their grandparents were dead, and they had an aunt and a couple cousins who lived in Canada, but they didn't really know them.

That was when Harper noticed the state of the house and decided to do something about it. There was really nothing else for her to do, at least not anything that could help her with Gemma or the sirens, and she had to put her nervous energy to work. She couldn't just sit there staring at the phone all day, willing it to ring.

So she cleaned.

Harper started with the laundry, since it was overflowing,

and then moved on to the living room. She threw away garbage, vacuumed, and dusted. In the kitchen she scrubbed the floors, cleaned out the fridge, and rearranged the pots and the pans in the cupboards.

Alex came over shortly after Harper decided to tackle the basement. Every Christmas, when they brought up the tree and the ornaments, Harper vowed to go through the old boxes and get rid of junk and organize the keepsakes. She finally decided that today would be the day.

"Harper?" Alex was upstairs calling her name, and, based on the creaking of his footsteps above her head, she guessed he was in the living room.

"I'm down here!" Harper shouted toward the basement steps, hoping he'd hear her.

She was sitting in an old lawn chair, which she'd had to steal from a very large daddy longlegs spider. Once the chair was clean of cobwebs, she'd sat down with an old box on her lap and started rummaging through it.

So far, the box's contents appeared to be papers and projects from when Harper and Gemma were little. All of the papers had their mother's writing on them, like *Harper—First Grade, Age 7* or *Gemma—Mother's Day Card, Age 3* scrawled across the back.

That also explained why the box only contained items from until Harper was in third grade and Gemma was in first. That was the year when Nathalie had been in the car accident, and although Brian loved his daughters, he'd never been as good about keeping things as their mother had.

Harper pulled out a photo that was bent and faded with age. It had been glued onto a piece of pink construction paper cut into the shape of a lopsided heart. In sloppy cursive across the top, it said *My Family* in Gemma's handwriting.

The photo showed the four of them, Brian, Nathalie, Harper, and Gemma, at the beach. Gemma and Harper were wearing matching bathing suits—purple, with white flowers and a ruffle around the bottom. Harper had nearly forgotten about that day, but it was eleven years ago.

They all looked so happy—even Gemma, who hadn't wanted to come out of the water for the picture. Nathalie had had to bribe her with an ice-cream cone.

"Harper?" Alex said uncertainly from the top of the basement steps, pulling her from her thoughts.

"Yeah." Harper put the picture back in the box, then set the box aside.

"Sorry, I just let myself in," Alex said as he came down the steps. "I knocked, but you didn't answer."

"No, it's okay." Harper stood up and brushed the dust from her knees. The boxes had been sitting down here so long, they'd collected a lot of dirt and cobwebs. "I must not have heard you knocking."

When Alex came downstairs, he glanced around the basement, which was dimly lit by a few bulbs hanging from the ceiling. He had a brown leather laptop bag slung over his shoulder, and he readjusted the strap before turning his attention back to Harper.

"What are you doing here?" he asked her.

"Just cleaning up." She absently wiped at her eyes, which had welled up a bit while she was looking through the box. "I've been meaning to reorganize this junk for a long time."

"I see," Alex said, but he didn't sound like he really did. "Anyway, I came over because I wanted to show you what I've been working on all morning."

"You've been working on something?" Harper asked.

When they'd spoken yesterday, neither of them had been able to come up with a concrete plan for what to do about Gemma. The best they'd come up with was Harper making a few phone calls. Alex had offered to help, but they both agreed it would sound better if the calls came from a family member instead of Gemma's boyfriend.

"Yeah, it's on my laptop." He tapped the bag hanging on his hip. "If you wanna take a look."

"Yeah, sure, of course."

Alex glanced around for a place to sit. Looking past the old lawn chairs, which still looked rather cobwebby even after Harper had wiped them off, he sat down on the basement steps. Then he pulled out his laptop, setting it across his knees.

"I know you were making calls, but I wanted to do something, too," Alex said as Harper walked over to him. She tentatively sat on the step next to him, peering over at his computer screen as he clicked away. "So I went to the Internet."

Within a few seconds a big picture of Gemma popped up, nearly filling the screen. She was smiling, with her long waves of hair shimmering in the sunlight. Harper had taken the picture a few weeks ago on the last day of school.

"I took the picture from her Facebook," Alex explained.

In large bold letters above Gemma's picture, it read ***Have you seen me?*** Alex scrolled down below the picture, where all the pertinent information was listed, like Gemma's age, height, when she was last seen, and a contact e-mail address given as info@FindGemmaFisher.com.

"What do you think?" Alex asked, watching Harper expectantly.

"This is her own Web site?" Harper asked, avoiding answering him right away.

He nodded. "Yeah, I got a couple missing kids sites to link to it, too. And I also set up a Facebook page for it."

He made a few more keystrokes, and the Facebook page popped up, displaying the same picture he'd used on her Web site. This one had the tagline *Have you seen Gemma Fisher?*

"A few people have already written on the wall," Harper remarked, and leaned in closer to read the messages.

The only people who had written on the wall so far were a couple girls Gemma had gone to school with and her swim coach, all of them sharing the same sentiment—that they hadn't seen Gemma, but they hoped she came home soon.

"Yeah, there's no great tips yet, but I just launched it," Alex said. "It'll take a little bit of time to take off."

"You think people will post if they see her?" Harper asked.

"I don't know," Alex admitted. "But I hope they do. They might." He sighed. "I mean, I don't know where else to look or what else to do. This way we can get other people helping us."

"That's true." Harper leaned back on the steps. "It's really good, Alex. I'm glad you thought of it."

"Maybe she'll see it," Alex said, his words softer, as if he were speaking to himself. "Maybe if she realizes how much we miss her, she'll come back."

Harper turned away from the computer to look directly at Alex. He wore a worried, heartbroken expression.

"Alex, she didn't leave because she doesn't care about us," Harper said gently. "Or because she doesn't think we care about her."

He lowered his eyes, and when he spoke, his voice sounded tight. "I know. I just thought . . . maybe if she realized how much I care . . ."

"Alex." Harper put her hand on his back to comfort him. "Those sirens have done something to Gemma. You didn't see her leave because you were knocked out, but Gemma didn't want to go with them. They had something over her, and she left to protect us, to protect you and me, because she cares about us."

"I should've done more," Alex said, growing frustrated. "I'm her boyfriend. I should be helping her."

"And you are," Harper said, then corrected herself. "Well, you're doing everything you can."

"It doesn't feel like enough."

She let out a deep breath. "I know. I feel the same way. But this is all we can do right now. So it has to be enough."

SIX

Sisters

Gemma sat on the beach with the sun beating down on her, but it didn't stifle the chill that ran through her. She'd been shivering all day, and wore layers outside, despite the heat.

Being this close to the ocean was the only thing that seemed to help at all. She sat with her knees pulled up to her chest a few feet from where the water splashed onto the shore, and for once, the watersong in her head was nearly silent.

The sirens were out in the ocean enjoying one of their daily swims, but Gemma refused to join them. Sawyer had gone out with them today, though, and she could hear him laughing along with the faint sound of Penn singing to him.

They were far enough out that she couldn't see them that well, bobbing above the surface. The sirens kept disappearing underneath, preferring to swim deeper and farther than a human like Sawyer could go, and Gemma kept getting paranoid that they were going to drown him.

She didn't know Sawyer that well, and she had a feeling she never really would. Thanks to the spell, he'd never really be able to be himself. But he seemed nice enough when she interacted with him, and he didn't deserve to die.

So when he didn't come up after a while, Gemma moved toward the water, but he surfaced just before she dove in, laughing and telling Penn how amazing she was. Gemma sighed, then sat back down in the sand.

To Sawyer, Gemma supposed, this all must seem rather magical. He saw them as beautiful mermaids, and their spell never let him question any further. They appeared to be what fantasies were made of, and he was completely enchanted with them. On the surface, it all seemed so beautiful and perfect, but Gemma knew about the dark underside.

While Penn and Lexi played far out in the ocean with Sawyer, who tried futilely to catch them, Thea made her way back to the beach. When she got in the shallows, Gemma could see the scales of her tail shimmering through the water.

Her own legs tingled at the memory of the scales, at the way it felt when her legs became a tail slicing through the cool ocean water. Her body craved the experience, but Gemma denied it.

Thea pulled her tail out of the water without checking to see if anyone might be around. Sawyer's house was on a secluded beach, hidden away from the rest of the world, so the sirens were free to frolic in the open as much as they pleased.

As Thea's scales shifted back into flesh, Gemma lowered her eyes and looked away. Thea wore a bikini top, but she was nude otherwise. She grabbed a sari that she'd left discarded on the sand and wrapped it around her waist as she walked over to where Gemma sat.

"You really are a bore," Thea said, and sat down next to her, stretching out her long tanned legs on the sand and propping herself up on her elbows.

"This is a curse," Gemma said matter-of-factly, and stared out at the waves. "So I'm treating it like one. I refuse to enjoy any part of it."

"This curse is your life," Thea said, looking at her seriously. "And you're going to live a very long time. You might as well enjoy it."

"What do you care if I enjoy it?" Gemma asked. "If I want to be miserable, what's it matter to you?"

"You're one of us," Thea replied. "I'm going to be stuck with you for a very long time. And it'd be nice to have someone to talk to that isn't an insufferable idiot."

Gemma thought of something, and she turned to look at Thea. The wind blew her long red hair back, slowly drying it of the salty water.

"What about your sister Aglaope? How long were you stuck with her?" Gemma asked.

Thea visibly tensed up at the mere mention of her sister. The sirens hadn't spoken much of her, but they'd said that Gemma was meant to replace Aglaope. When Gemma pressed to find out how Aglaope died or what had happened to her, the sirens hadn't been very forthcoming.

Well, it hadn't been the sirens so much as Penn. Whenever Gemma tried to find out more, Penn changed the subject or brushed her off. Thea had seemed much more open to talking about Aglaope, so while it was just the two of them, Gemma decided to use the opportunity.

"I wasn't stuck with her," Thea snapped. "And she's really none of your business."

"You just said that I'm one of you now," Gemma countered. "If I really am, shouldn't I know what it means to be a siren? That means knowing stuff about the past, about the sirens that came before me."

"She lived for a very long time," Thea said at last. "She was only two years younger than me, so she lived nearly as long as I have."

"She was an original siren, wasn't she?" Gemma asked. "Demeter turned her in the beginning, and she wasn't a replacement the way Lexi and I are."

"That's right." Thea took a deep breath and brushed sand off her bare knee. "Aggie was actually my full sister, unlike Penn, who is only our half sister."

"You had the same father as Penn but different mothers?" Gemma asked.

"Yes, but our mothers were actually sisters," Thea said with a wry smile. "It was all very incestuous back then. The gods often moved around, sleeping with each other's siblings and children."

Gemma wrinkled her nose. "That's gross."

"So it is," Thea agreed. "But that's how things were done."

"And you just went along with it?" Gemma asked.

Thea thought about that for a moment, then nodded. "I tried to."

"But Penn didn't," Gemma said, turning her attention back out to the water, where Penn and Lexi were still taunting Sawyer.

"Penn's never really been a go-with-the-flow kind of girl." Thea laughed, but it was a hollow, bitter sound.

"What about Aggie?" Gemma asked, using the same pet name that Thea had used for her. "What was she like?"

Something dark passed over Thea's face, and any trace of a smile fell away. She lowered her eyes, staring off at nothing.

"Aggie was kind," Thea said. Her voice was naturally huskier than the other sirens', but it became deeper now as she spoke, heavy with sadness. "Penn says that made her weak, and maybe it did. But compassion is still something that ought to be admired."

"So what happened?" Gemma asked. "Did Aggie die because she was nice?"

Thea stared out at the ocean, and her expression went dark again. "Aggie thought we'd lived long enough. We'd had more than our share of time on this earth, and we'd experienced more and seen more and enjoyed more than maybe any other being here.

"But all of that came with a cost," Thea went on. "And Aggie thought that we'd caused far more than our fair share of death. She said that we had enough blood on our hands, and it was time for us to go."

"Go?" Gemma asked.

"Yes," Thea said. "Aggie proposed we stop eating and go off into the sea to swim together until our bodies gave up and we died."

"She wanted you all to die together?" Gemma asked.

"Yes. That was her grand idea." Thea took a deep breath, and when she spoke again, her voice was totally flat and emotionless. "So Penn killed her."

Gemma waited a beat, thinking she'd misheard her. "She . . ." Gemma shook her head. "She just killed her?"

"There was no other choice, we didn't want to die." Thea spoke quickly now, all her words running together in one long string, and they lacked any conviction. "And we couldn't let Aggie kill us, so it was us or her, and it was going to be her either way. We had no other choice."

"How did Penn kill her?" Gemma asked, realizing she might have a chance to learn about a siren weakness. But Thea only shook her head.

"Just because I'm talking to you doesn't mean I'm stupid," Thea said. "I'm not going to tell you how to kill a siren."

"What happened after Aggie died?" Gemma pressed.

"The timing was the worst part of it," Thea said. "The full moon was coming, and we didn't have another siren planned. And when we finally found one, she died. Penn had her eye on you, but we thought you were too young. Things get more complicated when you get involved with underage girls. Their parents and family tend to pursue them more."

"So what happened to the other girl?" Gemma asked.

"*Girls*, actually," Thea corrected her. "There were two of them before you. We found them in nearby towns and tried them out the same way we did you."

"What do you mean?" Gemma asked.

"You remember," Thea explained, waving her hand vaguely. "We brought them out to the cove, wrapped them in the gold shawl, and they drank from the flask."

She did remember that, but not very clearly. The night she turned had been a blur. She'd been swimming out in Anthemusa Bay back in Capri, and as soon as she'd heard Lexi singing, everything seemed to stretch and distort.

The only thing she could remember with real clarity was the awful taste of the liquid in the flask. It had been thick, and burned going down her throat. And then she'd passed out, and in the morning she'd woken up on the rocks with a gauzy gold shawl wrapped around her.

Later, Penn had explained to her what the liquid had been—the blood of a siren, the blood of a mortal, and the blood of the ocean. That had been the mixture that had actually turned her into a siren, but until now she hadn't questioned the purpose of the shawl.

"What's the significance of the gold shawl?" Gemma asked.

"It was Persephone's," Thea said. "She was supposed to wear it in her wedding."

Persephone was the reason for them becoming sirens. Thea, Penn, Aggie, and their friend Ligeia were supposed to be watching Persephone, but instead they were off swimming, singing, and flirting with men. Persephone was kidnapped, and her goddess mother, Demeter, cursed them in punishment for not protecting her.

"What that has to do with the ritual, I don't really know,"

Thea admitted. "It was all part of Demeter's instructions, and we have to follow them."

"So then what happens?" Gemma asked. "You wrap the girls in the shawl, give them the potion, then what?"

"We toss them into the ocean," Thea replied simply. "The mixture is supposed to turn them into a siren, and that will protect them. If it doesn't take, then the girls drown."

"And you'd already drowned two girls before me?" Gemma asked, her heart hammering in her chest. "And you just tossed me into the water and hoped for the best?"

"Essentially, yes," Thea said. "You were our final hope. When you washed up on shore, *alive*, we were all so relieved."

"I nearly died!" Gemma said, indignant.

"Yes, but you didn't." Thea gave her a hard look, signaling her to stop the melodramatics. "And now you're one of us. It all worked out the way it was supposed to."

"But it almost didn't," Gemma said. "And I know that you all couldn't care less about me or the other two girls you killed, but don't you care at all about your own lives? If I had died, what would you have done?"

"I don't know," Thea snapped. "We would've found someone else."

"With only a few days before the full moon?" Gemma shook her head skeptically. "I sincerely doubt that."

"Then we would've died." Thea threw up her hands, exasperated. "But none of us did."

"Except for Aggie," Gemma pointed out. "I don't understand

that, either. Why didn't you wait until you found a replacement siren before you killed her?"

"*I* didn't kill her," Thea said pointedly. "It wasn't my idea."

A cloud moved in front of the sun, casting them in shadow. The breeze coming off the ocean suddenly felt cooler. Gemma couldn't see Penn or Lexi or even Sawyer anymore, but she didn't care.

"Penn couldn't wait," Thea said finally. "She couldn't stand to be around Aggie anymore, and she just . . ." She trailed off and shook her head.

"Penn's younger than you," Gemma said. "Why do you let your kid sister tell you what to do?"

"I don't—" Thea abruptly stopped midsentence, as if changing her mind about what she wanted to say. "There are many things you don't understand. You're too young. You haven't lived long enough or made any real sacrifices. You've never had to take care of anybody, not even yourself."

Penn, Lexi, and Sawyer suddenly surfaced, only ten or twenty feet from the shore. Sawyer was gasping for breath, but Penn and Lexi were completely silent.

"It's getting chilly," Thea said, and stood up. "I'm going in."

Gemma watched over her shoulder as Thea walked toward the house. Her sari was whipping in the wind, and she'd wrapped her arms around herself.

"Maybe we should go in, too," Sawyer suggested, and Gemma turned back to look at him. He was standing waist-deep in the water, the chiseled muscles of his torso visible above the waves.

"No," Penn said without looking at him. Her black eyes were

fixed on Thea, watching her figure retreat into the house. Penn's voice was normally like silk, but it had a harshness to it as she chastised Sawyer. "I'm not done playing yet."

"Sorry," Sawyer said, sounding genuinely upset, and he moved toward her, like he meant to touch her as part of his apology. "We can play as long as you want."

She turned back to glare at him. "I know that. I'm the one that makes the rules."

Before he could say anything more, Penn turned and dove under the water. Sawyer immediately tried to give chase, splashing roughly through the waves after her.

"Gemma!" Lexi called to her with that familiar singsong tone to her voice.

The sun had broken through the clouds, and a sliver of light managed to find Lexi's long golden locks, making them shine.

"Gemma," Lexi repeated when Gemma didn't answer. "Come swimming! Join us!"

Gemma simply shook her head no. Lexi let out a flirtatious giggle, then dove into the ocean, leaving Gemma alone on the beach.

SEVEN

Assiduous

Alex had his sites going, so far generating mostly useless tips, and between Harper and Brian, they had called every single person they could think of. Nobody knew where Gemma was, and there really wasn't much more that Harper could do.

So she went to work on Thursday. Brian had been reluctant to leave the house unmanned, but Harper pointed out that if Gemma came home, she probably wouldn't leave just because nobody was there. Besides that, Harper had her cell phone on her, and Alex was sitting in the house next door, keeping watch for his girlfriend.

"Have you figured out how to kill the sirens yet?" Marcy asked when Harper sat down at the front desk of the library.

"Not yet," Harper said.

She'd just punched in for the day, and she had to get ready to read a story to toddlers in twenty minutes. Marcy stood behind the desk, organizing the piles of recently returned books onto a cart so it would be easier for her to put them away.

"You could try holy water," Marcy suggested, and Harper looked back at her.

"What?"

"Holy water," Marcy repeated. "Although the sirens do love water. But it works on demons and vampires, so it should work on a couple of skinny little sirens."

"Maybe." Harper turned back to her desk, flipping through the calendar to see what story was scheduled for today. "But I'll have to find them first before I try it out."

"No luck on finding Gemma, then?" Marcy asked.

"Not yet." Harper sighed.

"That sucks. I was hoping that since you called in yesterday, maybe you had a lead on her."

"I have to go get ready for story time," Harper said, eager to change the subject. "Do you know if *Where the Wild Things Are* is on the shelf?"

"Uh, I think so," Marcy said. "It should be, at least."

"Thanks."

Harper pushed out her chair and hurried over to the children's corner. There were already a few little kids waiting with their moms or older siblings.

This was part of the summer reading program at the library. Harper or the librarian would read a book aloud to little kids a couple times a month, acting out the voices and engaging the audience as much as possible. Since the librarian was still traveling the world on her honeymoon, that left Harper to do it.

She didn't mind, though. In fact, she usually enjoyed interacting with the kids. It was fun getting them excited about reading, especially when they were so young. They didn't care if it was cool or not—they just liked a good story.

Today Harper liked it for a different reason. It kept her distracted. She needed to get her mind off Gemma, although the book *Where the Wild Things Are* didn't help much. It had been one of Gemma's favorites when they were kids, and Brian used to read it to them almost every night, acting out the parts.

At least she had that going for her. Harper already had her father's dazzling renditions of the characters to use as inspiration. This should be her best story-time performance.

She got the book off the shelf, then settled into her chair in the children's corner. As more kids came in, they sat around her in a circle. From where she was, Harper could see Marcy at the desk, loading up the book cart and directing children to story time as they came in.

When it was time to begin, Harper threw herself into her performance. All the kids came here today to have a good time, and it was her job to deliver, no matter how worried or distraught she might feel.

And as she read, Harper found herself having fun despite herself. She had the kids join in, and when they were gnashing their terrible teeth and roaring their terrible roars, she couldn't help but smile.

It was all going well until she was nearing the end of the story and heard the front door open. She lifted her head, expecting to see a late-arriving child, but instead it was Daniel, striding up to the front desk.

Her heart skipped a beat, and for a second Harper forgot how to read. She fumbled over the words, but she'd recovered by the time Marcy pointed back to the children's corner and Daniel turned around to smile at her.

Harper quickly averted her eyes, forcing a smile down at the little kids in front of her, and tried not to think about how foxy Daniel looked today.

What Harper found even more unnerving than her own feelings for Daniel was his banter with Marcy. He leaned against the desk, apparently waiting for Harper to finish the story, and chatted amiably with her.

Nobody chatted amiably with Marcy. Not even Harper, and Harper was pretty much her best friend.

It wasn't that she was jealous, but she couldn't imagine what they were talking about. Her real fear was that they were talking about her and Marcy might spill some hideously embarrassing secret.

Of course, Harper knew that it shouldn't matter what Marcy said to Daniel. In fact, it would be better if Marcy told him something that would turn him off of her forever. She didn't have time to get involved with him. Since he hadn't called and told her he'd found anything about Gemma in a voice mail, Harper thought it was a safe bet that this was a social call, and it probably would be better if Marcy got rid of him for her.

But then . . . Harper didn't want that, either. She knew she didn't have time to like him, but that didn't mean that she didn't like him. She just wished she didn't.

Harper did a slipshod job of the last quarter of the book, and she made a promise to herself that she would make it up to the kids at the next story time. But none of the kids complained. They seemed happy just to have an excuse to roar.

Some of the children and their parents tried to talk to her after she'd finished the story, and Harper did her best not to rush them. She smiled and reminded them about the next story time in July. When a mother told her how much she loved Maurice Sendak, Harper even recommended other books she should check out.

But the very second she could, Harper extracted herself from the children's corner and went over to the front desk, where Daniel was still talking with Marcy.

"No, I don't doubt that," Daniel was saying, laughing at something Marcy had said.

Marcy, for her part, wore her usual blank expression, giving Harper no indication of what they could've possibly been talking about.

"Hi," Harper said, and her voice sounded oddly high-pitched to her own ears, so she rushed to correct it. "Hi. Um, were you looking for a book?"

Daniel had been leaning forward, his arms resting on the desk, but he turned so he could face Harper, leaving one elbow on the counter. His smile widened when he saw her, and she noticed the fading cuts on his cheek.

When Penn had been that awful bird-monster on Bernie's

Island, Daniel had rushed in with a pitchfork to defend both Harper and her younger sister. But Penn had lashed out, scratching him across the cheek with her claws.

That memory both tightened her heart and warmed it. The horror of the monsters still frightened her, but knowing that Daniel had put himself in harm's way to protect her . . . it was hard not to feel something for him.

"What book were you reading them?" Daniel asked, pointing to where she'd been for story time. "Because that looked like a lot of fun."

"*Where the Wild Things Are.* I can get it for you, if you want." Harper moved like she meant to, and Daniel reached out, gently putting his arm on hers to stop her.

"Nah, that's okay," he said, letting his hand fall back to his side. "I think I've read it before. It is a good one, though."

"Yeah, it is," Harper agreed.

"I have to come clean with you," Daniel said gravely.

She swallowed hard. "Oh?"

"I didn't come in for a book," he admitted, and one corner of his mouth turned up slightly.

Harper glanced over at Marcy, who was standing on the other side of the desk, unabashedly watching the two of them talk. Harper raised her eyebrows, trying to give her friend a knowing look, and Marcy sighed.

"I guess I have some books to put away or something," Marcy muttered, and started pushing the cart out from behind the desk. "Because it's not like I don't have all day to put away twenty books. I need to do it right now."

Once Marcy was out of earshot, Harper turned her attention back to Daniel.

"What is it that brought you here, then?" Harper asked, hoping she didn't sound as nervous as she felt. Daniel had a way of making her completely flustered.

"I wanted to see why you've been avoiding me." Daniel was smiling when he said it, but he couldn't hide the hurt in his hazel eyes.

"I haven't been—" Harper began to protest, but he waved her off.

"You've been ignoring my calls, and you haven't been down to the docks to bring your dad his lunch," Daniel said. "The poor man is probably starving."

Brian worked down at the docks near where Daniel lived on his boat. Her father was notorious about forgetting his lunch, and Harper saw Daniel a lot when she brought it to him.

"My dad didn't work that much this week," Harper said. "He is today, but I honestly can't tell you if he remembered his lunch or not. I forgot to check."

"Oh," Daniel said. "Well, that makes sense. But that doesn't explain you ignoring my calls."

"I . . ." She stared down at the floor, unable to meet his gaze. "Daniel, you know what the situation is. Things are so strange right now, and I really don't have time for anything."

"I wasn't suggesting we run away together," Daniel said. "I know how crazy things are. That's why I was calling. I wanted to see how you were doing."

"Oh." Harper licked her lips and tried to think of something to say. "Well. Things are . . ."

"Why don't we go talk about it?" Daniel asked. "Let's go across the street to Pearl's and grab some lunch. I'll even let you pay for me."

"I can't just leave." Harper gestured to the library, which was now almost empty aside from one mother and her child looking through the kids' books. "I'm working."

"I can cover for you," Marcy said, poking her head out from behind a nearby bookshelf. "If you want to go have lunch, I've got it."

Harper sighed. "Thanks, Marcy."

Of course Marcy had to go and be helpful the one time Harper didn't want her to be. She knew Marcy was making a concerted effort to be nice, since Harper was going through a rough patch with Gemma missing, but still. This was insane.

"You may not have time to run off with a ruggedly handsome guy like myself, but I know you still have to eat," Daniel said. "And Marcy says that she has this under control. You have no reason to say no."

"Okay," Harper relented, because he was right. She couldn't think up an excuse, no matter how hard she tried. "But it's a little early for lunch."

"We'll have brunch, then," Daniel said.

He stepped back from the desk and waited as she prepared to go. When they left, he held the door open for her, and she smiled politely but tried not to let her eyes meet his.

"So, have you heard from Gemma?" Daniel asked as they waited on the sidewalk for a break in traffic.

"No." Harper shook her head. "Not yet."

"I'm sorry to hear that," Daniel said, and it sounded like he really meant it.

"Me, too," Harper said, and they crossed the street.

"It's a terrible situation," he said. "But I think she'll get through it and come home. She's a good kid. She's tough and can handle herself."

They'd reached Pearl's, and Harper grabbed the door so she could open it before he did.

"You always say that," she told him.

"And I'm always right. You don't give Gemma enough credit."

"I think this time I actually gave her too much credit." Harper slid into a booth in front of the window. "I never thought she'd get into any real trouble, and now she's turned into some kind of mythological beast."

"Mythological beast?" Daniel raised an eyebrow and leaned back in the seat across from her.

"Yeah." Harper glanced around to make sure that no one was close enough to hear, but they were early for lunch, so the diner was pretty empty. "Sirens. Alex and I did some research, and that's what we think they are."

"Sirens?" Daniel asked. "The mermaids that sing?"

"Something like that." Harper signaled him to be quiet because Pearl was approaching.

"How are you doing today?" Pearl asked.

"Good." Daniel grinned broadly at her, and even Pearl had

to feel the effects of it. When he smiled, it was a truly stunning thing. "How is my favorite waitress doing?"

"Better now that you're here," Pearl said, laughing a little at her own joke. "What can I get for you two today?"

Daniel looked to Harper, waiting for her to order first. Pearl's didn't have menus. She had a few specials written on a chalkboard hanging behind the counter, but with everything else, customers were just supposed to know what was served. It helped keep locals in and tourists out.

"Um, just a Cherry Coke and a cheeseburger," Harper said.

"I'll have the same," Daniel said.

"Coming right up." Pearl winked at them both before walking back to the counter.

"So." Daniel leaned forward, resting his arms on the table. "You're not ignoring Alex's calls, then?"

"That's different." Harper shook her head and stared out the window at the traffic passing slowly by.

"How is it different?" Daniel asked.

She groaned and rubbed the back of her neck. "You know how it's different."

"No, I don't. I can help you. I *want* to help you."

"But . . ." She sighed. "It's complicated with me and you."

Daniel laughed a little. "No, it's really not. You've made it perfectly clear what you're open for right now. I get it. You don't have time for anything more than friendship. But Harper, I'm not offering anything more than that."

She bit her lip and tentatively looked up at him. Hearing him say that actually stung a bit, and she was surprised. All this time she'd been saying she didn't want to get involved with him, and it hadn't really occurred to her that he might not want to get involved with *her.*

"Your sister ran off with some weird-ass bird-monsters," Daniel said. "Can you really afford to turn away somebody that wants to help you get her back? Especially someone that doesn't think you're insane for believing in weird-ass bird-monsters?"

"No," Harper admitted, smirking a little at his description of the sirens.

"Good." He smiled wider at that and relaxed more in the seat. "So, what's your plan for finding Gemma?"

"I don't have one."

"That's okay," Daniel assured her. "We'll come up with one."

EIGHT

Ungrateful

Gemma woke up while it was still dark out, and she barely made it to the bathroom in time. She leaned over the porcelain bowl, retching up what little contents she had in her stomach. It was Friday, and the last time she'd eaten anything had been days ago.

Once she'd finished throwing up, Gemma leaned back against the tiles of the bathroom wall and tried to catch her breath. Her mind swirled, dizzy and aching from the watersong.

Her skin felt too tight. Sweat clung to her flesh, drying sticky and making it feel as if she were shrink-wrapped.

A shower seemed like the best solution. It wouldn't completely erase the way she felt, but it might ease her sickness a bit.

Outside, the sky was starting to lighten, and dim blue light spilled in through the bathroom window. Gemma decided to leave the light off, preferring the semidarkness. That would probably upset her migraine the least.

When she turned on the faucet, she kept it cool, even though she still had the chills. The cold sweat left her shivering. But she thought a cold shower might clear her head.

Standing under the spray, she found it hard not to sing. She hadn't sung since she'd accidentally called to Alex back at her house in Capri, and she'd nearly hurt him. Even worse, it had left him more susceptible to the other sirens.

So though the lyrics played on her tongue until she had to bite her lip to keep them from escaping, Gemma didn't sing. She was too afraid of accidentally luring another guy into this mess.

If Sawyer weren't living here with them, she might have been tempted to try a soft lullaby or humming to herself. But it was bad enough that Penn and Lexi had him wrapped around their fingers. Gemma didn't want to control him, too.

At least the shower was helping. Her body craved water the way plants craved sunlight. The tap water wasn't exactly right, partially because of all the chemicals used to treat it, but mostly because it wasn't salt water from the ocean.

Normally, when her skin got wet, she'd feel this fluttering sensation in her legs as they tried to transform into a tail. It wouldn't work, not fully, because only the ocean induced the transition.

This time, she felt nothing. It was as if her body didn't even have the strength to attempt to change. But her headache had abated, and that was all she really hoped for.

Gemma moved on to washing her hair, and she caught herself humming despite her attempts not to. The sound of the running water would probably drown it out, though, so she decided to go with it.

As she was washing her hair, something tangled in her fingers. She pulled her hand out to inspect it in the ever-brightening morning light. It was a whole clump of her own hair, and Gemma yelped in shock.

She reached up and pulled at her hair. Without her even really trying, another chunk of hair came out.

While she'd never considered herself particularly vain, the sight of her hair falling out was a terrible shock. It wasn't about the way she would look so much as that she associated hair loss with people dying, like cancer patients.

The shower curtain flew open, and Gemma hurried to cover herself with her arms so she wasn't standing there so exposed.

Penn stood on the other side of the tub, glaring at Gemma in the way only Penn could glare. It was like her black eyes sliced right through Gemma.

Beyond that evil death gaze, Penn looked stunning, for the first thing in the morning. She wore a black silk nightie that stopped at the middle of her thighs, and her glossy black hair hung down her back.

"Penn!" Gemma shouted.

"Your fucking hair is falling out," Penn said, her tone going past annoyed to full-on bitchy.

"Yeah." Gemma swallowed back her fear and tried to cling to her indignation. "I'm also naked. So it'd be great if you could close the curtain and give me some privacy."

"You need to eat something," Penn said, ignoring her.

"I'm not gonna eat anything right now," Gemma said. "I'm in the shower."

She wanted to reach out and grab the curtain so she could pull it shut herself, but that would mean leaving herself out in the open. As it was, one arm was barely covering her chest while the other attempted to hide her nether regions.

"You are no good to me dead, Gemma," Penn warned her. "If you don't eat something, you will die. And then I will be royally pissed. Do you know what happens when I get pissed, Gemma?"

Gemma sighed. "No."

"I get even." Penn leaned in toward her and lowered her voice. "That means I'll go after that stupid boy you like and your ugly sister."

Gemma lowered her eyes. The cold water was still dripping down her body, and it took all her strength to keep from shivering.

All she wanted to do was protect Harper and Alex. That was why she'd left, why she'd agreed to any of this. But there were still some lines she wouldn't cross. Even if it meant risking the people she cared about most, Gemma wasn't sure that she could do it.

"I won't kill anyone," Gemma said finally.

"You can't even attract anyone to kill. You look like zombie Barbie right now." Penn gestured to Gemma, who was looking pale and ill, with hair still tangled in her fingers. "You need to swim."

"I don't want to—" Gemma began, but Penn cut her off.

"That wasn't a suggestion." Penn smirked at her. "That was a command, Gemma, and as I recall, you promised to follow all my commands."

Before Gemma could agree or disagree, Penn grabbed her arm and yanked her out of the tub. She tripped over the lip and fell to the floor, but that gave her a chance to pick up the spaghetti-strapped nightgown she'd slept in. Penn let go of her long enough for Gemma to slide it over her head, then she was pulling on her arm again.

"This has gone on long enough," Penn said as she dragged Gemma out of the bathroom.

Gemma glanced down the hall and saw that everyone had come out to see what the commotion was about. Lexi and Thea stood in front of a bedroom door. Sawyer looked like he'd just stumbled out of a room, his hair disheveled from sleep.

"Do you need help, Penn?" Sawyer asked as Penn led Gemma down the stairs.

"Not now, Sawyer!" Penn snapped.

His entire face fell. "Sorry, babe."

"The problem is that I've been too kind," Penn said, returning to her rant at Gemma. "I've let you into our fold. I've given you the greatest gift you could ever ask for, and you throw it all back in my face."

Gemma stumbled a few times, her wet feet slipping on the marble floor, but Penn never slowed down. If she didn't hurry up, Penn was liable to rip her arm out of its socket.

When they made it outside, it got harder for Gemma to keep her footing. The back door opened right onto the beach, and the sand made it nearly impossible for her to stand.

Penn must've tired of dragging her along, because she yanked Gemma's arm so hard Gemma stumbled to the ground. Gemma sat up but didn't get to her feet.

"What is wrong with you?" Penn shouted, glowering over her.

"I didn't ask for this!" Gemma shot back, trying to match Penn's glare.

"Neither did I!" Penn growled. "But I made the best of it! Why can't you?"

"How have you made the best of it?" Gemma asked. "What have you done that's so great?"

"Don't you dare question my choices!" Penn shook her head. "You have no right! And you know what? It doesn't matter what you think or what you want or if you're happy."

"Why don't you just let me go?" Gemma asked.

"You are a siren and I can't let you go!" Penn shouted. "The sirens have to stay together. If one of us leaves for more than a week or so, we all die. You have to stay with us. As you agreed. If you want to be miserable, that's fine by me. But you will not die. We had an agreement, and you will do what I say!"

As much as Gemma hated to admit it, she knew Penn was right. So she let out a deep breath and looked up at her. "Fine. What do you want me to do?"

"For starters, get in that ocean and swim before all your hair falls out and your skin starts to slide off." Penn pointed to the water lapping on the beach.

Gemma wasn't sure if Penn was exaggerating, or if the next step in her deterioration really would be her skin falling off. But she didn't want to find out, and she definitely knew it wasn't in her best interest to push Penn right now.

She got up and walked out into the ocean, giving in to the song that had been haunting her for days. The waves knocked her down, and she fell into them.

When her legs didn't turn, she began to panic. The familiar flutter of the transformation didn't come. The waves started pulling her out to sea. She tried to swim and fight it, but she was too weak. The water was taking over, pulling her under, and if she didn't transform soon, she would drown.

And then, when Gemma was beginning to think it was too late, it finally happened. It wasn't as smooth or as pleasurable as it normally was. Her legs thrashed for a while before they became a tail.

She breathed in deeply, grateful to be able to again, and then she swam off.

For a moment, all her cares evaporated. Her skin felt alive, tingling with the magic of the water. Even her scalp began to prickle, and Gemma realized that her hair was growing back. All of her aches and pains were washed away.

As she swam, darting around in the ocean like a dolphin at play, Gemma considered running away. Or swimming away, as it were.

She could leave this all behind, Penn and the sirens and the issues with feeding. Thea had told her of Aggie's plan to die that way, to just swim out to sea and let themselves starve. Gemma could do that. The other sirens would eventually die without Gemma, and this would all be over for everyone.

But then she thought of Alex and Harper. As soon as Penn realized what she'd done, that Gemma had left, Penn would go after them and kill them.

Penn may have been able to kill her own sister, but Gemma never could. She couldn't even stand the thought of Harper being hurt.

Gemma surfaced, and the sun was completely over the horizon now. She was quite a ways from the shore, but she could still make out Penn's figure standing on the beach, watching her swim.

That was when Gemma finally understood that Penn was a whole different kind of creature than her. Even when Gemma had been her maddest at Harper, she'd never have even dreamed of killing her. Or anyone, for that matter.

Penn might be evil, but it wasn't because she was a siren. Gemma would do as she was told and be a dutiful little siren, but she was determined not to let herself become the same kind of monster as Penn.

NINE

Funeral

The funeral was small, but Harper hadn't really expected it to be any different. Bernie McAllister had planned it himself, long before he died, and he was a simple man, so it made sense that his final wishes would be simple.

After Brian had found out about Bernie's death, he'd actually called the funeral home to set up something, only to discover that everything had been prepaid. According to the funeral director, Bernie had taken care of it all shortly after his wife died some fifty years ago.

As far as Harper knew, the only family Bernie had was one sister, and she lived in England, if she was even still alive. Bernie had spoken very little of his family, only mentioning his long-deceased wife on occasion.

The service was at the funeral home. Bernie had declined to have a wake, and the service wasn't very well attended. Bernie had been an old man who kept to himself, and many of his friends had already passed away.

Most of the people there were his former coworkers. Bernie had worked out at the docks for years, long before Harper's father had started, and according to Brian, Bernie had been very well liked down there.

The poor attendance was probably more a result of it being a Friday afternoon, when it was hard for people to get time off. Brian's foreman was pretty strict, and it had been a bit of a struggle for him to take the time, but Brian refused to miss the funeral.

Despite the solemnity of the occasion, Brian actually looked better than he had in days. He'd shaved today, and the dark suit he wore looked good on him, even if he looked uncomfortable in it. He always seemed ill at ease in anything other than jeans, but Harper thought her father cleaned up rather well.

Before the funeral got fully under way, people were milling around, speaking to one another in hushed tones. This was the time when they could pay their final respects to Bernie.

Bernie had a closed coffin, and Harper knew why. As hard as she tried to remember the wonderful, warm man he'd been, when she thought of him, the only image that came to her mind was the final one she had of him: his body torn open as he lay bleeding on the island he'd loved so much.

Harper had gone to the front of the room with her father, joining him as he said good-bye to the old man. Brian put his hand on the smooth wood of the coffin, awkwardly rubbing it for a minute before lowering his hand.

"I wish we'd spent more time with him these last few years," Brian said. He wasn't crying, at least not yet, but he sniffled and his voice was thick.

"Me, too," Harper agreed.

Brian shoved his hands in his pockets and shook his head. "Gemma should be here."

"Yeah. She should."

Harper had been hoping he wouldn't bring up Gemma today, but he was right. Gemma should've been here.

She didn't know if Gemma even knew that Bernie was dead. Gemma had been out on the island, but that didn't mean she'd seen him.

Then a new thought, a horrible, dirty one, wormed itself into her brain. Maybe Gemma had had something to do with Bernie's death.

As soon as she thought it, Harper dismissed the idea. There was no way her sister would have anything to do with hurting anybody, let alone someone she cared about like Bernie.

But then again, Harper had seen firsthand what the sirens had been able to do, not just to Bernie but to Luke Benfield and the other boys they'd killed. The sirens were evil, so it wasn't unreasonable to think that Gemma could act monstrous, too.

The service was about to start, so Brian and Harper took their seats. It was a small room in the back of the funeral home, filled with thirty or so folding chairs, and most of them were empty. Since they seemed to be the closest to Bernie during his last years, Brian and Harper sat in the front row.

The pastor gave his brief sermon, then invited people up to

say a few words. Harper didn't think that her dad had planned on saying anything, but when nobody else got up, Brian rose and stood in front of the casket.

"Um, I'm Brian Fisher," he said, and cleared his throat. "Most of you know me from working out at the docks, and I suppose that's how you knew Bernie, too."

Brian kept his eyes down when he spoke, and Harper knew it was because he didn't want anyone to see the tears pooling in them. When he glanced up at her, she smiled reassuringly, and that seemed to embolden him a bit.

"I've known Bernie for over twenty years." He gestured to the coffin behind him. "He was a hard worker and hardly missed a day in all the time we worked together. He took me under his wing, and outside of work he was a good friend.

"When my wife—" His voice caught in his throat, and he paused a moment to collect himself. "He, um, he took care of my girls when I couldn't, and for that I will be forever grateful. I don't know what would've happened to my family if it hadn't been for Bernie."

Tears filled Harper's eyes as she listened to her father talk.

"I had the pleasure of seeing him a few days ago," Brian went on. "And he was as spry and happy as ever. He still had so much life in him." He let out a long breath, then turned to the coffin. "At least you get to be with your wife now, Bernie. I know you've been waiting a long time to see her."

He looked back at the pastor awkwardly. "I guess that's all I have to say. Thank you."

The pastor thanked him as Brian hurried to his seat. He exhaled deeply as he collapsed next to Harper. She looped her arm through his and rested her head on his shoulder.

"That was very sweet, Dad," she told him. "Bernie would've liked that."

The service finished up shortly afterward. The pastor asked people to come out to the cemetery for the burial if they liked, but most of the attendees seemed to be leaving.

Brian and Harper got up with the intention of heading out to their car when a man in a gray suit approached them. He looked familiar, but everybody in Capri looked familiar. The town wasn't that big, so even if Harper didn't personally know certain people, she'd probably seen them around.

"You're Brian Fisher?" the man asked.

"That's right," Brian said cautiously.

"I'm Dean Stanton, Bernie's lawyer." The man stuck out his hand, but Brian was slow to shake it.

"Bernie had a lawyer?" Brian sounded genuinely surprised. "What did Bernie need a lawyer for?"

"I handled his will and his estate," Dean said. "And I've been meaning to get in touch with you."

"What for?" Harper asked, inserting herself in the conversation.

"He's named you, Brian, as his beneficiary," Dean said. "He didn't have much in the way of life insurance. What he did have only covers what he owed on the island, but at least now you get the property free and clear."

"What?" Brian shook his head, not understanding. "Property?"

"Yes, he's left everything to you," Dean explained. "The island and all of its contents, including the cabin, the boathouse, and the boat."

"He left me the island?" Brian appeared dumbfounded, and he exchanged a confused glance with Harper. "He never told me that."

"Well, he did," Dean said. "I'll need to have you come down to sign some papers.

"Here's my card," Dean said as he handed it to Brian. "Give me a call, and we'll set something up. But right now I'll let you get back to the funeral. I'm sorry for your loss."

"Thank you," Brian murmured, sounding distracted and dazed.

The funeral home director was wheeling the casket out the back doors so they could load it into the hearse, and Brian turned back to watch Bernie's departure as Dean walked away.

"We should get going if we want to be in the procession," Harper said.

Brian nodded and shoved the lawyer's business card in his back pocket.

Neither of them said anything about Bernie's will as they walked out to Brian's truck. In fact, neither of them said anything at all as they followed the hearse out to the cemetery. They were the only car in the procession, and other than the pastor, they were the only people who watched Bernie's coffin be lowered into the ground.

Harper was shocked that Bernie had left them the island, and she assumed her father felt the same way. But it did make sense, since he had no real family here, and Brian was one of his closest friends.

That also made her feel guilty, when she realized how little she'd seen Bernie lately. Before they went out to his island this past weekend, it had probably been months since they'd visited him.

Harper didn't want to see them pour the dirt onto his coffin, so she turned around to head back to the truck. As she did, she spotted Daniel standing several feet away, leaning against a bald cypress tree.

Harper walked over to Daniel, but her father lingered behind a few minutes. She wasn't sure if Brian was paying his final respects to Bernie or giving her a moment alone with Daniel.

"What are you doing here?" Harper asked.

"I read about his funeral in the paper," Daniel said. "I thought I'd come check it out."

"You seem a little underdressed for a funeral."

Daniel glanced down at his outfit. He wore a flannel shirt with the sleeves rolled up over a faded Led Zeppelin T-shirt, and his jeans had a hole in the knee.

"At least I put a shirt on," Daniel teased. Harper had once commented on the fact that he never wore a shirt, or so it seemed whenever she saw him on his boat.

"Hello again, Daniel," Brian said, walking up behind Harper.

"I'm sorry for your loss, Mr. Fisher." Daniel stepped away from the tree and held out his hand.

Brian shook it quickly and nodded. "Thanks," he said. "Did you know Bernie well?"

"No, not really." Daniel shook his head. "But I knew that Harper was close to him, so I wanted to see how she was holding up and offer my condolences."

"That's very thoughtful." Brian eyed him, as if he weren't quite sure what to make of Daniel, then turned his attention to Harper. "I really hate to do this, but I have to get back to work."

"I can give her a ride," Daniel offered. "If you need to get going."

Brian's eyes flitted over to Daniel before looking to Harper to see what she wanted to do. Her father would just be going home to change for work and then leaving right away, so it wasn't as if he needed her to go with him. And she wasn't really looking forward to spending another day alone in the house.

"You go ahead, Dad," Harper said. "Daniel can take me home."

Her father hesitated before nodding. "Okay. I'll see you later, then." He leaned over and kissed Harper quickly on the temple before walking away.

"So . . ." Harper said once her father had left. "Do you often peruse the obituaries for funerals?"

"No." Daniel stepped away, walking among the headstones, and Harper fell in step with him. "I've actually been checking the paper a lot for any info on Gemma."

"Oh, yeah," Harper said. "I've been doing the same thing."

"So you haven't heard anything from her yet?" Daniel asked, watching Harper as she spoke.

"No. Alex has gotten a couple e-mails, but they've been false leads so far." She sighed. "I have no idea where she is. And I don't know what I'll do if she never comes home."

"I hate to break it to you, but . . . you'll live," Daniel said solemnly.

"Why do you make that sound like bad news?"

"Because I'm under the impression that you want to curl up and die," he said. "Or at least that's what you think you're supposed to do if something happens to your sister. But the hard truth is that you won't. Life will move on, and you're strong and smart, so you'll move on with it."

Harper shook her head. "I can't imagine that. I can't ever give up on her."

"Nobody's asking you to give up," Daniel said. "I'm just suggesting that you keep things in perspective."

"How so?" Harper asked.

Daniel had stopped walking, so she stopped and looked up at him. The sun was shining brightly above them, and the day felt far too lovely for a funeral. He squinted in the light, then gestured to a headstone behind Harper.

"That's my brother John's grave," he said.

Daniel had told her about the accident he'd been in with his brother five years before. John had died, and Daniel had been left with scars covering his back and a few on his head, hidden by his hair.

"I'm sorry," Harper said.

"I visit him from time to time." Daniel stared down at the headstone, sounding uncharacteristically solemn. "I loved him a lot. But he's still dead, and I'm still here." He looked up at Harper, his eyes resting on her. "And so are you."

"I know." She smiled wanly at him. "And I don't plan on going anywhere."

"Good." He smiled at that. "Now come on. It's too nice out to spend the day at a cemetery. Let's get out of here."

TEN

Sirensong

Since going for a swim yesterday, Gemma was reenergized. Once she got past her guilt about enjoying any part of this experience, she felt pretty good. Penn hadn't spoken to her much after that, and that was fine by Gemma.

Penn had spent most of yesterday in her room with Sawyer, making all kinds of noises that Gemma had only thought existed in porn. Then Penn got up early this morning and declared that she and Lexi were going on another shopping trip, once again leaving Thea in charge of Gemma and Sawyer.

Gemma still didn't feel a hundred percent, but the watersong was hardly bothering her, and her chills and night sweats had gone away. So she decided to make the most of it. She put on a bikini and went out to the balcony to lie out in the sun. It was a beautiful day, and she wanted to enjoy it.

The problem was that Gemma had never really lain about before. She was always tan, but that was because she spent so much time in the bay. It didn't take long before she gave up; she just couldn't lie still that long.

The balcony outside her room hung about twenty feet from the ground. The ceilings on the first floor were tall, making the balcony exceptionally high. A railing of horizontal bars—painted white, of course— ran around the side of it to keep anyone from accidentally falling over.

Gemma went over to the edge and sat down, dangling her legs over the side and resting her arms on the lowest bar. She stared out at the ocean and swung her legs back and forth.

"I see you're feeling better," Thea said from the balcony next to hers. Each one of the five bedrooms that faced the ocean had its own balcony, and Thea's room was closest to Gemma's.

"Much better," Gemma admitted.

"It's the ocean that does it, you know," Thea told her. "Something about the transformation heals all your aches and pains."

"Yeah, I figured that."

"If you swim every day, you buy yourself some time," Thea said. "It'll help keep your body from completely falling apart. But eventually you will have to eat." She paused, running a hand through her hair. "But if you want to put that off, then I'd suggest you swim as often as you can."

"Thanks," Gemma said, genuinely surprised that Thea had offered her any tips.

Thea didn't say anything to that. She stayed outside a moment longer, then turned and went back into the house.

Gemma knew she should take Thea's advice, but she didn't want to just yet. She felt content. Or at least as close to content as she'd felt since coming here. She'd been in so much pain lately that just the absence of pain felt amazing.

She was about to get up and go down to swim when Sawyer wandered out to the balcony. He'd gone shirtless today, opting to walk around in drawstring pants. Not that Gemma minded all that much. Her heart might belong to Alex, but she wasn't blind.

"Do you care if I join you?" Sawyer asked.

Gemma shrugged. "It's your house. You can do what you want."

"Is it my house?" Sawyer sounded perplexed as he sat down next to Gemma, dangling his own legs over the edge of the balcony.

"Yeah, it's your house." Gemma gave him an odd look. "At least that's what you told me the other day."

"Right, right." He shook his head as if to clear it. "Of course. It's my house." He leaned against the railing, resting his chin on his arms. "It's just that lately it feels more like Penn's house."

"Yeah, I can understand that," she said. He sighed, and she turned to face him. "Do you even like her?"

"Penn?" Sawyer asked, then nodded quickly. "Yes. Of course I like her. I'm crazy about her. I don't think I can live without her."

"Why?" Gemma asked him directly.

"Because . . ." He furrowed his brow, seemingly finding it difficult to think of a single reason why. "I feel so restless when she's not around, like I can't get comfortable."

Gemma knew that Sawyer didn't really care about Penn, at

least not to the degree that he acted. But she thought he'd at least cite Penn's beauty or her voice as a reason for being so devoted to her.

She wondered what his absence of reasons meant. Maybe Sawyer didn't like Penn at all. If Penn took away the siren song, he might even detest her. But Gemma would probably never know how he really felt about Penn.

"I know I love her," Sawyer said finally. "But when I try to think of why, it's all a blur. All I can hear is her song."

"If you try to think, her song drowns it out?" Gemma asked.

"Yeah, kind of." He nodded. "Sometimes it's Lexi's, too, but mostly it's Penn's. She sings to me a lot. I don't think she likes when Lexi does."

"Why do you say that?" Gemma asked.

"She always tells me not to listen to Lexi's song," he said. "And that's really hard to do, because her song is the most beautiful I've ever heard."

"Yeah, I can agree with that."

Lexi's song didn't have the same power on Gemma that it once had. She still felt compelled to sing along with her, but she had no urge to do her or any of the sirens' bidding. Still, Lexi had the loveliest singing voice Gemma had ever heard.

"Do you think . . ." Sawyer's face scrunched up, as if he were in pain. "Does Penn love me?"

Gemma was shocked that he'd even asked her that question, and she didn't know how to answer. She briefly considered lying to him, telling him the kinds of things she thought he'd want to hear, but she didn't see the point.

"What has she told you?" Gemma asked, carefully avoiding answering directly.

"When I tell her I love her, she usually just laughs," Sawyer said. "She doesn't really say how she feels about me. She just yells at me a lot and tells me I'm an idiot."

"No, Penn doesn't love you," Gemma told him. "She's just using you. I don't know if she even likes you."

She turned toward him to watch his reaction. His blue eyes stayed locked on the view of the ocean, and he looked hurt but not surprised.

"Yeah. That's what I thought." When he spoke again, he sounded disappointed, but more with himself than with Penn's lack of affection.

"She put a spell on you," Gemma said, trying to ease his sadness. "She's a siren, and she's used her songs to trick you into thinking you feel a certain way about her. But you don't."

"No," Sawyer said quickly. "No, that's not true. I really love her. It's not some spell."

"Well, you can think what you want, but it is a spell." She turned back to the water.

"You really think Penn's a siren?" Sawyer asked.

"Yep."

"Lexi and Thea, too?"

"Yep."

He thought about it, then asked, "What's a siren?"

"A siren is sorta like a mermaid, but they can enchant people with their voices, usually men," Gemma said.

The explanation was longer than that, but she didn't think

Sawyer needed to know all the details. The Cliffs Notes version would do.

"Oh," he said. "Are you a siren?"

"Yeah, I am," Gemma said, her voice heavy with regret.

"But you're not like the others."

"Because I'm not as pretty?"

"No, no, you're all pretty." He waved off that idea. "But when I'm around you, I can actually think. You *feel* different."

"I *feel* different?" Gemma raised an eyebrow. "You've never touched me."

"No, not the way you physically feel. The way you . . . are, I guess," Sawyer said. "Your presence when you walk into a room. You feel real. The other girls, they feel like dreams I made up in the night. Or sometimes they feel like nightmares.

"And I don't know why you said you're not as pretty," Sawyer said. "You're just as pretty as they are, maybe prettier when you smile."

Gemma smiled. "Thanks."

"If me and Penn don't work out, do you think that we could go on a date sometime?" Sawyer asked.

"Me and you?" Gemma laughed. "No, I don't think so."

"Why not?" Sawyer asked. "Do you have a boyfriend?"

She kept smiling, but it became pained. Gemma had been trying not to think about Alex that much, since it wouldn't do her any good, and it still broke her heart a little every time she did.

"Yeah," she said thickly. "I do have a boyfriend."

"Then why isn't he here?" Sawyer asked. "I don't think I could stand to be away from you if I was your boyfriend."

"He, um . . ." Gemma licked her lips and looked down at the beach below her. "He had to stay back home. It's safer for him there."

"Oh. You mean 'cause of Penn?"

"Yeah." She nodded once. "Because of Penn."

"Do you love him?" Sawyer asked.

"Yeah, I love him." Gemma laughed again, this time to keep from crying. "I love him so much."

"Does he love you?" Sawyer asked.

Gemma thought back to the last kiss she'd shared with Alex in the cabin before she'd left with the sirens. It had felt real and true, shooting through her like electricity. Penn insisted that Alex wouldn't be capable of loving her now that she was a siren, but Gemma knew Alex, and he couldn't fake the way he felt about her.

"Yeah," Gemma said finally, with tears in her eyes. "I think he does." She sniffled. "Sorry for getting so emotional."

"It's okay. I probably won't remember this conversation anyway," Sawyer said, displaying a surprising bit of self-awareness.

Gemma wiped at her eyes and looked at him. "What do you mean?"

"I can't seem to remember much of anything anymore." He shook his head. "Everything's a blur of images."

"I'm sorry," she said sadly. "For all of this. I'm sorry that the sirens are doing this to you. You seem like a nice guy, and you deserve better than this."

"I don't know. I'm not sorry. It's kind of fun." He smiled, but the smile seemed sad. "Four beautiful girls in my house, and I'm in love with Penn. Some things are strange and my memory isn't so great, but it's still . . . fun."

"I hope that's true," Gemma said.

Sawyer let out a long breath. "Me, too."

ELEVEN

Runaway

Where is she?" Nathalie shouted, her voice taking on a feverish pitch.

"She's not here, Mom," Harper said, and rubbed her forehead.

This was not at all how she imagined their weekly visit going. She'd actually considered not coming today, but her father was busy meeting with Bernie's lawyer, Dean Stanton. Harper had even thought about hanging out with Daniel, but he was busy working on a job repairing someone's fence.

So Harper had mistakenly thought seeing her mother at the group home would be better than spending the day alone at the house.

But things had been rough from the start. As soon as Nathalie ran out of the house to greet Harper and saw that Gemma wasn't with her, she'd gotten agitated, demanding to know where her younger daughter was.

The really weird thing was that Gemma had skipped Saturday visits with Nathalie before. Gemma loved their mom and always wanted to see her, but with all her swim meets, sometimes skipping a visit couldn't be helped. Sometimes she just wasn't able to make it.

Usually, when Gemma had to go to a meet, Harper would still go see Nathalie. Brian would go watch Gemma swim, so it wasn't like she wouldn't have anyone cheering her on. But Brian would never visit Nathalie. He just couldn't handle it.

When Harper visited her mom alone, she would explain where Gemma was, and Nathalie would be fine with it. Sometimes Nathalie didn't even seem to notice.

But this time it was as if Nathalie knew something was wrong. She *knew* Gemma should be here, and she wasn't. So she freaked out.

Harper and Becky, one of the staff who worked at Nathalie's group home, managed to get her in the house before she totally lost it. But now it was only Nathalie and Harper in her bedroom, with Harper futilely attempting to contain the situation.

"No, no, no," Nathalie repeated over and over, shaking her head rapidly.

Today Becky had done Nathalie's hair in two long braids with a red feather woven into one. When Nathalie shook her head, Harper had to be careful to move out of the way because the braids were like whips.

"What, Mom?" Harper asked gently.

"This isn't right," Nathalie insisted. She paced her room,

which was hard to do, since she'd thrown everything around in the room.

The staff had informed Harper that Nathalie had done it yesterday during some kind of tantrum. Her clothes and stuffed animals were all over the floor, along with her stereo and her beloved Justin Bieber CDs.

The policy here was that if Nathalie made a mess, she had to be the one to clean it up. She struggled with responsibility, and the staff were trying to make her understand the consequences of her actions. If her stuff got broken because she threw it on the floor, then she had to deal with it.

"Mom, everything's fine," Harper lied. "Gemma's fine. She's just at a swim meet."

Telling the truth wouldn't do her mother any good, at least not right now. And Harper just wanted to get her calmed down before she hurt herself.

"No, she's not!" Nathalie insisted. "I'm her mother. I'm supposed to protect her. She told me where she was going, but I can't remember where."

"What?" Harper asked, and her heart stopped beating for a second. "Gemma told you where she was going?"

"She told me when she came before, and I can't remember." Nathalie hit herself in the head, rather hard by the sound of it. "My stupid brain doesn't work!"

"Mom, don't hit yourself." Harper went over to her mother and gently touched her arm to prevent her from hitting herself again.

"I should know this, Harper!" Nathalie wriggled away from

her. In her attempt to escape, she tripped over a tennis shoe on the floor and fell.

Harper bent to help her up, but Nathalie swatted at her, pushing her away.

"Mom, please," Harper said, crouching down next to her. "Let me help you."

"If you want to help me, tell me where Gemma is," Nathalie said. "I've lost her." She started crying then, heavy tears falling down her cheeks. "I can't find her. Something's happened to my baby, and I don't know where she is."

Harper wrapped her arms around her mother, holding her as she sobbed. She stroked her hair, and all the while Nathalie kept repeating over and over that she'd lost her baby.

Her mother cried for a long time, and when she finally stopped, she seemed exhausted. Harper helped her into bed, and Nathalie passed out almost immediately.

When Harper left the room, she closed the door quietly behind her so as not to wake her mother. Becky was in the kitchen, setting the table for lunch, and she gave Harper a knowing smile when she saw how weary Harper looked.

"She's sleeping now," Harper said.

"Good," Becky said. "Maybe she'll be in a better mood when she wakes up."

"I hope so," Harper said. "And I'm sorry about all that."

It wasn't her fault that Nathalie acted out and got out of control sometimes. Deep down, Harper knew that. But she still felt responsible for all of her mother's bad behaviors. Whenever the family would get word about Nathalie treating the staff badly or breaking things, Harper would instantly feel guilty, like she should somehow be able to make her mother act better.

"Don't worry about it." Becky waved off the idea of guilt. "She's been having a rough week anyway."

"What do you mean?" Harper asked.

"She's been asking about your sister a lot, which is strange because she doesn't ask about either of you all that often," Becky said, then instantly looked apologetic. "I know she loves you both very much. It just doesn't occur to her to ask about you."

"No, I understand," Harper said. "What exactly has she been asking about Gemma?"

"Mostly just where is she and when is she coming to visit," Becky said. "I kept telling her that Gemma would be here today, and I was really hoping that when she came today, it would calm Nathalie down."

"Sorry. I should've called and told you, I guess," Harper said. "But Gemma's not . . . Gemma ran away."

"Oh?" Becky's eyes widened with concern.

"Yeah, she left earlier this week, but we hadn't planned on telling my mom," Harper said. "At least not yet. I didn't want to worry her."

"Of course, I understand." Becky nodded. "But, gosh, that's so weird. It's like Nathalie knew that Gemma was missing."

"Yeah, I know," Harper agreed. "I was wondering if maybe Gemma said something to her when she visited last Sunday? Did my mom say anything about where Gemma might be going?"

Last week, they'd skipped their Saturday visit, because Gemma had been comforting Alex over his friend Luke's death. Harper and Gemma had gone out to see their mom on Sunday instead, and Harper had planned on going in with her, but Gemma asked to visit Nathalie alone.

"No, sorry," Becky said sadly. "The only thing your mom said after Gemma visited was that she was going to live with mermaids, and we didn't put much stock in that. Maybe it means something to you?"

"Um, no." Harper shook her head. She couldn't very well tell her mother's assisted living staff that Gemma had turned into a siren.

"Sorry," Becky said again. "Wish I could be of more help."

"No, you're plenty of help, thanks." Harper smiled faintly at her. "I'll see you next week, then."

Harper wasn't surprised that Gemma had told their mother about what she'd planned on doing. Nathalie would've been the only person who wouldn't think she was insane or try to stop her from doing something stupid.

As hard as it had been seeing her mother act the way she had today, there was actually something sweet about it. Nathalie couldn't remember what Gemma had said, but it had gotten through to her that her daughter was in trouble. All week she'd been worrying about her.

Harper didn't want her mother to be upset, but she wasn't always sure that Nathalie still loved them. Her mother had a severe traumatic brain injury, and when it came to love, everyone always told her that Nathalie loved them "in her own way" and "as best as she could."

And Harper accepted that. She just didn't know exactly what that meant, but today it became a lot clearer.

She left feeling even more drained than she normally did after visiting Nathalie. Along the drive home her eyes blurred with tears, and she had to blink them back so she could see the road.

When she finally got home, she noticed her father's truck was gone, so he was presumably still at the lawyer's. Harper pulled in the driveway behind Gemma's beat-up Chevy. It hadn't moved since it had died on Gemma, and now she wondered dimly if her sister would ever drive it again.

Harper shook her head, trying to clear it from that kind of thinking, and she knew she couldn't spend the afternoon alone in the house.

She got out of the car and was headed toward Alex's house when she spotted him in the backyard. Dark clouds were gathering overhead, looking almost black on the horizon, and Alex was staring up at them.

This wasn't the first time Harper had caught Alex gazing up at the sky. He'd always been fascinated by the weather and the stars. In recent years, his fascination had turned into career aspirations.

He'd even started working with storm chasers this past spring, tracking thunderstorms, tornadoes, and even hurricanes, which Harper was actually surprised to learn. She'd always thought that Alex would prefer analyzing things from the comfort of his home, but apparently he didn't mind danger as long as he was passionate about what he was chasing.

"What are you doing?" Harper asked when she walked up behind him.

"Oh, hey." Alex turned around, looking surprised to see her, and gave her a half smile. A gust of wind came up, blowing his hair back. "I didn't see you there."

"I didn't mean to sneak up on you," she said. "I just came to see what you were up to this afternoon."

Alex shrugged. "Not a whole lot."

"It seems like a storm is coming," Harper said, hugging her arms to her chest to shield herself from the chill of the wind.

"Yeah, but the worst is going to be farther west." He pointed to the line of clouds. "We'll get rain and wind, but I'm thinking there might be hail farther inland."

"Are you gonna go out and chase it, or whatever it is you do?" Harper asked.

"Nah." He shook his head. "Some of the people I've gone with before are out. They think there might even be a tornado, but I don't think it's likely."

"So why aren't you with them?" Harper asked. "I know you love that kinda thing."

"I do," he agreed. "It just doesn't feel right. Not with Gemma still being gone."

"Oh." She let out a deep breath. "Have you heard anything new on that?"

"Not really," he said, then corrected himself. "Nothing useful, anyway."

"That sucks."

"I went to the police today," Alex admitted, sounding sheepish about it.

"Did you really?" Harper asked. "What for?"

"I just wanted to know what they were doing to find Gemma."

"What *are* they doing?" Harper asked.

"Not a whole lot," Alex said. "I mean, I can't really blame them. They're still looking into the murders of Luke and those other boys, and Gemma just ran away from home. She's not exactly their top priority."

"Yeah." Harper hadn't really expected any different, but she'd hoped for more than that. "Do they have any leads on the murders?"

"I don't think so." He shook his head. "They asked me a couple more questions about Luke, but I didn't tell them anything." He paused for a minute, thinking. "The sirens killed him and the others, right?"

Harper hesitated before answering him, then nodded. "Yes, they did."

"But I can't tell the cops that." Alex sounded exasperated. "They'd think I was crazy, and if they didn't, they'd think Gemma was involved. And she wasn't."

Harper swallowed hard when Alex said that, but she didn't respond. Not for the first time, she wondered exactly what Gemma's involvement with the sirens was.

"You should go, then," Harper said.

"What?" Alex turned to look at her, confused.

"If there's nothing new on Gemma, you should go," Harper

told him. "I'm home, so I'll be here if she gets back. There's nothing more you can do. You can't sit cooped in your house all the time, waiting for her to come back. You need to do something."

He hesitated before asking, "Are you sure?"

"Yeah." She nodded. "Go on. Go track your storm. Have fun. I'll be here."

"You're right." He gave her a small smile. "I'll have my cell phone if you need me."

He hurried back in the house to gather his things, and it was almost as if he'd been waiting for permission. Harper knew he cared about Gemma a lot and didn't want to do anything to betray her, but he couldn't stop living just because she was missing.

Thunder boomed in the distance, and Harper watched the approaching storm. She thought back to what Alex had said about the sirens, and she couldn't shake her new fears.

She didn't believe that Gemma had hurt anybody. At least not yet. But if the sirens were monsters, how long would it be before her sister acted like a monster, too?

TWELVE

Compulsion

"Today is the first day of the rest of my life," Gemma told her reflection. It was her attempt at a pep talk, but it wasn't that effective.

What Penn had said to her the other day had finally gotten through to her. Gemma had made a choice to be with the sirens, and since they were immortal, it was a very long commitment. She couldn't spend the rest of eternity moping because this wasn't what she'd wanted. She'd been living with them for nearly a week, and that was enough sulking.

Admittedly, she'd had to leave behind everything she cared about, her friends, family, boyfriend, and the swimming career she'd worked so hard for. Those were plenty of reasons to be heartbroken, but she'd given herself time to grieve. Now it was time to make the best of things.

Since she'd started swimming every day, she felt much better. Not great, but better. She was no longer nauseated, which made the hunger more intense, but she was managing it so far.

Thea had told her that Aggie had been kind, and Thea herself didn't seem so bad. That meant that while being a siren might not be a choice, being evil was. So Gemma would simply choose not to be evil, and try to make the best of everything else this life had to offer.

She woke up determined to have a new attitude about the whole thing. She got up, showered, got dressed, and went downstairs to see what the sirens were up to for the day.

Gemma found all three of them and Sawyer in the living room watching *Splash* on the giant flat-screen. Thea was sprawled out on her belly with her chin propped up on her hands, while Lexi and Penn were sitting on the white sofa with Sawyer between them.

Lexi kept laughing at what was happening on-screen, but Gemma couldn't tell if it was because she thought the movie was funny or because of the way mermaids were portrayed.

"Hey, guys," Gemma said.

Penn turned to her. Her eyes were as dark and sinister as ever, but a seductive smile played on her lips. "Look, girls, it's alive!"

Sawyer looked confused for a minute, but when Lexi laughed, he joined in.

"Since you slept all morning, Penn thought you might be dead," Lexi explained with a giggle.

"Well . . . I'm not."

"What do you need?" Penn propped her elbow on the back of the couch so she could face her.

"Nothing." Gemma tried to smile widely. "I just wanted to see what you were up to today."

Penn narrowed her eyes. "Why?"

"I wanted to see if maybe I could join you," Gemma said.

Thea turned to look at her for the first time, and for a few moments all three of the sirens just stared at her. Sawyer was too busy watching the movie to notice.

"We're just watching a movie," Lexi said finally, breaking the staring contest. "That's probably what we're going to do all day, if you want to hang out with us."

"Sure, that sounds fun."

Gemma planned on sitting on the other couch in the room, but Lexi scooted over, sliding up right next to Sawyer. He'd been sitting closer to Penn with his hand on her thigh, but when Lexi moved over, he smiled and slid his arm around her.

"Here you go." Lexi tapped the empty spot on the couch. "You can sit by me, Gemma."

"There's not enough room," Penn said, and glared at Lexi.

"Penn, there's plenty of room." Lexi gestured to the spot next to her, and really there was more than enough room for Gemma. In fact, Lexi hadn't even needed to slide over, and there would've been room for her.

"No, there's not," Penn growled.

"Fine." Lexi sighed and turned back to Gemma. "Sorry, I guess—"

"No, Lexi, there's no room for *you*," Penn corrected her.

Lexi's head snapped back around so she could look at Penn. "What?"

"You know, I'm fine sitting over here," Gemma interjected as she edged back to the empty couch on the other side of the room. "I can see the TV great from here."

"Sit on the floor, Lexi," Penn commanded, ignoring Gemma.

"*Penn,*" Lexi tried to protest, but Penn just kept glaring at her. "Whatever." Lexi rolled her eyes, then got up and flopped down on the floor next to Thea.

With Lexi banished to the floor, Penn smiled sweetly up at Gemma. "Why don't you sit with us on the couch?"

"Uh, sure?" Gemma sat down tentatively on the couch, careful to put as much room between her and Sawyer as she could manage.

Truthfully, she didn't care where she sat. But this was obviously some sort of power play on Penn's part, and she didn't want to get caught in the middle of it. Especially not when she'd just decided to make the best of the situation. She didn't want to start by pissing off Penn *or* Lexi.

"Oh, my god." Sawyer laughed and pointed to the TV. "She thinks the video cameras are trapping her in the box. That's so funny."

Eventually, in large part to Sawyer's oblivious commentary on the movie, the tension in the room seemed to ease. Gemma settled into the couch, and she ended up kind of enjoying the movie. She'd never seen it before, and it had its moments.

The funniest parts probably were Sawyer's reactions. Most of the time, when Thea, Lexi, and Gemma were laughing, it was at something he'd said. Penn never laughed once, though.

Every now and then Gemma would glance over to see Penn's

eyes fixed blankly on the screen. Despite that, Gemma couldn't shake the feeling that Penn was watching her out of the corner of her eye, making sure that Gemma was behaving herself.

After the movie ended, the girls argued about what movie to watch next, and finally Lexi put in *Mannequin*.

Gemma started to relax then. So what if Penn was watching her? It wasn't like she was doing anything wrong. She was watching a movie, same as everybody else.

Seemingly out of the blue, Gemma's hunger flared up. The ravenous one that seemed to radiate from her belly all the way through her. She bit her lip and struggled to swallow the feeling down.

Then Sawyer laughed, and Gemma turned to look at him. But it was almost as if she'd never seen him before. He had to be the most attractive person she'd ever seen. His smooth tanned skin, the hard contours of his chest, the strong line of his jaw, even the way his blond hair just touched the nape of his neck.

Her whole body tingled as intense heat spread through her. A kind of primal lust that started in her belly traveled down her thighs.

Gemma wanted nothing more in the world than to touch him and kiss him and taste him. Her hands trembled at the thought of it, and she licked her lips.

"You okay, Gemma?" Penn asked, barely breaking the trance that Gemma was under.

"What?" Gemma asked.

She blinked, trying to clear her head, but all her thoughts still involved kissing Sawyer and ripping off his shirt. He was so close to her that she could nearly do it, and that was when Gemma realized she'd somehow moved closer to him. She was nearly touching him, the smooth, warm skin of his arm.

"Gemma," Penn repeated, her tone harder this time. "Are you enjoying the movie?"

"Uh, yeah." Using all her willpower, Gemma forced herself to scoot away from Sawyer. To be on the safe side, she tucked both her hands underneath her so she was sitting on them. "It's a good movie."

The next few minutes seemed to stretch on for hours. All Gemma could think about was Sawyer. He was so gorgeous and so close, and she was certain that she'd never wanted anyone more. She tried to think of Alex, but just then she could barely even remember his face, let alone how she felt about him.

Without warning, Penn leaned over and started kissing Sawyer. And not just a gentle peck on the lips. Penn climbed over, straddling him between her legs, as she kissed him deeply. She pushed her body against him, and he moaned.

"Holy crap," Gemma muttered to herself, and then stood up.

Watching Penn make out with Sawyer was messing with her head. It somehow managed to both increase her lust and repulse her at the same time.

Fortunately, the logical part of her won out, and she backed away from the couch.

"I think I'm going to go for a swim," Gemma said, and for some reason she was nearly shouting.

"I'll join you," Thea said, jumping to her feet.

Lexi was still on the floor, but she'd turned around to watch

Penn and Sawyer make out, which Gemma thought was rather creepy.

Thea walked with Gemma through the house and out the back door. As soon as Gemma felt the ocean breeze, she felt like she could think again. The bizarre lust had retreated, leaving behind confusion and shame as she tried to make sense of her feelings.

She'd never felt like that before, or had such extreme thoughts before. It had to have something to do with being a siren. It definitely wasn't Gemma. She loved Alex and thought he was a super fox, and yet she'd never wanted to attack him the way she had wanted Sawyer.

"I'm so glad you're swimming now," Thea said as they walked down the beach toward the water. "I was getting sick of watching you sulk."

"How come Lexi didn't join us?" Gemma asked when they reached the water. "What is she doing in there with Penn and Sawyer?"

"Honestly?" Thea turned to face her so she walked backward into the waves. "I don't even want to know what Lexi and Penn do when I'm not around."

"Gross," Gemma said, and Thea laughed in agreement.

THIRTEEN

Sanitize

Harper stared at what had become of Bernie's house and tried not to let it overwhelm her. She put her hand on her hip and took a deep breath.

"It's really not *that* bad," Daniel said from behind her, sensing her unease and trying to calm her. "It's mostly junk thrown around. We can pick that up, no problem."

"Yeah, you're right." She nodded to convince herself.

Daniel brushed past her, carrying a box of cleaning supplies she'd brought from home. "Do you want to start with the living room, since that looks a bit easier than the kitchen?"

The kitchen wouldn't have been so bad if the sirens hadn't emptied the fridge. Apparently there wasn't much in there, but a jug of milk had been spilled on the floor for nearly a week, along with some fresh veggies that had begun to rot in the heat.

"Why don't you take the living room?" Harper suggested. "I'll start with the kitchen."

"I can help you," Daniel offered. "I mean, that is why I came out here today."

"I know." She smiled at him. "But you're already helping me enough. I think I can handle scrubbing up some sour milk."

Harper's father had gone to see the lawyer yesterday to sign the papers. The lawyer had made a special point of meeting Brian on a Saturday since it was hard for him to get off work during the week. The house wasn't theirs yet, not officially, but it was only a matter of the papers being processed. So Harper thought she'd get a jump start on cleaning the place. She'd asked Daniel to help her, since she needed a boat to get out to the island and they were working on being friends.

The police had released the crime scene a few days before, but there was still yellow tape stuck to the door and around the trees where they'd found the body. Other than that, the place didn't look like it had been disturbed much since Harper had seen it last, so she wondered how much digging around the police had even done.

If they did any fingerprinting, Daniel and Alex would have to make up a story. Gemma and Harper had plenty of reasons to have fingerprints there, since they'd both been out to Bernie's many times.

But Harper wasn't too worried about that. She, Alex, and Daniel had come up with an alibi for that night, which they'd already told the police: they were arguing with Gemma, and then she ran off with Penn, Lexi, and Thea.

Alex and Daniel could easily come up with logical reasons

for being at Bernie's place. Alex had visited with Gemma once, maybe. And Daniel delivered groceries to Bernie.

Both of those excuses would work, and the police would probably go back to pursuing the three unidentified sets of prints in the cabin. Harper seriously doubted the sirens had ever been fingerprinted.

"So are you moving out here, then?" Daniel asked, drawing Harper from her thoughts as she scrubbed milk off the kitchen tiles.

"What?" She glanced back to see him picking up all of Bernie's books and putting them on the shelves.

"Now that you own the place, I was wondering if you're going to move out here," Daniel said. "Is that what we're cleaning it up for?"

"No, I'm not moving out here." She'd gotten the milk off the floor, so she stood up and wrung out her washcloth in the sink.

"Why not?" Daniel asked. "It's a nice place."

"No, I know. I just . . ." A strand of hair had come loose from her ponytail, and she tucked it behind her ear. "I'm leaving for college soon. And even if I wasn't, there's too many memories here."

"Too many memories?" Daniel had finished putting all the books back on the shelf, and he moved on to uprighting the coffee table. "Aren't they mostly good memories?"

"Well, yeah," she said. "But that last night was . . ."

She grabbed a garbage bag so she wouldn't have to talk about the last time she'd been here, when she'd seen Bernie's dead body and the horrible monsters attacking her and her sister.

"So what are you going to do with this place?" Daniel asked.

"I don't know," Harper replied as she filled the bag with spoiled food and the garbage strewn about the floor. "Sell it, I guess."

"Sell it?" Daniel scoffed. "Why would you do that? Why wouldn't your dad just move out here?"

"He can't," Harper replied. "I mean, I guess he could, but he can't sell his house, and he can't really afford the upkeep on two places, especially on an island like this."

"Why can't he sell his house?" Daniel asked.

"He has, like, three mortgages on it," Harper explained. "Nine years ago my mom and I were in a car accident, and she had a ton of medical bills. It was a drunk driver with no money or insurance, so all the bills fell on my dad."

"Wow." He grimaced. "I'm sorry about that."

"It's not your fault. It's just the way things are."

She'd filled the garbage bag, so she stopped to survey the house. They hadn't even been cleaning that long, and it already looked so much better. It almost looked like when Bernie had lived here.

"It will be so weird to think of somebody else living here," Harper said, more to herself than to Daniel. "I mean, this is *Bernie's* Island."

"It'll always be Bernie's Island," Daniel assured her. "No matter who lives here, this will always be Bernie's."

They spent the rest of the afternoon cleaning up the place as best they could. If Brian did sell it, they would eventually have to get rid of all Bernie's possessions, but Harper didn't want to do that right now. She just wanted to get it clean.

The sun was starting to set when Harper flopped on the couch and called it quits.

"I think we did a good job," she said.

"Are you kidding?" Daniel asked, grinning down at her. "We did an amazing job. You scrubbed a ring out from the bathtub that I'm certain had been there since that tub was installed."

Harper laughed, but she didn't argue with him. "Hey, when I do something, I do it right."

"That you do."

Daniel sat down on the couch next to her, closer than he needed to, but Harper didn't say anything. There had been little moments like this all day long, and she didn't know how to react to them. When he'd hand her something, his touch seemed to linger a little too long. Or when he helped her lift something, he'd reach around her, nearly hugging her in the process.

She kept telling herself that he was just being helpful, the little touches meant nothing, or it was all in her head. But still, every time he brushed up against her she found her heart beating a bit faster.

There were more than a few times when she'd meant only to glance over at him and she found her gaze lingering. Especially when he'd been working in the bedroom.

The whole bed had been flipped over, the headboard smashed, the dresser completely destroyed. Bernie didn't believe in AC, so it was about a hundred degrees in the bedroom. Daniel had taken off his T-shirt as he strained and lifted the broken wood, tossing it out an open window before he took it to the woodpile to chop up for the fireplace.

Harper had offered to help him, but Daniel had insisted that he had it under control. She'd been sweeping the living room, and she'd found herself stopping to stare at him far more often than she should have.

There was something about the way he looked when he moved. The muscles in his back and arms flexing as he lifted the dismantled furniture. And that tattoo, which Harper had first thought was evidence that Daniel was bad news, she now found so appealing.

It was a thick black tree, with the roots growing out from the waistband of his boxers that were showing just above his jeans. The trunk grew upward, over his spine, then twisted to the side so the branches extended out over his shoulder and down his right arm.

He'd once caught her staring, and she looked down in a flash, blushing, but he'd only laughed at her. Daniel said that she ought to think about getting a tattoo, and then she hurried off to clean something far away, so she wouldn't be able to gawk at him.

"Thank you for coming out to help me today," Harper said, now that they were finished and he'd unfortunately put his T-shirt back on. "Not everybody would want to spend their Sunday cleaning up a house."

"No problem." He stretched his arms out so one rested on the couch behind her, but it wasn't exactly around her. "I told you I'm always happy to help."

"I know, but I really appreciate it," she said. "I needed to get out and do something instead of moping about Gemma or worrying about her or talking about her with Alex or my dad."

"Well, I was happy to help you keep your mind off her." He looked over at her. "And I'll be more than happy to help you keep your mind off anything anytime you want."

"Thanks." She smiled when she looked over at him, but something about the look in his eyes made her smile fall away.

His arm had moved, so she could feel his hand on her shoulder. It felt strong and rough on her skin, and he was holding her, moving her closer to him as his hazel eyes stared into hers. She leaned in to him, and just when she thought he was about to kiss her, he spoke.

"We should probably get going before it gets dark," he said.

"We should," Harper agreed when she found her voice.

He turned away from her and rather abruptly got up and walked away, leaving Harper dismayed on the couch.

"I'm going to start carrying the garbage out to my boat." Daniel walked away and didn't look back.

"Yeah, um, I'll help you." Harper jumped to her feet and hurried after him, but he'd already grabbed all the bags by the time she reached him.

When they got on his boat, he barely spoke a word to her.

FOURTEEN

Cravings

Gemma spent the whole morning in the ocean, swimming with Thea, Penn, and Lexi. Penn told Sawyer to stay behind, because she wanted to swim out farther and faster than he could go. And though she hated to admit it, Gemma was glad for that.

Penn led her out farther than she'd ventured on her own before. Gemma had set limits, afraid of enjoying herself too much, but with her new vow to heed Penn's advice, Gemma let herself enjoy the exploration.

The four of them swam together, flitting between one another like they were performing an underwater ballet. Penn swam quickly, driving them forward, and now they had to be miles from shore. Not only that, but they went deeper down than Gemma had gone before.

The sunlight barely broke through the water, and it was so dark Gemma could hardly see. Fortunately, the iridescent scales of the sirens' tails managed to shimmer in what little light made it down here, so Gemma could keep track of them.

When they finally surfaced after darting around the ocean, chasing each other and whatever sea life crossed their path, Gemma was relieved. The deeper they went, the colder the water got, until Gemma was nearly shivering. Now the sun warmed her skin as she stared out at the waves around her.

"I told you it was a great day for a swim," Lexi said, grinning broadly as she floated next to Gemma.

"Everything's so much easier when you play along," Penn said, her voice an odd mixture of silk and contempt. "Isn't it, Gemma?"

"It is," she admitted, and wiped the salt water from her eyes. "But I think I'm going to head back to shore."

"You're such a party pooper." Lexi pretended to pout, but Gemma couldn't imagine that she actually cared all that much if Gemma stayed or not.

"Sorry, guys. I've had enough swimming for today."

Penn narrowed her eyes at her, as if trying to decipher something. "You aren't getting tired, are you?"

"No." Gemma forced a smile at her. "I'm just getting a little cold. I think I want to go lie out on the beach."

Penn didn't seem convinced, but she shrugged noncommittally. "Suit yourself. Thea, head back with her."

Thea sighed and didn't argue with Penn, but Gemma thought she looked disappointed. Thea had seemed to be enjoying herself. She'd chased a sea turtle for a while, and Gemma didn't want to make Thea leave if she was still having fun.

"No, that's okay," Gemma said. "Thea can stay with you guys. I know my way back to the shore."

Thea and Gemma both turned to Penn, waiting for her response, and at length Penn nodded.

"Fine," Penn said. "We'll see you when we get back."

Gemma turned and headed back toward the beach house, a little surprised that Penn had let her go. Apparently Gemma had proven herself enough that Penn had begun to trust her. That was probably a good thing.

She stayed close to the surface of the water as she swam, letting the sun warm her back as she headed toward the land.

When she'd said she was getting cold it hadn't been a lie, but that wasn't the only reason she'd wanted to go back. She was getting tired. It was hard for her to keep up with the other sirens, and she had a feeling that it had to do with the awful gnawing hunger in the pit of her stomach.

Her fins were slow to transform back to legs when she reached the sand, and her stomach lurched. Thea had told her that the daily swims would only hold off her need to feed for so long, but Gemma was determined to put it off as long as she could.

She swallowed hard and forced herself to her feet, though her legs felt wobbly underneath her. When she pulled on the bikini bottoms she'd left on the beach, she nearly fell over. She waited a minute, steadying herself, before slipping on her sundress over her head.

By the time she made it to the house, she felt a bit better. Her strength seemed to be returning, and the hunger pains in her stomach had abated. The transformation had just been unusually grueling today. That was all.

Gemma planned on heading upstairs to her room to lie down for a while, but Sawyer caught her just as she reached the steps.

"Hey, Gemma." He smiled at her in a way that had only seemed mildly dazzling a couple days ago. But since yesterday, she'd been unable to completely shake this strange new attraction to him.

To make matters worse, he was shirtless and walking over to her.

"Hi, Sawyer," Gemma mumbled, and looked away from him.

"The other girls are still out swimming?" Sawyer asked.

She nodded. "Yep. They're out there. And I was just gonna head up to my room."

"Oh, cool." He moved toward her, like he meant to walk up the stairs with her. "I was just heading that way, too."

"Why?" Gemma blurted out.

Sawyer stood on the bottom step next to her, and it was impossible not to look at him. Or to ignore the proximity. His eyes were so unbelievably blue, and his arms looked so strong. She breathed in deeply. He even smelled like the sea.

"I was going up to my room." Sawyer cocked his head, maybe noticing the change taking over Gemma. "Did you want to join me?"

"*No!*" She hadn't meant to sound so forceful, but he didn't seem to notice. He seemed just as entranced by her as she was by him.

It wasn't lust and it wasn't hunger, but some dangerous combination of the two. She *craved* him in a way she hadn't known it was possible to crave a human being. Her mind was filled with the same thoughts as yesterday, of all the things she wanted to do to Sawyer, but then it all turned into a blurry haze. She couldn't think, and all she could feel was a blazing heat that threatened to consume her.

She reacted on instinct, doing what her body told her to do. She didn't even realize what she was doing until she felt Sawyer's lips pressed against hers. She'd thrown her arms around him, pressing her body as tightly as she could against the warm contours of his, and kissing him ferociously.

The only reason she stopped kissing him was that she needed to breathe, and she felt his lips on her neck, trailing down her collarbone. Hot tingles radiated through her, reminding her of when her legs shifted into a tail, and dimly she wondered if she was transforming into something else.

Then suddenly Alex flashed into her mind. When the hunger/lust had first taken over her, it had blocked him from her thoughts, but now she remembered him again. She loved him, and she still thought of him as her boyfriend, even if she wasn't sure that she'd ever see him again.

So this with Sawyer, this was cheating on him. Maybe for a second she'd lost control, and that could be forgiven. But she remembered now, and she had to get back in control before she did something with Sawyer that she'd regret forever.

"No," Gemma said. She started pushing against his chest, but Sawyer ignored her, still kissing the spot just above her heart. "I said *no*!" She pushed more forcefully then, and he went flying back, slamming hard against the railing behind him.

"Did I do something wrong?" Sawyer asked in a daze.

"Yes!" Gemma shouted, then shook her head. It was a struggle for her to keep from attacking him again. "No. I don't know. But I have to get out of here."

"I'm sorry." He moved toward her in some attempt at an apology, and Gemma jumped off the step, getting away from him before she gave in to her urges.

"Where are your keys?" Gemma asked, realizing the house was far too small for her to stay away from him. Sawyer stared blankly at her, not understanding. "I need to get out of here! Where are your car keys?"

"They're on a hook by the garage."

She turned and ran toward the garage, but Sawyer followed, asking her where she was going and apologizing for upsetting her. She never answered him, though. She just grabbed the keys off the rack and dove into his convertible.

Gemma sped off without knowing where she was going or how to get there, but the wind was in her hair, helping clear her head of the bizarre lust that had consumed her inside the house. She wasn't sure if she was ever going back to the house, or if she could ever handle herself around Sawyer again. All she knew was that she had to get the hell away from that house as fast as she could.

FIFTEEN

Superstitious

The idea had been Marcy's, and Harper thought it was idiotic. Harper had woken up Monday morning with renewed vigor and determination to find Gemma. She'd been gone for a week already, and Harper had yet to hear anything from her.

Before going to work this morning, she did her morning routine of making phone calls to everyone she could think of. Alex continued to scour the Internet, not just with his FindGemmaFisher pages, but searching for any news stories that might relate to the sirens at all.

The problem was that Gemma could literally be anywhere. She could've swum across the Atlantic, for all Harper knew, which made it impossible to pin down any type of location. So until Harper got some kind of clue or lead, she was stuck making phone calls, searching the Web, and going about her daily life and hoping that Gemma was taking care of herself.

It was while Harper was at work that Alex stopped by the

library, and the two of them began lamenting the lack of search options for Gemma. Then Marcy came up with her brilliant idea.

"Why don't you ask Gemma where she's at?" Marcy asked.

Harper was standing at the copy machine, making flyers for the new July summer reading program. Alex was sitting in Harper's chair at the desk, and both of them were completely caught off guard by Marcy's question.

"What?" Harper asked, and turned around to look at her.

Marcy was sitting on top of the desk, even though there was a perfectly good chair next to it, and was focused on making herself a necklace out of paper clips.

"You keep saying that Gemma could be anywhere, like Spain or Japan or Kentucky."

"I never said Kentucky," Harper corrected her. "The sirens wouldn't go to the middle of the country. They'd want to be by the ocean."

"Well, exactly." Marcy bit her lip in concentration as she tried to unhook a paper clip that had gotten bent. "She could be anywhere. So the easiest way to find her is to ask her."

"We can't just ask her," Alex said. "We have no idea how to contact her. She left her cell phone behind, and I've been checking her Twitter and Facebook, but she hasn't been on them."

Marcy rolled her eyes. "I don't mean call her or drop her a postcard."

"Okay . . ." Harper said after Marcy went several moments without saying anything. "How do you propose we contact her?"

"We use the spirits," Marcy said.

"The spirits?" Harper raised an eyebrow. "You mean like Capri Liquor Wine & Spirits?" Marcy looked up from her paper clips to glare at Harper.

"Gemma's not dead, though." Alex leaned on the desk and looked up at Marcy. "She's not a ghost, so we can't just ask her."

"*She* isn't," Marcy agreed. "But that friend of yours is, and so is Bernie."

"My friend?" Alex questioned. "You mean Luke?"

"Right." Marcy finished her necklace, and she dropped it around her neck. "Both Bernie and Luke were murdered by the sirens. At least one of them has to be a restless spirit, haunted by the fact that their murderers got away with it, and I bet they're keeping tabs on the sirens, too."

Harper rolled her eyes. "Oh, come on, Marcy. That's ridiculous."

"You really think that Luke would know where Gemma and the other girls are hiding?" Alex asked, oblivious to Harper's comments.

"Probably." Marcy nodded. "I mean, if Penn had killed you and ripped out your heart, then run off to frolic in the ocean, wouldn't you be pissed off and stalk her?"

"I probably would," Alex reasoned. "So how do we go about this? How would we try contacting them?"

"Alex!" Harper said in disbelief. "You can't really be buying into this."

"Your sister is a siren," Alex said, looking back at her. "She can turn into a mermaid. But ghosts seem unbelievable to you?"

Harper crossed her arms over her chest and leaned back

against the copier, but she didn't say anything. Alex had made a point she couldn't really argue with, but that didn't mean she still didn't think this was all stupid.

"Do I need to get like a Ouija board or something?" Alex asked.

Marcy scoffed loudly. "Ouija. Pfft. That's all hokum."

"Okay," Alex said. "So how do we contact the spirits?"

"Why don't I meet you at your house after work, and I'll bring everything we need?" Marcy suggested.

Even though Harper thought it was dumb, she didn't have any better ideas, so she went along with it. Alex went home, and after work Marcy went home to get her stuff, then was going to meet them at Alex's house.

Harper waited outside with Alex, sitting on the front steps of his house. He wasn't sure what to bring, if anything, so he'd grabbed the video camera he used to record storms and a pocketknife in the shape of Batman's batarang.

"You really think this will work?" Harper asked, watching him as he flipped the blade in and out of the pocketknife.

"I don't know," Alex admitted. "But I don't know what else to try. I've got to do something, and I'm running out of options."

"Can I ask you something?"

Alex shrugged. "Sure."

"Why do . . ." Harper tried to choose her words carefully. "You're really passionate about finding Gemma, and I'm glad. It's just . . . it's a little strangely intense, since you and Gemma haven't been together that long."

"Is that your question?" Alex asked, looking over at her.

"Kinda. I just don't fully understand why you care *so* much."

"But I've known her practically my whole life," Alex pointed out. "And it's not like I suddenly started having feelings for her the day we started dating. I mean, I've liked her for . . ." He trailed off, as if realizing he'd admitted more than he wanted to.

"When did you start liking her?" Harper asked.

He shifted uneasily. "I don't know the exact date."

Harper had known that Alex and Gemma liked each other for a little while, possibly longer than the two of them knew themselves. Alex would be over watching a movie with Harper or doing homework with her, but as soon as Gemma came in the room, he could barely pay attention to the task at hand.

That eventually had put a strain on her friendship with Alex. She didn't mind so much that he liked Gemma. It just weirded her out that they'd be hanging out in her room, and Gemma would be across the hall in hers, and Alex would suddenly get up and go hover in Gemma's doorway. It was obnoxious, so Harper had stopped hanging out with him as much.

"I think I noticed it a few months ago," Harper said. "You kept making eyes at her."

"I did not," he said quickly. "I don't even know what that means."

"There's nothing wrong with it," Harper said. "I'm just curious about how long you've had a crush on my sister."

"I don't know." He sighed, and when he spoke, his voice got quieter. "Maybe years."

"Years?" Harper asked loudly, thinking she must've heard wrong.

"I don't know." He lowered his eyes and looked uncomfortable. "I mean, it wasn't like a crush. It was just I really liked her, and she always thought I was such a dork. But then in the last year or so, something changed, and she started looking at me like I was a person, and not some geeky guy running around with her older sister. And then I think . . . I don't know."

"So you've been into Gemma for a really long time?" Harper asked, still trying to process what he was saying.

"I guess so," he admitted. "Sorry."

"Why are you sorry?" Harper asked.

"Because we were friends, and I didn't tell you?" Alex said as if he weren't sure why he was apologizing. "I feel like I wasn't supposed to have a crush on your sister."

"Honestly, I'm fine with you about it," Harper said, smiling at him to prove it. "It's just strange to me that I didn't realize you did."

"So that's why I'm kinda being such a freak about all of this," he said with a sad smile. "I *finally* get to be with Gemma, and then she's . . . gone."

"That would make me crazy, too." She twirled the bottle of water in her hands, staring down at it as she asked him the next question. "So . . . are you in love with Gemma?"

"I . . ." He ran a hand through his brown hair and hesitated to answer.

Marcy pulled up in front of the house, honking the horn on her Gremlin loudly as she parked. She got out of the car, carrying a book bag with Captain Planet on it as she walked up to the house.

"You cats and kittens ready to contact some spirits?" Marcy asked, but before anyone could answer, she noticed Alex's pocketknife. "Is that a batarang? Are you planning to batarang the spirit of your dead best friend?"

"No." He flipped out the blade to show her. "It's a knife."

"Oh, so you're gonna stab a ghost," Marcy said. "That's so much better."

"I didn't know what to bring. I thought we might need something to defend ourselves," Alex said.

"Well, we don't," Marcy said. "Now come on. Let's do this thing." Marcy turned and started walking away.

"Where are you going?" Alex asked, jumping up.

"Yeah, where is this *thing* taking place?" Harper asked as she followed Marcy and Alex away from their houses.

"Luke's body was found in the wooded area by the bay, right?" Marcy asked. "That's where we're going. His connection to the earth will be the strongest there. That'll make him easier to contact."

The trees where Harper and Alex had found the bodies weren't far from where they lived. Neither of them had been back there since they'd shown the police where to go. It wasn't someplace where Harper ever wanted to go again, so she slowed her steps when Marcy told them that was where they were headed.

"Are you coming, Harper?" Alex asked, glancing back over his shoulder at her. He hadn't slowed down even slightly. Harper knew that finding the bodies had really freaked him out, too, but apparently he was braver than she'd thought.

"Uh . . . yeah." She sighed and caught up to them.

Fortunately, when they got to the small cypress forest that ran along Anthemusa Bay, they didn't go into it. Marcy stopped abruptly before going in and declared that it gave her bad energy, and that apparently would interfere with contacting the spirits.

"We'll set it up here." Marcy motioned to a grassy patch just outside the trees. "Sit down in a circle."

"Shouldn't it be nighttime or something?" Alex asked, but he still did as he was told. He sat with his legs crossed underneath him, and Harper and Marcy sat on either side of him so they formed a small circle.

"Shouldn't what be nighttime?" Marcy asked. She set her book bag on her lap and began rummaging through it.

"It just feels weird to be doing a séance or whatever outside in the bright sunlight," Alex said.

"Yeah, I feel like we should be in a spooky room with candles and incense," Harper agreed.

"That's because you guys are idiots," Marcy told them.

"This coming from the girl who carries voodoo stuff in a Captain Planet backpack," Harper muttered.

Marcy glared at her. "Nobody messes with Captain Planet. He keeps looters, plunderers, and evil spirits at bay. *And* I don't practice voodoo. That's not my thing."

"What *is* your thing?" Harper asked.

"This." Marcy pulled out a handful of black stones, a faded book, and a thick white candle.

"I thought you said people who brought candles were idiots," Alex pointed out.

"No, I said you were idiots."

Marcy put the candle in the center of their circle, then carefully laid out the smooth black stones around it. When Alex reached out to touch one, Marcy slapped his hand. Then she set the backpack aside and opened the book on her lap.

"Now what?" Harper asked when Marcy appeared to be finished laying out everything.

"I'm going to read from this book," Marcy explained. "The incantation is in Latin. I don't know why. I guess the dead all speak a dead language. It's important that you don't interrupt me and you don't speak. Just sit quietly until I'm finished."

After Harper and Alex both nodded in understanding, Marcy flipped open the book and began reading from it. Harper had no idea what most of the words meant, but every now and then she'd catch one like "necro" and "terra."

As soon as Marcy finished, the candle lit up. A bluish flame burned from the wick, and even though the candle was white, the wax that dripped down the sides was black.

"How'd you do that?" Harper asked.

"I'm magic," Marcy said matter-of-factly, and closed the book. "So it's all set. We should be able to talk to Luke now."

"Really?" Alex asked. "I can just . . . talk to him?"

"Yeah. I would start by saying his name and seeing if he's around and wants to talk."

"How will we know if he wants to talk?" Alex asked. "Will he just talk back?"

"The stones will vibrate if something's present." Marcy motioned to the black rocks. "And then we talk to him and decide how he's going to answer. It's usually stuff like, *Knock once for yes, twice for no.*"

"How will he be able to name a place, then?" Alex asked. "If we say, *Where's Gemma?* it's not like he can knock once, and we'll go, *Oh, right, Toledo.*"

"Let's just see if he's here, and we'll take it from there," Marcy suggested. "You start, Alex, since you were closest to him."

"Okay. Um . . ." He took a deep breath, then cautiously said, "Luke? Uh, Luke Benfield? It's me, your friend Alex. Um, I wanted to know if you wanted to talk."

They waited a few minutes, and when there was no response, Alex tried again. Even Harper joined in, and eventually Marcy retried the incantation. But no matter what they said, they got no response.

All afternoon the three of them tried communing with Luke. The hot sun beat down on them, and Marcy grumbled about the heat a few times, but she stuck with the séance. The stones ended up vibrating twice, but Marcy could never make any contact beyond that.

"So that's it?" Alex asked when Marcy began packing up her stuff. "We're giving up?"

"Sorry, loverboy," Marcy said as the sun began to set. "There's nothing more I can do. We'll just have to go back to looking the old-fashioned way."

SIXTEEN

Wanderlust

Gemma reached a town about a half hour after leaving Sawyer's house, but she drove around in it for a long time before she stopped. She needed to be sure that her head was clear and her hunger was under control.

That was actually what made her finally decide to stop. She figured that eating people food would at least do something about her appetite.

The only thing Gemma knew about what sirens were supposed to eat was what Lexi had told her back in the cabin on Bernie's Island. Penn had wanted her to eat Alex, and Lexi had tried to convince her that eating him would be delicious.

But Gemma wasn't sure exactly how much truth was in that. Based on the way the sirens spoke, she assumed that they needed to feed on humans somehow, but she wasn't sure what that meant. Maybe they just drank blood like vampires. Or maybe they swallowed an entire person whole.

The only thing Gemma knew for certain was that she didn't want to find out. She wasn't yet at the point where cannibalism was an option, and she hoped she never got to that point.

But she still had to eat something, so she parked behind a restaurant. She'd wanted to park in front, but it was packed. Like Capri, this was another seaside resort, only much larger. The restaurant was a steakhouse, and that was why she'd picked it. She thought maybe eating a rare steak would be the best substitute for eating a person.

Before getting out of the car, Gemma checked herself in the mirror. She'd driven here with the windows open, and even though her hair had been blowing around for more than an hour, it still looked great. Gemma had to admit that she looked stunning. The glow that had grown dull the last few days had brightened up.

She wondered if maybe her kissing Sawyer had something to do with it. It occurred to Gemma that that was maybe what the sirens meant. Maybe they didn't eat boys literally, but it was a figure of speech. Maybe they were like a type of succubus that fed on lust and sex.

Honestly, Gemma wasn't too thrilled about that, either. She felt guilty enough just kissing Sawyer. She couldn't imagine how awful she'd feel if she had to sleep with him. She was in love with Alex, and even if she never saw him again, being with someone else would always feel like she was cheating on him.

Besides that, she'd always imagined her first time as being romantic, with someone she loved, not because she'd die if she didn't have sex.

But if it came down to killing someone or having sex with him, Gemma would pick the latter.

Of course, she had no idea if it would even come to that. She'd seen the kind of monster Penn had turned into, all fangs and claws. She doubted that that form was just for fun. Those teeth probably served a purpose, like devouring boys.

Gemma's stomach rumbled, and that spurred her into action. She wasn't wearing any shoes, but at least she'd put on a sundress over her bikini, otherwise she'd have real trouble trying to get a table at the restaurant.

Since Penn and Lexi were always off shopping, Gemma decided to check the trunk of Sawyer's car and see if the sirens had accidentally left any shoes behind. When she popped the trunk, it turned out better than she'd hoped.

There were several bags with clothes spilling out. She found a pair of flip-flops pretty early on, and then discovered the real prize—a purse containing several hundred dollars and one of Sawyer's credit cards. That was great, since Gemma hadn't thought to grab money when she made her escape.

The steakhouse seemed kind of fancy, so Gemma continued to search through the clothes in hopes of finding a nicer dress than the one she wore. She grabbed some fabric with a flower print on it, and before she'd pulled it out enough to determine if it was a skirt or a dress, she saw dark red splotches all over it.

It was unmistakable. The fabric was stained with blood.

Her heart thudded dully in her chest. Once she realized what she was holding, she dropped it in a hurry, not wanting to touch the blood. Hurriedly, she slipped on the flip-flops, grabbed the purse, and slammed the trunk shut.

Gemma stared down at the trunk, swallowing hard and slowing the panic rising in her chest. She knew the sirens were monsters. She had to assume that they did bad things. But she couldn't think about it. She couldn't do anything about it, at least not right now.

The best she could do was get herself under control, eat something before she freaked out, and then decide how she was going to deal with the situation.

She had to walk through a long alley to get around to the front of the restaurant, and that gave her time to calm down and cool off. By the time she reached the front door, she felt normal enough to smile at the maître'd.

The straps of her bikini were showing, and she was clearly underdressed. It wasn't a super-upscale place, but it was nice enough that flip-flops and a sundress shouldn't have cut it. The maître'd looked as if he were about to tell her just that, but then she smiled at him, and everything changed.

He apologized profusely that he couldn't find her a table right away and asked her to wait at the bar until one opened up. Gemma told him not to hurry, afraid he might actually kick people out to make room for her.

The sun was setting when she'd arrived, and based on the crowd, she guessed she'd hit the dinner rush. People were finally leaving the beaches and heading indoors to eat.

As she walked through the restaurant up to the bar, she could feel people looking at her. The room seemed to grow more hushed as she walked by. The power of the siren was still something she wasn't used to.

"What can I get for you?" the bartender asked her before she even had a chance to sit down on the stool.

"Um, just a Cherry Coke would be fine," Gemma said.

"Coming right up," he said, smiling brightly before dashing off to fill her order.

A guy was sitting two stools down, nursing his Long Island Iced Tea. Gemma happened to glance over at him, and she caught him looking at her. He apparently took that as some kind of invitation, and he moved next to her.

"Hey," he said with a Southern drawl. "What are you drinking?"

"Cherry Coke." No sooner had the words left her mouth than the bartender appeared in front of her with the drink.

"I gave you a couple extra cherries." The bartender winked at her and motioned at the three maraschino cherries in the glass.

"Thank you," Gemma said.

Another patron called to the bartender from the other end, and he reluctantly stepped away to do his job.

"So . . ." The guy next to her leaned on the bar, moving closer to her. "Are you from around here?"

"No." Gemma deliberately stared straight ahead and stirred her drink with the straw. She wanted to eat the cherries, but she was afraid it might be construed as seductive somehow, and she didn't want the guy next to her to get the wrong idea.

"Me neither," the guy went on. "It's a nice town, though."

"Yep."

"Yeah." He took a long sip of his beverage before turning back to her. "I'm Jason, by the way."

She smiled thinly at him, doing her best to be polite. "Gemma."

"It's nice to meet you." He held out his hand to her, but she didn't shake it.

Jason was a little cute, but he appeared to be in his early thirties. Not to mention the fact that she definitely wasn't looking to hook up with anyone. She'd run away from the sirens and Sawyer to avoid that. Besides, Jason wasn't Alex.

"Are you here alone?" he asked.

"I'm having dinner alone," Gemma clarified. "I wanted some time to myself."

"Oh." He scratched his head, and for one glorious moment she thought her rebuff was going to sink in. "A pretty little thing like you should never dine alone. Why don't you have dinner with me?"

"Don't you think I'm a little young for you?" Gemma asked. The guy was probably twice her age.

"Is that what's bothering you?" Jason laughed jovially, as if he'd solved a problem that Gemma didn't even know needed solving. He leaned in closer to her then, almost whispering to her. "The younger the better, that's what I always say."

"Wow," Gemma said. "That's actually really creepy."

"Aw, come on, honey." He brushed his hand against her arm in a way that was probably meant to be flirtatious, but it made her skin crawl, and she pulled away from him.

"Is he bothering you?" the bartender asked, leaning over the bar and glaring at Jason.

"We're just having a little fun, that's all." Jason laughed and moved away from Gemma, trying to look more innocent than he actually was.

"Is he bothering you?" the bartender repeated, and this time his eyes were fixed on Gemma.

Out of the corner of her eye, Gemma had seen the bartender hovering around her, sometimes ignoring the other patrons. Now at the other end of the bar a young man kept leering at her, much to the annoyance of his date. And Jason was next to her, stealthily trying to put his hand on her thigh under the bar.

Gemma had hoped to sit quietly, eat her meal in peace, and think about what she should do. But this was obviously not the place to do it. It was too busy, and she was drawing too much attention.

"You know what? I think I should just go," Gemma said. Jason pouted, and she ignored him and jerked her leg away from his hand.

"You haven't even finished your Cherry Coke," the bartender said. "And if he's bothering you, I can have him thrown out."

"Oh, come on!" Jason protested, and threw his arms up in the air. "I wasn't bothering anybody! We was just talking!"

"You're always harassing ladies," the bartender insisted, glaring at Jason. "We should have you banned from here."

"How much do I owe you?" Gemma asked, interrupting their argument.

"Nothing." The bartender smiled at her.

"I can get your drink," Jason hurried to supply.

"I got it," she snapped. "How much is it?"

"There's no charge," the bartender said, softening. "You didn't drink any, anyway."

She wanted to argue with him, but she wanted to get out of there even more.

"Thank you," she said simply, and slipped off the stool.

Gemma hurried out of the restaurant. She wanted to jog, but she forced herself to keep her pace to a normal speed. Her stomach rumbled, and she knew she'd have to find someplace else to eat. It was nearly dark now, and she didn't know the town, so she wanted to hurry.

She'd nearly made it around the corner when she heard footsteps pounding behind her, and she looked back over her shoulder to see Jason running to catch up to her.

"You sure took off like a flash." Jason grinned as he fell in step next to her. "Sorry if I said something to offend you in there."

"No, you were fine," she lied, and shook her head. "I just didn't realize how late it was. I have to be getting home."

"You haven't eaten anything yet," Jason reminded her. "Let me take you out somewhere. I'll find you something real special."

"No, I'm all right," Gemma insisted. She turned down the alley that led to the lot where she'd parked her car, and Jason stayed at her side.

"Please, Gemma," he entreated. "I was a jerk inside. Come back in. Get something to eat with me. Let me make it up to you."

She softened a bit and slowed down, but she still didn't want to go back in there or eat with some stranger. Really, she just wanted to get out of there.

"Sorry." She smiled up at him. "I'm not hungry anymore. I should go."

"Wait." He grabbed her arm when she started walking away, and while his grip wasn't exactly painful, she didn't like it. "If you're not hungry, there's plenty of things we could do."

"I need to go home." She tried to pull her arm away, but he hung on tighter.

"I know I'm older, and that scares you, but that's no reason to be shy." He smiled at her, but there was something menacing in the smile that made her recoil.

Thanks to her siren strength, she could overpower him, but just then he caught her off guard. He pushed her back against the brick wall of a building, putting an arm on either side of her and pinning her there with his body.

"Move," Gemma insisted. "Jason. Please. Move."

Just because she could overpower him didn't mean she wanted to. It would be easier and create much less of a scene if he just stepped away on his own. Not that there was anyone there to watch the scene. The alley was deserted.

"Move?" He laughed darkly. "Honey, I'll show you some moves."

He rubbed his body up against hers, and something flared inside her. It wasn't the lust she'd felt before, not like back at the house with Sawyer. At first it reminded her of when she went swimming, when the ocean hit her flesh and her body began to transform. It was that same kind of tingle running through her.

But instead of feeling the tingle in her legs, she felt it in her arms, and her mouth. Her lips trembled, and her vision changed. She couldn't explain it exactly, but it was almost as if her eyes shifted and her pupils dilated, so she could see better in the dark.

Jason had been rubbing himself on her and trying to kiss her neck, his mouth moving gruffly against her flesh as with one hand he clumsily pawed at her chest. He looked up, maybe to see if Gemma was enjoying this as much as he was, and his eyes widened.

"What the fuck . . . ?" he muttered, and those were the last words Gemma heard him say.

SEVENTEEN

Repercussions

I did something bad," Gemma said, her voice quavering as she spoke. "Something really, really *bad*."

She stood in the foyer of Sawyer's house, her arms covered in blood up to her elbows. Most of it had dried on the drive home, but some of it still dripped wet on the white marble floors. Her clothes were splattered red, and her mouth was filled with a sweet metallic taste that was somehow both delicious and nauseating.

When she'd parked the car haphazardly on Sawyer's front lawn after a frantic drive home, she'd caught a glimpse of herself in the rearview mirror. The entire bottom half of her mouth was covered in blood, except for the lines that were clean from her tears. She'd been sobbing so hard as she drove, it was amazing that she'd been able to see where she was going, let alone remember how to get there.

The commotion of her car skidding through the front yard

had drawn everyone to see what was up. Sawyer was already in the foyer when Gemma entered the house, and Lexi and Thea arrived shortly after.

"Are you okay?" Sawyer rushed over to her, inspecting her for wounds. His concern made sense, since she was covered in blood, but none of it was her own. Still, she was in such a state of shock, she let Sawyer touch her and look her over.

"So you finally ate?" Penn smiled, walking into the room. She stared at Gemma with a bemused expression.

"I told you she would come back," Lexi said proudly as she went over to Gemma.

"You did, but she's a mess," Penn said.

"She's fine, you nitwit. It's not her blood," Lexi said as she pushed Sawyer away and looped her arm around Gemma's shoulders.

"Whose blood is it?" Sawyer asked, sounding confused.

"That's a very good question." Penn walked up to Gemma, standing directly in front of her. Gemma just wanted to collapse and sob. "Where's the body?"

"The body?" Gemma asked, dazed.

"Yes, you killed someone and ate their heart," Penn said, as if it should be obvious. "Now, where is the body?"

"I, um . . ." Gemma gulped back her vomit and tried to think. "I don't know. It was outside a steakhouse in town. It happened in the alley next to it."

"A steakhouse?" Penn turned to Sawyer. "Do you know where she's talking about?"

"Marcel's Steakhouse?" Sawyer asked.

"I think so, maybe." Gemma nodded numbly. "I don't know for sure."

"Go clean it up," Penn directed Sawyer. "Take care of the mess before anybody finds it."

"His name is Jason," Gemma told him, as if that would help him find the body somehow.

"Nobody cares what his name is," Penn said. "Just take care of it."

"Okay." Sawyer nodded and hurried out the front door to follow Penn's wishes.

"I'm sorry," Gemma said as silent tears slid down her cheeks. "I didn't know what to do. I didn't know where to go."

"You did the right thing coming back," Penn said. "But next time, take the body with you. You can't just go leaving your scraps around. It makes the humans suspicious, and that's a headache you don't want to deal with."

"The convertible is covered in blood!" Sawyer called from the front yard.

"Then take one of the other cars in the garage!" Penn shouted at him, and rolled her eyes. "He's so lucky that he's handsome and rich, because he is a friggin' moron."

"He is cute, though." Lexi squeezed Gemma's shoulder, trying to reassure her. "We should get you cleaned up, huh?"

"Yeah," Gemma agreed.

Lexi leaned over, then licked her cheek. Gemma recoiled and pushed Lexi back hard, causing her to fall back into the front closet.

"Did you just lick blood off my cheek?" Gemma cried. She

tried to wipe Lexi's saliva from her face, but she probably only ended up smearing blood on her cheek. "You're a psycho!"

"You're the one covered in blood!" Lexi countered, clearly offended by Gemma's reaction. "I just tasted it! At least I didn't rip out his heart!"

"Lexi, that really was inappropriate." Penn looked at her in disgust. "Thea, go help Gemma get cleaned up. When Sawyer gets back, we'll talk about how we're going to deal with all of this."

"Come on." Thea took Gemma's hand and started pulling her away. "You'll feel better once you get cleaned up, and you'll think better once the food settles."

"That wasn't food," Gemma muttered.

"It's what you eat now, so it's food," Thea countered.

In the upstairs bathroom, Thea filled the bathtub with warm water. Gemma stripped down to her bikini, then climbed inside. The water quickly turned pink as the blood mixed with it, but Gemma barely even noticed.

She pulled her knees up to her chest, resting her chin on them, and Thea sat next to her, rinsing the blood out from the tangles of her hair.

"I'm a monster," Gemma said quietly.

"We all are, sweetie," Thea said as gently as she could. She used a cup to pour the warm water over Gemma's hair and ran her fingers through it. The blood had really matted into it on the drive home in the convertible.

"I don't even really remember what happened," Gemma

said, wiping at the tears that fell from her eyes. "It's all kind of a red blur."

"You don't remember the first couple times," Thea said. "You're not really in control of your body or your transformation. And since you were avoiding eating, you were probably especially out of control."

"But I . . . I ate his heart?" Gemma asked.

"That's what we do," Thea said. "That's how we survive. We have to eat boys' hearts."

"That's so messed up."

Thea laughed darkly. "That's all Demeter's sick sense of humor. She was one twisted bitch when she made the curse."

"I don't think I can do this." Gemma hugged her knees tighter as her stomach lurched. "I can't kill people like this."

"The good news is that you only have to eat four times a year," Thea said, trying to comfort her. "Once before every solstice."

"What?" Gemma sniffled and turned to look back at Thea. "You eat more than that."

"I don't," Thea said. "Not really. Have you noticed how my voice isn't as silky as Penn's or Lexi's?"

"That's because you don't eat as often as they do?" Gemma asked.

"That's part of it." Thea nodded. "I once went a whole year without eating. It nearly killed me. And now my voice is like this. If I ate more, the huskiness would eventually go away, but I don't need to eat more, so I don't."

"You can go a whole year without eating?" Gemma turned in the tub to face her. "Could you go longer?"

"No, Gemma, it nearly killed me," Thea repeated. "It was excruciatingly painful, physically and emotionally, and eventually I started going mad. When I did finally eat, I was so out of control I nearly slaughtered everyone around me. You have to eat more than that."

"If you hurt so bad, then why didn't you eat?" Gemma asked. "Why'd you go a whole year without eating?"

Thea lowered her eyes. "That's a story for another day." She leaned over and reached into the tub, pulling out the stopper so the water would drain. "Why don't you turn on the shower to rinse off, and I'll go grab you a towel?"

After Gemma got out of the shower, she hated to admit how awesome she felt. Emotionally, she was a wreck, but physically, Gemma had never felt better. She'd never done drugs, but she imagined that this was how a really good high felt.

Thea came back with a huge towel, and Gemma wrapped herself in it.

"You feel better now?" Thea asked.

"I guess," Gemma said, trying to downplay how good she felt, and started walking to her room.

She lay down in her bed and pulled her blanket over her. It made her uncomfortably warm, but she kept it on, wanting to bury herself in it. Thea had followed her, and she stood tentatively at the end of the bed before sitting down.

"Why are you being so nice to me?" Gemma asked Thea. "You used to be such a bitch."

"I'm still a bitch," Thea replied. "But this is hard enough to go through. Lexi and Penn are too dumb and selfish to help. I just don't think anyone should go through this alone."

"How do you live with it?" Gemma asked.

"What?"

"The guilt."

"You mean from killing people?" Thea asked.

"Yeah." Gemma pulled back the blanket a bit so she could look at Thea. "I just can't stop thinking that he was a person, and . . . and he didn't deserve that."

"If it makes you feel any better, it didn't hurt," Thea said.

"How can you say that? I ripped out his heart!"

"Yes, but you're a siren," Thea said. "When you feed, you make a kind of purring sound. It's like a cross between a cat and a lullaby. It has an anesthetizing effect on your prey. So it's like they're in a coma almost. They don't know what happens. They die peacefully."

"Still." Gemma settled back down in her blankets, and while she found that fact a bit more comforting, it didn't erase her guilt. "I still killed a man tonight."

"That's the part that's the hardest to get over," Thea said. "That we do the actual killing ourselves. You would probably be a wreck if you murdered a cow, too, but you don't think twice about eating a hamburger."

"That's different," Gemma insisted.

"For you now, it seems that way," Thea said. "But the longer you live, the more your perception of humans changes. They die all the time, over the simplest things. Life is very, very fleeting for them. The best they can hope for is a painless death, and we provide that for them."

"You can't honestly believe that," Gemma said. "You can't really think that you're doing them a service by killing them."

"Sometimes I can." Thea sounded sad, staring down at Gemma's comforter and picking at a stray thread. "What helps me is trying to find people that deserve it."

"People that deserve to die?" Gemma asked.

"Yeah, pedophiles, rapists, that kinda thing," Thea said. "We seem to have the strongest effect on them, anyway, so it's easy to find them."

"Luke wasn't a pedophile or a rapist," Gemma countered. "I bet those other boys that you killed back in Capri weren't, either."

Thea shook her head. "That wasn't me. That was Penn, and even she was feeding more than she normally does. She was collecting human blood to create a new siren."

"She killed all those boys for one flask?" Gemma asked. "I doubt that."

"We had two failed attempts before you," Thea reminded her. "Penn saved Aggie's blood in a jug, because she knew we only had one siren that we could get blood from. But she was more wasteful with the humans. She knew she could always get more. So she took what she needed, then left them, and when the girls died, she needed more blood and a new boy."

"So you didn't eat them?" Gemma asked.

"No, Penn doesn't like sharing anyway," Thea said. "And

that's fine by me. I prefer going after people that deserve it, not lovesick teenage boys."

"You don't have the right to decide who deserves it, though," Gemma insisted. "You don't get to decide who lives and dies. You don't get to play God."

"People decide who lives and dies every day," Thea said flatly. "And in the end, it doesn't matter if you agree with what we do or whether you think it's right. I do what I need to do to survive, and you will, too."

"Am I interrupting girl talk?" Lexi asked, appearing in Gemma's doorway.

She leaned back against the doorframe, arching her back a little. She'd changed, so she was wearing a white nightie now, and her long blond hair hung down, covering up her chest in a way the fabric didn't.

"No, Gemma was just getting some rest," Thea said, and stood up.

"I just thought I'd let you know that you're in big trouble, Gemma." Lexi laughed when she said it, a strange flirty giggle.

"I'm in trouble?" Gemma sat up a little, propping herself on her elbows.

"Sawyer just called Penn, and cops are swarming the alley," Lexi said. "They found the body."

"What does that mean?" Gemma asked, feeling a new fear at possibly getting caught.

She didn't exactly want to get away with murder. On one hand, she thought getting arrested might be the best thing to happen to her, because then she couldn't hurt anybody else. But on the other hand, getting life in prison would be really terrible if she lived forever.

"Nothing." Thea shook her head. "Penn and Sawyer will take care of it. It's just more work for them. That's all."

"And Penn hates extra work," Lexi said, smiling down at Gemma. "But that's not the only reason you're in trouble. Penn found out about your little make-out session with Sawyer today."

"Lexi," Thea groaned, and started pushing Lexi out of the room. "Just leave her alone. She needs to rest."

"She called me a psycho!" Lexi insisted as Thea forced her out of the room. "She can't talk to me that way without getting in trouble!"

"Lexi, you *are* a psycho." Thea shut the door behind her, but Gemma could still hear them talking outside the room. "And Gemma's one of us now. You'll just have to learn to get along with her."

"She shouldn't be making out with Penn's boyfriends," Lexi insisted, her voice getting quieter as she and Thea got farther away.

"Neither should you, but you do it," Thea reminded her.

"But I get in trouble for it!" Lexi whined.

"I'm sure Gemma will get in trouble," Thea said. "Just not right now."

EIGHTEEN

Lost

Their afternoon of trying to summon spirits hadn't led them any closer to finding Gemma, but it had left Marcy with a nasty sunburn that she kept complaining about at work the next day.

"I hope your sister appreciates what I did for her," Marcy muttered.

She sat at the desk, resting her head against the cool laminate. Her arms were spread out, looking beet-red against the light color of the faux-wood, and she'd hardly moved since she'd come in this morning.

While Marcy was busy doing nothing, Harper went through the books that had been left in the drop box last night, scanning them back into the system.

"I'm sure she does," Harper said. "As soon as we find her, I'll tell her of your heroism in battling the sun. Gemma will be thoroughly impressed and eternally grateful."

"If it didn't hurt so much for me to lift my arms right now, I would totally be flicking you off," Marcy told her.

Instead of replying to that, Harper grabbed the stack of books she'd just scanned, and headed back to the shelves to put them away. If there had been a lot, she would've used the cart, but there weren't that many and they were mostly children's books, so they were lighter anyway.

"Are you and Alex planning on doing anything tonight?" Marcy asked, raising her voice to be heard as Harper walked away.

"Um, I don't know."

She crouched down in front of the kids' shelves. They were lower, so little kids had easier access to them. The books had been left in a bit of a mess, since they'd left quickly last night and neither Marcy nor Harper had straightened them up.

Harper started organizing them, putting them in the right order and uprighting the books that had slumped or were shoved in the wrong way.

"What do you mean, you don't know?" Marcy called from behind Harper.

"That's what I mean," she replied tersely.

Harper's enthusiasm was waning. Everything they had done, all the phone calls, all the searching, it hadn't led them any closer to finding Gemma. And not only did they not know where she was, they weren't even completely certain *what* she was.

Yes, Alex had a hunch that Gemma was a siren, and Harper was inclined to think there was something to that, but she didn't even know what that meant. In her spare time, Harper was still looking up everything she could on sirens and mythology in general, but she hadn't found anything particularly helpful.

In fact, most of the information she'd read would contradict information she'd read earlier. A lot of the texts seemed to assume that the sirens were already dead, having been killed when a ship sailed past without stopping to hear the siren song.

None of it made sense, and none of it brought her any closer to Gemma. In the end, everything she'd done felt like busywork. The hard truth was that she wasn't helping her sister, and she had no idea how to.

"So, what?" Marcy asked. "Are you just giving up, then?"

"Of course I'm not giving up." Harper roughly shoved a book onto the shelf. "I'll never give up."

"Then what's the plan?" Marcy asked.

"Why do you even care?" Harper snapped.

Her legs ached from the way she'd been crouching, so she stood and turned back to face the desk. The bookcases in the kids' section only came up to Harper's waist, and she stared over them at Marcy, who blinked at Harper from behind thick-rimmed glasses.

"You're my friend," Marcy said, sounding surprised by Harper's tone. "She's your sister. I want to help."

"So your plan to help is to bitch about everything we do all the time?" Harper asked. "Because that's all I ever see you doing."

"What's your problem?" Marcy sat up straighter. "I know I'm not the greatest in these situations, but at least I'm trying to help. I'm doing the best I can."

"So am I, Marcy!" Harper yelled. The few library patrons turned to look at her, but she didn't care. "I'm trying and I'm trying, and it doesn't matter! I'm not doing anything to help anybody!"

"I am sorry that you can't find her," Marcy said. "I truly am. But it's not my fault."

"I know!" Harper started shouting again, then softened. "I'm sick of all this." She let out a deep breath to fight back a sob. "I just want to know that she's okay. I want her to come home."

The fight had gone out of her, and she leaned back against the shelf behind her. She fought back tears, and wiped at the few that managed to fall.

"I feel like this is the time I'm supposed to come over and hug you," Marcy said from where she sat behind the desk. "But I'm not really the hugging type. Plus, the sunburn."

"It's okay." Harper sniffled and forced a smile at her. "I think I just needed to let off some steam."

A couple of patrons were still staring suspiciously at her, so Harper offered them an apologetic smile.

"Sorry about my outburst, folks," she told them, and straightened up. "It won't happen again. You can go back to your browsing."

She crouched down to pick up the books she'd left on the floor, the ones she still had left to put away. She'd honestly meant to pick them up and go about her work, but as soon as she was safely hidden behind the shelves, it hit her.

Gemma might never come back, and even if she did, Harper

had no idea if Gemma would even still be her sister. No matter what happened from here on out, the little sister Harper had always known and loved was gone. And nothing Harper could do would bring her back.

She put one hand over her mouth to keep quiet as tears spilled down her cheeks, and she put her other hand on the shelf to steady herself. Her whole body shook as she cried, but she managed to stay relatively silent.

"Hello?" a voice said behind her.

She turned her head to the side, hiding her face as best she could from whoever stood behind her.

"Um, Marcy's at the desk," Harper said, swallowing back tears. "If you need help finding a book, check with her."

"Harper, I don't need help finding a book," he said. She glanced back over her shoulder to see Daniel.

"Daniel." She turned away from him and rushed to wipe her face as inconspicuously as possible. "Of course you would come here now." He didn't need to see her all snot-nosed and sobbing.

"Are you okay?" he asked.

"Yes, I'm fine. Everything's fine." She sniffled, grabbed the books, and stood up, realizing that she probably looked the best she could hope for, and turned to face him. "What can I do for you?"

"Were you crying?" he asked, his voice warm with concern.

She lowered her eyes, refusing to look up at him, but she could feel his eyes searching her. He moved even closer to her, so he was mere inches away, but Harper just hugged the books to her chest and stared down at her feet.

"I'm working, Daniel, so if you don't need anything from me, I should probably get back to it," she said.

"I know you're working, and I wouldn't bother you if it wasn't important," Daniel said. "Can you take, like, five minutes to go somewhere and talk with me?"

On her list of wants, being with Daniel right now only came second to finding Gemma. What Harper really wanted to do was go someplace dark and quiet with him, to give in to the warmth of his voice and the strength of his arms. To have him hold her and kiss her until she couldn't feel anything but him, until she'd forgotten about the ache inside, all the pain she felt about losing her sister and disappointing her family.

And that was exactly why she shook her head. She wanted to use Daniel as an escape, and that wasn't fair to him or to her. She needed to deal with the mess of her life instead of hiding from it, even if hiding sounded far more pleasant.

"I don't think that's a good idea," Harper said.

She wanted to lift her head, to steal a look at his expression, but she settled for looking up from his battered Converse shoes to his torso. He wore a T-shirt today, the dark black lines of his tattoo traveling out from underneath his sleeve down to his elbow.

Ever since he'd helped her at Bernie's house on Sunday, Harper had a weird urge to trace her fingers along the dark lines of that tattoo. Last night, she'd even dreamt about it.

She and Daniel were lying in a bed, probably the largest bed she'd ever seen. It nearly took up the whole room. The room itself was white. Everything was pure, stark white.

Harper could hear the ocean outside, and she could smell it in the breeze. French doors that presumably led out to the beach were wide open, and sheer curtains billowed in the wind.

Daniel was lying next to her in the bed, shirtless, with the sheets up to his waist. He wasn't facing her, but instead had his head turned toward the ocean. Harper rested her head on his bare shoulder and ran her fingers along his tattoo, tracing the dark lines that ran along the scars. He said nothing, but Harper sang him a sweet lullaby.

Then she heard her sister's voice, coming from everywhere and nowhere at all. Gemma simply said, "Wake up," and then she did. Harper had opened her eyes to find herself lying in her own bed, alone.

Maybe that was why everything was hitting her so hard today. It was as if Gemma were telling her that she was running out of time, and that Harper needed to stop wasting her time on a silly crush and get back to what mattered.

"Harper." Daniel sighed, frustrated. "We need to talk. It's about Gemma."

Her eyes shot up then, and she finally met his gaze. His face was solemn, but there was something hopeful in his eyes, like he might have good news. But really, almost any news about Gemma would be good at this point.

"What about her?" Harper asked. "Have you heard from her?"

"Not exactly." He reached behind his back and grabbed a rolled-up copy of *USA Today* that he'd jammed into his back pocket. "But you should take a look at this."

"What?" She dropped the books she'd been holding on top of the bookshelf and snatched the paper from him before he could explain further.

The cover story was about some politician being caught in a tawdry affair with a celebrity, and the smaller features on the bottom half were about the economy and how people were planning to spend Independence Day this upcoming weekend.

"What does this have to do with Gemma?" Harper demanded.

"It's not—here, just give it to me."

Daniel took the paper from her and laid it out on top of the bookshelf. He opened it to the third page and smoothed out the crinkles as best he could before pointing to a small column on the side of the page.

"Boys Don't Die" was the headline, with a subhead reading "Why the Media Doesn't Care When Boys Are Killed."

"This is about sexism in the media?" Harper scoffed, and looked at Daniel.

"Will you just keep reading?" Daniel asked.

She stared at him uncertainly before turning her attention back to the paper. As soon as she started reading, she saw the connection, but didn't completely understand how it would help find Gemma.

The reporter had picked up on the dead boys in Capri and wrote a little about the brutal murders of four teenage boys. But the story wasn't about the murders so much as why nobody was covering them.

Even Harper had to agree that the story had been largely ignored. Other than a few local reporters, she hadn't seen much in the way of media. Which seemed odd, especially since they were labeling it as the work of a serial killer.

The article went on to name several high-profile murder cases that all involved beautiful young women, then speculated why this case, which consisted of multiple murders, garnered so little attention. The writer of the article clearly thought there was some kind of gender bias involved.

Harper was just about to ask Daniel why he wanted her to read this when she realized the answer was in the last few paragraphs.

The murders no longer appear isolated in Maryland. Just yesterday, in a small seaside community 45 minutes south of Myrtle Beach, a young man was found murdered in much the same fashion as the previous victims in Capri.

Thirty-three-year-old Jason Way was found with his chest cavity ripped open in an alleyway outside a busy restaurant. Despite the heinous nature of the crime, no witnesses have come forward as having heard or seen anything.

With this fifth murder of a young man, perhaps the media will start giving these serial killings the coverage they deserve. So far, however, that seems unlikely. Local authorities in South Carolina are hesitant to connect this murder with the previous ones in Maryland.

Jason Way also has a long history of domestic violence, sexual harassment, and a rape conviction, so retribution from previous victims hasn't been ruled out, a representative for the police force has said.

For now, mothers need to watch out for their sons, because it seems that nobody else is going to.

"Oh, my gosh," Harper said, exhaling shakily after she finished reading. "That's them, isn't it? This has to be the sirens."

Daniel nodded. "I think so. I mean, that guy sounds like he might have been a douche, so it could be some kind of copycat killing. But it's worth checking out, at least."

"When is this paper from?" Harper flipped to the front with shaking hands to check the date.

"It's from today," Daniel answered.

"So that guy, he was really killed yesterday?" Harper pushed her bangs back from her forehead and tried to think, but her mind was racing too fast. "They might still be there. Gemma might be there. How far away is it?"

"Myrtle Beach is about a ten-and-a-half-hour drive from here," Daniel said. "So a little over eleven hours, if we hurry."

"Do you know what town that was?" Harper looked back at the paper, scanning the article to see if it had named the exact town where the body had been found.

"I Googled it on my phone before I came here," Daniel said. "It's right on the coast. We should have no problem finding it."

"Good." Harper nodded, then she realized what he had said. "You're coming with?"

"Well, duh," Daniel said, like it should be obvious. "I saw

what those sirens are capable of. There's no way I'm letting you go up against them alone."

She wanted to argue with him, but he had a point. She needed all the help she could get if she wanted to rescue Gemma.

She smiled gratefully at him, but that was all she had time for. They needed to hurry if they wanted to catch the sirens before they moved on.

"I'm taking off, Marcy," Harper said as she walked toward the front door.

"Wait!" Marcy stood up, and when Harper turned back to her, she saw Marcy holding her purse outstretched toward her. "You probably need your car keys and stuff."

Harper ran back and grabbed her purse. "Thanks, Marce. And sorry about earlier."

"Don't sweat it." Marcy shrugged it off. "Just go get her. And be careful."

NINETEEN

Warning

Gemma hated how good she felt when she woke up. The effects of feeding yesterday hadn't worn off. If anything, they'd only grown stronger. Her body was like liquid. Every movement she made was smooth and fluid, and she felt like she was gliding everywhere she went.

When she got out of bed, she actually danced around the room, unable to help herself. And while she'd never had any formal training of any kind, she moved like a ballet dancer. As if elegance had suddenly become part of her DNA.

She didn't have to look in the mirror to know that she was glowing. She could feel it. Her skin was positively luminous.

And despite her best efforts to feel guilty and mourn the loss of the man she'd murdered yesterday, her sirenness was at full blast, and happiness radiated through her.

The sadness was still there, because she had done something absolutely horrific and could never forgive herself for it. But it was buried down deep inside her, hidden with the rest of her negative emotions that the new siren powers didn't want her to feel.

She went down the stairs two steps at a time, simply because she felt like it, and nearly bumped into Sawyer, who was standing at the bottom.

"Good morning, Gemma," he said, sounding even more dazed than usual. He looked almost awed by her beauty, and Gemma felt a sharp pang of self-loathing that she had that effect on him. Or any guy, for that matter.

"Morning," she replied, smiling at him anyway.

She was pleased to find that the insatiable lust she'd been feeling for him had disappeared. Sure, she still thought Sawyer was attractive, but she had absolutely no urge to jump him.

"Do you need anything?" Sawyer asked, following her into the kitchen.

"Dear God, Sawyer, stop drooling on the poor girl," Penn said with an exaggerated eye roll. "She doesn't need to deal with you acting like a dog in heat first thing in the morning."

Penn was sitting on a stool at the kitchen island. A trashy magazine was spread out before her, showcasing the best and worst beach bodies, and a half-empty glass of orange juice sat next to it.

"Sorry." Sawyer stared down at his feet, looking ashamed.

"I see you slept well," Penn said, turning her attention to Gemma as she languidly flipped the pages in the magazine.

"I slept fine," Gemma replied noncommittally, and opened the fridge. There wasn't much in the way of food, but she grabbed an apple, then shut the door.

"Well, you look radiant," Penn said without looking at her. "Being a siren obviously suits you."

Gemma leaned against the fridge and bit into the apple, ignoring its unpleasant taste, because she didn't know how else to respond. That was obviously some kind of compliment, but Gemma really didn't want to take it that way. She still didn't want to be a siren.

The house was suddenly filled with the sounds of music as Lexi turned on a stereo in another room. Adele came wafting out, and Lexi joined in, somehow managing to sound even lovelier than Adele when she sang.

Sawyer had still been staring down in shame, but as soon as Lexi started singing, he turned toward her. He even started walking toward her, moving slowly, like he was drawn to her song.

"Shut the hell up, Lexi!" Penn shouted, with an unsettling undercurrent to her normally sweet voice. When she was angry, she had a monstrous tone that she couldn't seem to control, sounding like some awful creature from a horror movie. "Nobody wants to hear you squawking!"

"Ugh!" Lexi groaned loudly, and the music fell silent. Not just Lexi, but the stereo that played along with it. "I'm going out for a swim since you're being a killjoy!"

"Can I go swim, too?" Sawyer asked, looking over at Penn.

"Did you get all the blood out of the convertible last night?" Penn asked, still staring down at the glossy pages in front of her.

"Um, no?" He furrowed his brow as he thought now. "No. You told me not to worry about it and just to come to bed with you."

"Well, you're up now." She smiled thinly at him, not even attempting to hide her contempt. "Go clean out the car."

"Sure, yeah, of course." He nodded quickly, then left the kitchen to do her bidding.

"So how did it feel?" Penn asked, resting her hand on her chin as she flipped a page.

Gemma swallowed the bite of apple in her mouth before answering her. "What?"

"Taking a human life." Penn kept her head tilted down, as if she were still examining the beach bodies, but she lifted her eyes to meet Gemma's. Penn's were black as usual, but they were dancing at the thought of murder.

Gemma forced herself to take another bite, even though she felt nauseated at the talk of murder, and she refused to answer Penn's question.

"You really are one of us now," Penn went on, smiling as she spoke. "You're a monster now. Just like me and Lexi and Thea. You've had a taste of the human heart, and you won't be able to stop yourself."

"I'll never be like you." Gemma shook her head and stared down at the apple in her hands. "I made a mistake last night, but I'll never let myself be out of control like that again. I'll never be a monster."

Penn laughed. "You said you'd never kill anyone in the first place. These little moral compromises you keep making with yourself. You'll find that eventually morality will mean nothing to you. We chose you for a reason."

"You chose me because you were running out of options,"

Gemma pointed out. "Thea told me that I was your last chance."

"You were my first choice, though," Penn said, but her smile had faltered. "Do you know why I wanted you?"

Gemma toyed with the fruit in her hands, not wanting to admit to Penn that she didn't really know, and she actually wanted to.

"I saw the evil in you," Penn said.

"That's not true." Gemma shook her head. "I'm not . . . There's no evil in me. Or at least there wasn't before I became a siren."

"Whatever you say." Penn threw up her hands as if it were of no concern to her. "You're not evil. You killed that man last night out of the goodness of your heart."

Gemma tossed the half-eaten apple in the garbage can. "I'm not hungry."

"Oh, hey, Gemma," Penn said as Gemma was about to leave the kitchen. She paused in the doorway and glanced back over her shoulder at Penn. "I heard about your little rendezvous with Sawyer yesterday."

When Gemma didn't say anything, Penn turned to look back at her.

"He told me," Penn explained, as if Gemma had asked how she had found out. "He has no secrets from me. He can't have secrets."

"That's the basis for a really healthy relationship," Gemma said dryly.

"He's an attractive guy, isn't he?" Penn went on as if Gemma hadn't said anything. "He's downright gorgeous. He'd have to be, right? Otherwise you wouldn't have cheated on your beloved Alex."

Gemma chewed the inside of her cheek and looked away from Penn. "Yep. He's a very foxy guy. You're one lucky lady, Penn."

"You know luck has nothing to do with it," Penn said, and slipped off the stool. "I make my own luck. I create my own destiny."

She walked over to Gemma and stood right in front of her, but Gemma refused to look at her. She just stared down at Penn's pedicured toes.

"If you ever want to join Sawyer and me, I understand," Penn said, her voice turning low and sultry. "As a siren, you have all sorts of new urges, and they're hard to contain. Sawyer would be happy to show you how to handle them, as long as I'm there to guide you."

"What?" Gemma wrinkled her nose in disgust when she realized what Penn was talking about. "That's a really weird offer, and also gross. Seriously. Ew, no."

"You're a prude now, and I don't care," Penn said, waving it off. "But the point is that if you ever touch Sawyer again when I'm not around, I'll rip off your filthy little hands."

Gemma looked up at her then, and saw that, though Penn had kept her tone sexy and almost cheerful, her eyes had shifted. They were no longer her usual black eyes but the odd yellow eyes of an eagle.

"You can't have what isn't yours," Penn said, and Gemma

could hear the monster under her words, the beast inside her growling. "Don't touch things without my permission."

Before, Gemma would've been afraid of this, and part of her knew she should be intimidated by Penn. She'd killed her own sister, so she would obviously think nothing of tearing off Gemma's head. But Gemma didn't care anymore. If she was going to live with Penn forever, she wasn't going to kowtow to her. She'd rather end up dead than as Penn's slave.

"Sawyer's not yours, and he's not a thing," Gemma said. "Just because you have a spell over him doesn't mean he's not still a human being with feelings and thoughts of his own. You just won't let him use them."

Gemma had expected Penn to yell at her, but instead Penn threw back her head and laughed. When she'd finished, her eyes had gone back to normal.

"Oh, Gemma, that just shows how little you know about humans." Penn turned back and walked toward the kitchen island, still giggling to herself.

TWENTY

Complications

They'd picked up Alex on their way out of town, not just because he would kill Harper if she went after Gemma without him, but because he might be useful.

Harper called her dad, leaving a message on his cell phone letting him know that she wouldn't be home that night. She thought about telling him that she was going after Gemma, but if Harper wasn't successful in finding her, that would only break Brian's heart more.

They took Harper's car on the road trip because Daniel didn't have one and Alex's car was so small. He sat in the backseat while Harper drove, and Daniel gave him the newspaper to read.

Both Alex and Harper couldn't believe that they'd missed the article in the first place. Alex especially had been scouring the Internet for clues on Gemma, but he'd gotten bogged down with pointless e-mails. He felt obligated to follow every "lead" he got, but they all led nowhere.

Harper had probably missed it because she'd been out of sorts. After she'd woken up from that dream about Daniel that ended with Gemma saying, "Wake up," she hadn't been able to get into any kind of routine. Everything felt off, and she hadn't done her usual search on the computer for the sirens.

Fortunately, while Harper and Alex had been relying on technology, Daniel had been looking the good old-fashioned way. He'd been going to Pearl's every morning and buying a copy of each paper she had. And eventually it had paid off.

Unfortunately, the article hadn't been very specific. The only real information they'd gotten from it was that a body had been found near a restaurant. Daniel had figured out what town it was, but that was still a fairly large area to search.

Harper didn't even know where the sirens had been living when they were in Capri. She'd heard something once about them staying in a beach house that used to belong to the mayor, but she wasn't sure if that was true.

Her worst fear wasn't that they wouldn't find Gemma. Or that the sirens would try to stop Harper from taking her. She would figure out how to fight them if she needed to. No, her biggest worry was that they would find Gemma, and she wouldn't want to come back with them.

What would she do then? Gemma was sixteen and had new mythical powers. It wasn't exactly like Harper could drag her home and force her to stay in her room. If Gemma wouldn't come back with them on her own . . . then she wouldn't come back.

As they drove on, Harper didn't voice any of these fears, though. Alex probably shared some of her concerns, but he wasn't talking about them, so she didn't think she should, either.

Besides that, she had more important things to focus on—like figuring out exactly where they were going. The drive started out okay, but things quickly went downhill.

Before they'd even made it past the state line, they got stuck in traffic for nearly an hour because of an accident ahead of them on the highway.

Daniel tried to keep things upbeat, but Alex and Harper were too nerved up for it to really work. After several failed attempts at making conversation, he settled for tuning the radio to a classic rock station and air-drumming along to "Immigrant Song" by Led Zeppelin.

Once the car got moving again, things went smoothly for a while, and then they were off course again. Harper's '96 Sable lacked any kind of GPS, so they were relying on the maps app on Alex's phone.

It would've been a straight shot down the coast, but after getting stuck in traffic, Alex tried to find an alternate route that would get them there more quickly. Unfortunately, it only succeeded in leading them to a dead end, but not until they'd been driving off course for fifty miles.

That led them to stop at a gas station, where Daniel got an atlas and mapped out the route. Harper fumed quietly about the unnecessary detour for a few hours, while Alex sulked.

According to Daniel's earlier calculations, they should've reached Myrtle Beach around midnight. Thanks to all the stops and starts, it was almost twelve and they were still over two hours away.

That was when the length of the trip started wearing on Harper. She would've thought that her excitement and nerves would've kept her awake, but she'd slept terribly the night before, and the whole situation simply exhausted her.

In the backseat, Alex snored fitfully. He'd nod off, but almost as soon as he did, he seemed to become aware of it and would wake himself up again.

"He should've gotten a Red Bull at the gas station," Daniel said, referring to their pit stop about an hour before.

"What?" Harper blinked. She'd been spacing out and had barely heard him.

"Alex." He gestured to the backseat, and Harper glanced behind her.

Alex's chin had fallen to his chest, and he swayed slightly in motion with the car. He snorted loudly, but didn't wake up this time.

"Yeah, I guess, he's really out," Harper said, stifling a yawn, and turned her attention back to the road.

"How are you holding up?" Daniel asked.

He sat next to her, appearing surprisingly chipper. The map was on his lap, folded in just the right way so their path was sitting faceup, and he had a can of Red Bull in his hand. So far on the trip, he had yet to yawn or sleep or even complain of being tired.

"Great," Harper said, but that was at least partially a lie. She was fading, and the highway seemed to stretch on in an eternal blackness that made her eyelids heavy.

"You sure?" Daniel asked. "Because I can take the wheel. You've been driving this entire time, and it wouldn't hurt to trade off."

She shook her head. "I'm fine."

There was no real reason not to let Daniel drive, except that it made her feel a bit more in control of the situation. She wasn't, really. Gemma had run off and turned into a monster, and there was nothing Harper could do about it.

But she could drive the car. She could keep them moving in the direction of her sister, and that was the best she could do right now.

"Let me know if you do get too tired," Daniel said. "I'll be happy to take over."

"I'm fine," Harper repeated.

There were hardly any cars on the road. It was a completely open stretch of highway, devoid of streetlights or houses. The car window was down, and Harper could smell the nearby ocean.

The moonlight shone down on them, and the yellow lines in the middle of the road began to blur.

"Whoa!" Daniel said loudly. The car suddenly jerked to the side, and Harper's eyes flew open. His hand was on the steering wheel, guiding it so they didn't drive off the road.

"What's going on?" Alex asked, sounding panicked in the backseat. "Is everything okay?"

"Yeah, Harper's just pulling over now," Daniel said, his hand still on the wheel.

"I'm fine," Harper repeated, now wide awake after nearly crashing the car.

"Nope, you're falling asleep at the wheel," Daniel said. "Pull over." He wasn't demanding, exactly, but there was a forcefulness to his tone, and Harper was too tired to argue with him. Besides, he was right.

"Who will check the map?" Harper asked as she parked the car on the side of the road. "I don't want to get lost again."

"Alex can handle it," Daniel said. "He's had a nap, and I have an extra can of Red Bull he can drink."

"What's going on?" Alex asked, still groggy and confused.

Daniel had opened the passenger door to get out, but he turned back to Alex. "Hop out. You're up. It's your turn as navigator. Harper's gonna sleep in the backseat for a while."

Reluctantly, Harper got out of the driver's seat, and before she slid in the back, she warned Alex that if he got them lost again, she would literally kill him. She sprawled out in the backseat, expecting sleep to come slowly, but she was out within minutes.

Up front, Daniel and Alex started talking, and Harper would drift in and out of sleep, catching bits of their conversation. Most of it was mundane, and there was a bit where Daniel was apparently attempting to explain some kind of sporting event to Alex, and then Harper was asleep again.

She woke up again, and would've fallen right back to sleep like she had before, but then she heard her name, and she opened her eyes.

"Harper's just that way," Alex was saying. "You can't take it personally."

"I'm not," Daniel said, but he sounded a bit defensive. "Well. I don't know. I try not to."

"She's just a control freak," Alex said. "And I mean that in the nicest way possible."

"Is she sleeping?" Daniel asked.

Alex turned to look in the backseat, and Harper closed her eyes quickly before he could see that she was awake. If they were talking about her, she wanted to hear what they had to say.

"Yeah, she's out," Alex said. "I kinda can't believe she's sleeping. The last week must've been really hard on her."

"It definitely has," Daniel agreed. "Every time I see her, she just seems so exhausted and sad."

"Hopefully, when Gemma comes home she'll feel better," Alex said.

"Yeah, I hope so."

The boys lapsed into a silence, and Harper decided to try to sleep again. If they weren't saying anything interesting, it would be better for her to get some rest. She wanted to be wide awake when they found Gemma.

"How long have you known Harper?" Daniel asked, and the sound of her name perked her up again.

"Um, I don't know exactly," Alex answered. "I think, like, ten years or so. Why?"

"I don't know," Daniel replied quickly. "No reason. I was just curious."

"Oh," Alex said. "How long have you known her?"

"A few months," Daniel said, then fell silent for a minute before asking, "So . . . you and Harper have been friends that whole time?"

"Pretty much," Alex said. "We haven't been talking as much since I started dating Gemma."

"How come, do you think?" Daniel asked. "Is Harper sorta jealous?"

"Nah, I don't think so," Alex said. "Harper isn't a very jealous person. I think she's just kinda weirded out because Gemma's her kid sister and me and Harper have been friends for so long."

"But you guys were just friends, right?" Daniel asked. "I mean, it was never . . ." He trailed off.

"Are you asking me if Harper and I ever dated?" Alex asked.

"Yeah, I guess," Daniel said, sounding uncomfortable. "Or, you know, if you ever hooked up or anything."

"No, never," Alex said.

"Why not?" Daniel asked.

"I don't know." Alex sighed. "We just didn't. It never occurred to us. It's like asking why you never hooked up with your sister or something."

"I don't have a sister."

"You know what I mean," Alex said.

"I do, but that's so . . . strange," Daniel said.

"Why is that so strange?" Alex asked.

"I don't know. She's a pretty girl, you're a teenage boy. I guess I just don't understand how you could just be friends for so long without anything happening."

"Guys and girls can be friends. It happens. I mean, you and Harper are friends." Then it finally seemed to dawn on Alex what they were talking about. "Oh. You and Harper aren't *just* friends."

"No, we are," Daniel replied quickly. "I mean . . . we . . . I . . . It's complicated."

"How is it complicated?" Alex asked.

"Well, for starters . . . I think she hates me," Daniel said.

"She does *not* hate you," Alex assured him.

"Yeah?" Daniel sounded hopeful. "How do you know?"

"You wouldn't be in this car," Alex said. "She wouldn't even let you near her car if she hated you. And you'd know. Harper can be a bitch when she wants to."

"So, then . . . what's the deal?" Daniel asked.

"I have no clue," Alex said. "I don't know anything about your 'complicated' relationship. But Harper's not that big into dating."

Daniel sighed loudly at that. "Yeah, I got that from her." He turned to Alex. "Was she burned by a past boyfriend or something?"

"No, I don't think so. She just . . ." Alex paused, thinking. "You know how nuts she's going over Gemma missing?"

"Yeah?"

"Well, she'd be like that if I went missing or Marcy or her dad," Alex said. "Well, probably not quite as bad for me or

Marcy, but she'd still do everything she could to find us. She feels like she needs to take care of everybody. And as much as she loves Gemma and her friends, I think she just looks at a boyfriend as another person she'd have to take care of, and she doesn't feel like she has time for that."

"But I don't want her to take care of me," Daniel said. "If anything, I want to take care of *her*."

"That's not how Harper works," Alex said. "If she wasn't worrying about everyone and trying to make sure everything was all right, she wouldn't know what to do with herself."

"So what you're saying is that I can't change her mind?" Daniel asked.

"It is incredibly difficult to change Harper's mind," Alex allowed. "But what I'm saying is that I've never dated her, and I have no idea how one would go about doing that." He let out a deep breath. "Hell, I don't even know how to date my own girlfriend."

"I don't know," Daniel said. "I thought you were doing pretty good. Gemma seemed super into you. If she hadn't gotten turned into some bizarre mythical creature, I'm sure the two of you would be doing just fine."

"This is just how my life goes," Alex said. "I have enough trouble dating girls, and now I have to figure out how to date a mermaid."

"Sorry, man," Daniel said, laughing a little. "But if anybody can handle it, I'm sure you can."

"Thanks for the pep talk," Alex said, laughing himself.

"Anytime," Daniel said. "How far away are we anyway?"

"Um . . ." Alex rustled the map. "I think we're almost to Myrtle Beach now, and then it's roughly forty-five miles after that. So we're getting close."

Things were quiet after that, and Harper felt guilty about the way she treated Daniel. She didn't want to stop hanging out with him, but she wondered if she was being fair to him.

Eventually she fell back to sleep while debating what she should do about Daniel. Alex woke her up when they finally reached the town. The sky was just beginning to lighten with very early morning sun, and Harper stretched in the backseat.

"Stay close to the beach," she directed Daniel. She let him continue driving, preferring to look around and scope out the area. "They're probably staying in a house by the ocean."

"How will we know when we find it?" Daniel asked.

"I don't know." Harper shook her head. "We'll have to keep a lookout for the girls themselves. We probably won't be able to find their house, but we'll be able to see them on the beach or in the water."

"They have that song, too," Alex pointed out. "We should listen for that."

They drove around for a long time, with all three of them growing frustrated the longer the search went on. They ended up driving out of town, hugging the coast as the sun rose higher in the sky.

"Stop!" Harper shouted abruptly, and Daniel put on the brakes.

"Do you see them?" Alex asked, craning in his seat.

"No, but that's the house," Harper said, pointing to a massive white mansion. It was surrounded by huge rocks, so they couldn't even see the ocean from the road. The house was set back at the end of a long driveway, partially hidden by trees that filled the yard.

"What house?" Daniel asked, confused.

"The house from my dream," Harper said, and she didn't even know how she knew it. In her dream, all she'd been able to see was the room where she and Daniel had been lying together. It didn't make any sense, but somehow, deep inside, she knew it. "That's the house that Gemma is in."

TWENTY-ONE

New Hope

Gemma had probably woken up a thousand times that night. She tossed and turned horribly before finally giving up on sleep. It was still dark out, and based on the silence in the house, everybody else was still asleep.

It was a feeling inside her chest that she couldn't shake. Like something was happening or something was coming. It reminded her of how she felt before going to bed on Christmas Eve, only mixed with nausea and a touch of dread.

To calm herself, she decided to go out for a swim. In reality, Gemma had been using night swims to self-medicate for years. It was the way she dealt with any kind of anxiety or unpleasant feelings. She'd tried to give it up when she became a siren, but that'd only made things worse.

Discarding her bikini bottoms on the shore, Gemma dove into the cold water, swimming out under the stars.

She tried to explain the feelings away. It was probably residual guilt from feeding the other day.

Thea had tried talking to her more about it, but there was no consolation for her. She knew what she'd done was wrong, and nothing anybody could say to her would change that.

But it was something she'd have to learn to live with. She couldn't take it back, and whether she liked it or not, this was part of who she was now. It was part of how she stayed alive, and that was what she'd agreed to do to protect Alex and Harper.

All of the water in the ocean couldn't wash the blood from her hands, but it did calm her slightly. She swam far away from shore, and then floated on her back, letting her tail flick through the water to steady her, and she stared up at the stars above her.

She tried to make out the constellations that Alex had shown her. The only ones she could really decipher were Orion and Cassiopeia. The sun was starting to rise, and soon the sky had gotten too light for her to see them anymore.

When the sky turned bright pink, Gemma decided to head back to shore. Sawyer seemed to get up rather early, and he might alert Penn if he noticed that Gemma was gone. She didn't want to get in trouble with the sirens for swimming without telling Penn.

She swam back to shore languidly, relishing the water. As much as she hated everything else about being a siren, there was truly something magical and amazing about being able to swim like this.

Gemma had to remind herself to be grateful for it. She might have given up everything else, but she would always have the ocean.

She stayed close to the surface, bobbing up and down in the water like a dolphin. Once when she leapt out, she thought she heard someone call her name.

She stopped swimming and just treaded water, so her head and shoulders were above the waves. And then she saw him, a figure waving his arms on the beach and running out toward the ocean.

"Alex?" Gemma breathed.

Once she got over the shock of it, she dove in the water, swimming as quickly as she could. She needed to reach him before he yelled again or he might wake the sirens, if he hadn't already. She didn't understand how he'd gotten here or what he was doing, but she didn't care. All she could think about was how much she missed him, and how she couldn't wait to be in his arms again.

Alex had run out into the water, and he'd gone out deep enough for it to crash over his waist when Gemma finally reached him.

They didn't even speak when she got to him. She pushed herself out of the water and threw her arms around him. She was cold from the water, and when his arms wrapped around her back, they felt hot against her skin.

He held her tight to him and kissed her more fiercely than he'd ever kissed her before. There was this panicked insistence to it, like he couldn't kiss her deeply enough, and Gemma loved it. She put her hands on his neck, pulling him closer to her.

He was lifting her out of the water as they kissed, and her tail pressed against his legs and stomach. Gemma clung to him desperately, and she never wanted to let him go.

Eventually they had to stop so they could breathe, but Alex still held her close to him. He rested his forehead against hers, his eyes closed as he breathed her in.

"I missed you," he murmured, and kissed her on the mouth again, more gently this time.

"I missed you, too," she said, wanting to sob. She'd been so certain she'd never see him again, and now she was afraid that she'd never be able to let him go.

At that thought, she returned to kissing him frantically. In the back of her mind, she knew the sirens were nearby in the house, and Alex would have to leave very soon if she wanted him to live. So if she only had a few moments with him, she had to make them count.

His hand moved down, pressing against the smooth scales of her tail, which rose up to the small of her back. Nobody had ever touched her tail before, and the warm touch of his skin sent pleasurable shivers down to her fin.

"Wow." Alex stopped kissing her so he could look down at the iridescent scales, which shimmered in the early morning light. "So . . . you really are a mermaid now?"

"Yeah." Gemma laughed and looked him in the eyes. "I kinda am."

"So you two are done making out now?" Harper asked, and

Gemma looked over Alex's shoulder to see Harper standing behind him. She'd been so excited about Alex that she hadn't even noticed her sister there.

Harper had gone out far enough so the water was just lapping against her feet, and Daniel was standing a bit farther back on the shore, looking uncertainly from Gemma to the stark white house on the beach behind them.

"You have to go," Gemma said. Seeing Harper and Daniel's unease had snapped her out of her romantic notions, and she realized how dangerous this could get.

"Alex gets a kiss, and you tell me to get out of here?" Harper raised an eyebrow. "No way. We didn't come all this way to leave you behind."

"I appreciate that, and I'm glad to see you—all of you," Gemma said. She'd pulled back from Alex enough to comfortably talk to Harper, but his arms remained around her. "I truly am. But you need to get out of here."

"We're not leaving without you," Harper said. "I don't care if I have to drag you out of here kicking and screaming or stab those horrible she-devils in the eyes, you are coming with me when I leave."

"You have to go," Gemma insisted.

"Gemma, I'm not leaving without you," Alex said, and she turned to look at him, staring up into his deep brown eyes. "Last time you left, I was unconscious and couldn't stop you. But this time I'm wide awake, and I'm not letting you go."

"You don't understand," Gemma told him plaintively. "They'll kill you if they find you here."

"Then we should really get going," Alex replied.

"No, I can't go with you," Gemma said. "They'll come after me, and then they'll hurt you and Harper and Daniel to punish me."

"Gemma, you're not listening to me," Alex said. "I am not leaving you. So if you stay, I stay."

"Alex!" Gemma wanted to push away from him, but his arms felt too good and too strong around her. "They won't let us be together. If they see you, they will kill you."

"Come with us," Alex said. "Leave with us right now, and we'll find a way to stop them."

"I don't know if there is a way to stop them," Gemma admitted sourly.

"There's a way to stop everything. We just have to figure it out," Alex assured her.

"You don't know what the sirens are like," Gemma said, but her resistance was wearing down.

"Do you want to stay here?" Alex asked. "Do you want to be a siren?"

"No," she said emphatically.

"Then let's get out of here." He lowered her into the water, and stepped back away from her, toward the shore. "We'll find a way to get you free, but the first step is leaving here."

She bit her lip and glanced up at the house. It was dangerous to leave, that was for sure, but it was also probably the only chance she had of ever figuring out how to break the curse. Penn sure as hell was never going to tell her how.

But maybe if Gemma worked with Harper and Alex, the three of them could figure out how to change things. It was the best chance she had to escape this life.

And based on the way both Harper and Alex were looking at her, Gemma wasn't sure if there was anything she could say or do to get them to stop looking for her. She knew Alex was dead serious when he said he wouldn't leave without her.

If she wanted to keep him alive and rid herself of the curse, the best way to do it would be to leave. And if she was going to leave, she ought to hurry and do it before the sirens woke up.

"Let's go," Gemma said, and Alex smiled widely at her. He pulled her close to him again, kissing her quickly. "But we really do need to hurry."

Alex pulled her toward the shore, but when the water got shallow enough that her tail began to tingle, she stopped him.

"You need to go ahead and turn around," Gemma said.

"What? Why?" Alex asked, alarmed.

"Because my tail doesn't change into bikini bottoms when it turns back into legs," Gemma told him.

"Oh." Alex blushed slightly when he realized what she meant and quickly turned around.

"What's going on?" Harper asked. She was standing just far enough away that she hadn't heard Gemma's explanation.

"Turn around," Alex said, walking over to where Harper and Daniel were standing. "Gemma's naked and needs to put on bottoms."

"Oh, crap," Daniel said, and immediately turned around.

Harper turned away from Gemma more slowly, as if she didn't trust Gemma not to disappear in the waves while they had their backs turned. But Gemma had no plans to do that.

She pulled herself out of the water, willing her legs to speed up. The transformation from tail to legs had never seemed so slow. Since she'd decided to leave, she wanted to get out of here as quickly as possible.

Gemma actually stood up before her legs had completely shifted back. One of her feet was still more fin than foot, and she almost tumbled in the sand, but she caught herself. She rushed over to her bikini bottoms, and by the time she'd slipped into them, her legs were normal.

"Okay," Gemma said, and ran over to where Alex was waiting. "We need to get out of here."

Alex took Gemma's hand, and the four of them ran through the sand. They had to go a ways down the beach to get around the boulders. The house was sandwiched right between the rocky outcroppings, so the quickest way to the front road was through the house, but they weren't about to take that path.

Daniel had parked in the grass about a quarter mile from the house. When they finally reached the car, Harper popped open the trunk and pulled out an old hoodie for Gemma to toss on so she wasn't running around in a bikini.

Gemma was standing behind the car as she slipped it over her head, and Harper stood beside her. As soon as she had it on, Harper grabbed Gemma and hugged her.

"I'm so glad you're safe," Harper said, hugging her so tightly it actually hurt.

"Thank you," Gemma said, her voice strained because of the intensity of Harper's hug.

Then Harper released her, and her eyes were grave as she stared at her. "If you ever run away like that again, you won't need to worry about the sirens. Because I'll be the one to kill you. Do you understand?"

"Yes." Gemma nodded meekly. "But in my defense, I did it to protect you."

"I don't care why you did it," Harper said. "Don't do it again."

Harper went around the car and got in the driver's seat, while Gemma hopped in back with Alex. She sat as close to him as she could, and he put his arm around her. As Harper sped off, Gemma settled back next to him, and she honestly couldn't tell if she'd made the right decision by leaving with them or not.

"How did you find me?" Gemma asked.

"It was in the paper," Daniel said.

"The paper?" Gemma arched an eyebrow.

Daniel handed the newspaper back to her and pointed to the article about the murdered boys. Gemma read it quickly, and when she got to the part about Jason Way, her heart pounded so hard she thought she might have a heart attack. She was afraid she might throw up or pass out.

Did they know that she'd done this? She tried to slow her breath and couldn't even look at them. They couldn't know. They wouldn't have rescued her if they realized what a monster she was.

"We knew the way the body was torn open was the sirens' trademark," Alex explained when Gemma didn't say anything.

"And we thought if they were here, you were probably close by."

"That was a good guess," Gemma said. She forced a smile at him and tried to slow her earlier panic.

The one consolation she did have was that Thea had been right about attracting rapists. According to the paper, Jason Way had been a rapist. Gemma had actually theorized that before. If she hadn't been able to turn into a man-eating beast, there was a good chance that Jason would've actually raped her.

That still didn't make it okay, though. It wasn't up to her to exact punishment on people, and killing him had been a bit more than self-defense.

But she didn't want to think about that right now. She was with Alex and Harper after thinking she'd never be with them again, and she wanted to enjoy it while she had the chance.

"How did you know where I was?" Gemma asked, folding up the newspaper and shoving it aside. "At that exact house on that beach?"

"That was all Harper." Alex motioned to her.

"How did you know?" Gemma asked her sister.

"I just knew," Harper said, trying not to elaborate further. "I don't know how to explain it more than that. I just knew you were there."

The car ride went smooth and rather fast. Or maybe it just seemed that way to Gemma. Admittedly, she did spend a bit of time making out in the backseat with Alex, until Harper threatened to hose them both off.

Most of Gemma's attention was focused on Alex, but while she was curled up next to him in the backseat, she watched Harper and Daniel interact. Daniel was trying to get Harper to relax and cheer up, and Harper tried to resist, but she ended up laughing with him more times than she'd have wanted to.

When they got back to Capri in the evening, Harper decided to drop Daniel off at his boat before heading to their house. She pulled up to the docks to let him out.

"Thanks," Harper said, and she seemed to avoid looking directly at him. "For coming with and helping look for Gemma, and for everything, really."

"Yeah, it was no problem," Daniel said. He sat in the car for a moment, then opened the door. "Well. I'll see you around."

"Yep," Harper said.

"'Bye, Daniel," Alex added, and Daniel waved at him as he got out.

"Wait a sec," Gemma told Harper, and then she hopped out after him. He was walking away, so she called after him, "Daniel. Hold up."

"Yeah?" He turned back around to her.

Gemma threw her arms around his waist, hugging him. It took him a second to hug her back. It was short and slightly awkward, but she smiled up at him when she took a step back.

"I just wanted to thank you properly for helping me out and for being concerned and all that," Gemma said.

"It's really not a problem," Daniel said, waving it off.

"And I wanted to thank you for Harper," Gemma said.

"For Harper?"

"Yeah," Gemma said. "She needs you more than she thinks she does, and I'm really glad that you can see that."

"Uh . . ." Daniel looked like he didn't know how to respond to that. "Um, you're welcome?"

"Yeah, anyway." Gemma waved at him as she stepped back. "See you later."

She ran back to the car, and Harper asked her what that was about. Gemma just shrugged, and Harper drove them back home.

TWENTY-TWO

Reunion

Being in her own room again felt so strange. Gemma stood in the doorway for a long time, just staring at the mess of things she'd left behind. It gave her a weird sense of being in a time warp. She hadn't been gone that long, not really, but with the insanity of the past few weeks, it felt like it had been a lifetime ago that she'd been the girl who lived in this room.

It was also a bit weird to see so much color. The pale blue of her walls, the bright colors of her bedspread, even the Michael Phelps poster on her wall. It all seemed so vivid after the constant whiteness of Sawyer's house.

She flopped back in her bed, a twin-size that felt so much better than the empty space of the big bed she'd been sleeping in. Everything about here felt so much better, even though the house was small and worn down and completely lacked the grandeur of the beach house.

But that didn't matter. This was home.

She looked over at her bedside table, expecting to see the picture of herself, her mom, and Harper that had occupied that space for years. When she saw it was gone, she sat up in a panic, but then remembered that she'd taken it with her when she left. She'd left it at the sirens' house, hidden in the top drawer with her clothes.

Harper knocked gently on Gemma's open bedroom door, and Gemma turned to look at her. Once they got back, Alex had gone home. Gemma hadn't really wanted him to leave, but Harper pointed out that they had spent the last eleven hours together, and their father would be home from work soon. He'd picked up overtime to compensate for his time off the previous week, and wouldn't get done until after seven.

"How does it feel to be back?" Harper asked.

"It's pretty strange, actually," Gemma admitted. "But I'm glad to be here."

"And I'm glad you're back." She smiled a little at that and walked into the room.

"What's the plan now?" Gemma asked. "Did you have one, beyond finding me?"

"Not really." Harper leaned back against the wall next to the closet. "I was kind of hoping that you might have some ideas. Alex and I have been doing tons of research on sirens, but we can't find anything." She paused. "You are a siren, right?"

"Yeah, I'm a siren," Gemma said with a heavy sigh. "So are Penn, Thea, and Lexi."

"So what does that mean exactly?" Harper asked. "You turn

into a mermaid, and then there's that bird-monster thing that Penn changed into. You can sing and enchant people."

"It's kind of a lot of things." Gemma lowered her eyes. She didn't want to explain it all to Harper, at least not right now. That would mean telling her about the whole curse, and about how she had to kill to survive.

"We've got time to talk about it later," Harper said, apparently noticing Gemma's hesitance. "If you want to shower and relax a bit before Dad gets home."

"Thanks." Gemma smiled wanly at her.

"We do have time, right?" Harper asked. "How long do you think we have before the sirens come after you?"

"I honestly don't know," Gemma said.

She thought back to when she'd gone into town the other day and killed Jason. She'd been gone for several hours, after basically stealing Sawyer's car. But when she came back, the sirens and Sawyer were all there, looking nonplussed.

Since Gemma hadn't taken anything with her, they probably wouldn't think she'd run away, so it would be a little while before they began a search for her. And even when they did, they wouldn't know where she'd gone. It wouldn't be too hard for them to figure out she'd gone back to Capri, but it might take them a few days before they went after her. They would probably expect her to come back to them, since she knew what it meant if she left.

Eventually, though, the sirens would find her. They had to. Part of the curse was that they had to be near each other at all times.

If they didn't find her, Gemma would die within a couple weeks. And if the sirens couldn't replace her, then Penn, Thea, and Lexi would die, too.

"We probably have a few days," Gemma said finally. "Maybe a week, tops. But that's it. They will come after me, and they will take me away with them." She swallowed hard when she realized it. "If we haven't found a way to break the curse by then, I have to go with them."

"We'll find a way," Harper insisted, and Gemma wished she shared her sister's conviction. "But for now, why don't you just shower and change? Dad'll be home soon."

"What should I tell him?" Gemma asked as Harper turned to go. "I can't tell him that I'm a siren, can I?"

"No," Harper replied, but she looked uncertain. She furrowed her brow, then shook her head. "No, it won't do him any good. It'll just make him worry, and he won't be able to do anything to help you."

"So what do I tell him?" Gemma asked.

"Just . . ." Harper shrugged. "I told him you left with Penn, but I didn't know why. So . . . just tell him you ran away because . . ." She shook her head. "I don't know. Don't give him a reason. You're a teenager and were rebelling. That should be enough, right?"

"It'll have to be, I guess."

Harper turned to leave and began shutting the door behind her.

"Hey, Harper," Gemma said, stopping her.

"Yeah?" Harper leaned in the half-open door to look back at her.

"Thank you for coming to get me and all that," Gemma said. "No matter how this all turns out, I want you to know that I really appreciate all the stuff you do for me. Including but not limited to rescuing me from monsters."

"Anytime." Harper smiled at her, then closed the door, leaving Gemma alone to get ready.

Gemma had just gotten out of the shower when she heard her father come home. She was still in the bathroom, brushing her hair, when the front door slammed shut. Then she heard Brian's booming voice telling Harper that he was home.

Gemma knew he'd be mad at her. He was going to yell at her a lot, and while she was dreading that, it suddenly didn't seem to matter. She'd missed her dad. She hadn't realized precisely how much until she heard his voice.

"Dad!" Gemma yelled as soon as she opened the bathroom door, and then she raced down the stairs.

Brian was standing in the living room, still wearing his work clothes, which were stained with oil and smelled vaguely of fish. When he saw Gemma running down toward him, his eyes widened and his jaw dropped.

She threw her arms around him, and he hugged her gruffly. He held her tightly to him for a moment, then moved so he could get a good look at her. He touched her face, his callused hands feeling especially rough on her smooth skin, and his blue eyes were brimming with tears.

"I love you so much, Gemma," he said. "You had me worried sick."

"I'm sorry, Dad," Gemma said, stifling her own tears. "I love you, too."

"Where were you?" Brian asked.

"I don't know." Gemma lowered her eyes and stepped back from him, because she still didn't completely understand how to answer that question.

"What the hell were you thinking?" Brian asked, and he started yelling. "What in god's name did I do that was so terrible that you needed to run off for *over a week* without telling me? I've been searching all over for you! The police have been looking for you! Do you have any idea what you've put me and your sister and even Alex through?"

"I'm sorry." Gemma stared at the floor, unable to look him in the face anymore.

"Sorry doesn't cut it, Gemma!" Brian shouted. "There's no excuse for what you did! You can't just leave without telling anybody. That's not okay, and you know it."

"I do know, Dad, and I'm really sorry," she repeated.

"And with everything that's going on, with the serial killer on the loose," Brian went on. "That was so dangerous and irresponsible. You could've been hurt or killed! And Harper and I had no idea what was happening to you. Do you know how terrifying that is?"

Gemma swallowed hard and shook her head. "No."

"And you missed Bernie's funeral," Brian said, but his tone had softened a bit when he said it.

"What?" Her heart dropped, and she finally looked up at her father. "Bernie's dead?"

When she'd gone to Bernie's Island and discovered the sirens there, tearing up his house, she'd suspected that something had happened to him. But she'd been hoping that maybe he'd been knocked out somewhere or had fled the island. Now Brian was telling her that her worst fears were true. The sirens had killed him.

"Yeah." Brian had his hands on his hips, but his stance relaxed, and he looked apologetic. "He was found dead early last week. The funeral was on Friday."

"Oh." A tear fell down her cheek, and she hastily wiped it away. "I'm sorry I missed that."

"I know how fond of him you were," Brian said, and he put a gentle hand on her shoulder. "But that's why you shouldn't leave like that. You don't know how much time you have left with the people you care about, so you shouldn't waste any of that time running away for no good reason."

"You're right." Gemma nodded. "And I'm sorry."

Gemma was crying softly, so Brian pulled her into his arms, letting her cry against his chest. He kissed the top of her head and held her until she'd calmed down.

"I need to go make some phone calls," Brian said. "Let everybody know to call off the search, since you're home and you're safe. But you and I will be talking more later. Do you understand?"

"Yes." Gemma sniffled.

"And you are grounded until you turn eighteen," Brian said.

"You are not to leave the house without my permission, and you're not to have anyone over unless I say you can. That includes Alex. Do you understand?"

"Yes." She nodded.

"Okay." He stepped away from his daughter. "But I do love you, and I am glad you're home safe."

"Thanks." Gemma smiled meekly at him. "I really am sorry about all the trouble I've caused everybody."

"Good. Maybe you'll think twice about running away again," Brian said. "Now why don't you go up to your room?"

Gemma ran back to her room almost as quickly as she'd come down. She slammed the door shut and leaned back against it, trying hard not to break down in tears.

She hated knowing she'd scared her dad like that and all the crap she'd put Harper, Alex, and everybody through. She hated it even more that she might have to do it again. If she didn't find a way to stop the sirens, she'd have no other choice. She'd be forced to leave with them to stop them from hurting someone else the way they'd hurt Bernie and Luke, and the way she'd hurt Jason.

The problem was that Gemma saw no solution. There was no way out of this without somebody getting hurt.

TWENTY-THREE

Admissions

Gemma was still sleeping when Harper left. After Gemma had talked to their dad the night before, she'd stayed in her room. Both Harper and Brian checked on her many times, but each time, Gemma was sound asleep. Whatever Gemma had been up to while she was with the sirens, it had obviously exhausted her.

Harper had slept a lot, too. The twenty-plus-hour drive had been very tiring. But Harper woke up often, certain that Gemma had left again, and would rush across the hall to peek in on her.

Even leaving today had been hard. Harper had called in to work, because she wasn't ready to leave Gemma for that long. It wasn't that she didn't trust Gemma not to run away. It was that Harper was afraid the sirens might come and find her.

She'd called Daniel a couple times, and he hadn't answered the phone. For some reason, that made Harper nervous. With possible revenge-seeking sirens on the loose, she didn't like the idea of anybody involved with rescuing Gemma not answering the phone.

It wasn't like she could leave Gemma home alone, though. Harper had called Alex, and he came over to help watch out for her. Since Gemma was still sleeping, Alex got comfortable on the living room couch.

He'd brought his laptop with him, and he immediately returned to doing his Internet search on how to break the sirens' curse. When Gemma woke up, they both hoped she'd be able to help out, since she knew more about the mythology than either of them did. But for now they thought it'd be better if Gemma rested, and Alex was left to his own devices until she woke up.

Harper thought about warning him that his job was to guard Gemma, not make out with her, but honestly, she didn't really care much about upholding Brian's attempt at grounding Gemma, and he was at work so he couldn't enforce it. Usually Harper would back him up, but this time she understood that Gemma didn't need to be punished for what she'd done.

Besides that, she didn't think Alex should be punished. He'd worked hard to find Gemma, so at the very least he deserved to be an exception to the rule. And he could help protect and watch over Gemma when Harper wasn't around.

Still, Harper didn't plan on making her trip down to the dock a long one. She just planned to see Daniel, make sure he was all right, thank him again for his help, and then leave. If she could do all that without getting on his boat, that would be even better.

After overhearing his conversation with Alex the other night, Harper had become convinced that she couldn't be around him anymore. She couldn't become involved with him, not right now when so much was going on with Gemma, and it wasn't fair to lead him on like that.

But more than that, things were becoming increasingly dangerous for everyone around Gemma. Harper had seen what the sirens could do, and she had a feeling that if they did find Gemma, and Harper and the others couldn't stop them, the sirens would seek vengeance on all the people who had tried to help Gemma. That included Daniel.

Or it would, if he stayed a part of Harper's life. It would be much safer for him if she stopped talking to him.

So today she would just check on him, and maybe tell him good-bye. No, definitely tell him good-bye. She just didn't know how to word it yet without it sounding weird.

As Harper walked down the docks to where Daniel's boat was moored, she tried to go over what she planned to say to him. Red, white, and blue flags tacked onto the docks' posts waved wildly in the wind, preparation for the Fourth of July celebration this weekend.

When she reached Daniel's boat, she was surprised to see a flyer taped onto the side, right next to the boat's name, *The Dirty Gull*.

It was warped and faded from the sun and water splashing

on it, even though it had only been there for a few days, but the words *Have you seen me?* were still legible above a large picture of Gemma. Alex had printed up a bunch of flyers and hung them around town.

Harper leaned over and grabbed on to the boat with one hand. She had to get the flyer down. For one thing, she didn't want the reminder of Gemma being missing, but more important, she didn't want the sirens to spot the connection between this boat and Gemma.

She grabbed one corner of the flyer, and had just started to pull when a boat zipped by, creating a wave that made *The Dirty Gull* rock hard to the side.

"Oh, no," Harper groaned.

She gripped the boat tighter to steady herself, but that only succeeded in causing her to lose her tenuous foothold on the dock. She tried to wrap her arm around the railing so she could hang on, but she couldn't get a handle on it.

Just when she was about to slip and splash into the water, Daniel's arm appeared over the railing and grabbed her.

"I'm seriously starting to wonder how you survived without me," Daniel said, grinning down at her.

"Much better, actually," Harper said as his strong hands held both of her arms. "I wasn't always trying to climb onto boats, so I very rarely fell into the ocean."

Once he'd lifted her up and set her safely on the deck, she lingered in his arms for a moment before remembering why she'd come here. It was hard to do when he looked at her like that, his hazel eyes full of something that created heat in her belly.

And he was shirtless—again—which only made matters worse. It was getting harder and harder for her to reject someone who looked like Daniel did when he wasn't wearing a shirt.

"What can I do for you today?" Daniel asked, his arm still wrapped around her waist so her chest was pressed to his. His abdomen and chest felt so firm against the soft contours of her own body, like he was made of concrete instead of flesh.

"I, uh . . ." Harper couldn't remember what he could do for her, so she shook her head and stepped away from him. It was impossible to think or even breathe when he held her close to him like that.

"Are you okay?" Daniel wrinkled his brows in confusion as Harper backed away from him.

"A flyer!" Harper announced excitedly when she remembered. "I was peeling a flyer off your boat."

She'd actually managed to rip off half of the flyer. But in her attempt to hang on to the boat, she'd dropped it into the water, where the scrap of paper was presumably floating out to sea.

"You mean the missing poster for Gemma?" Daniel's expression grew even more confused. "You came out to tear that off my boat? How did you even know that I had one?"

"I didn't." Harper leaned back against the railing behind her, trying to put some space between her and Daniel. "I happened to see it when I came out here, so I was trying to take it off, and then I slipped, and here we are."

"Yes, here we are," Daniel agreed as a bemused smile spread across his face. "The question is, why are we here?"

"I tried calling you earlier, and you didn't answer the phone," Harper said. "I thought maybe . . . I don't know. Something might have happened."

"You were worried about me?" He stepped closer to her, and his smile grew wider.

"Yeah. So?" Harper shrugged and tried to seem casual. "I worry about people. There's lots of crazy stuff going on right now. It makes sense that I would worry. I worry a lot. That's not a big deal. It's just how I am."

Another wave came up, and since Harper had been leaning against the rail, she almost fell backward over it. She caught herself at the last second, and Daniel grabbed her arm, just to be safe.

"Why don't we go down inside and talk about how natural it is for you to worry?" Daniel asked. "It's much less likely that you'll fall overboard down there."

"Yeah, sure." Harper stepped back from the edge and followed Daniel down into the boat.

This was actually going against her original plan, which was to avoid getting on the boat in the first place, and, if she did go on the boat, not to go down into his living area. But it was better than standing on the deck and getting tossed around so he'd have to catch her.

When Harper went down, she noticed his tiny quarters appeared a bit cleaner than when she'd seen them before. A stack of neatly folded clothes was at the end of his bed, and his bed was actually made. There was an empty bottle in the tiny sink, but that was about all that constituted a mess.

"So?" Daniel leaned against the small dining table that sat between padded benches. "You were saying that you were worried about me?"

"No, I was saying that with everything going on, it makes sense that I would worry in general." Harper sat down on the bed, since it was the farthest away from him that she could sit. "Why didn't you answer your phone?"

"I was sleeping," Daniel told her. "I went on this really long road trip yesterday, and I was awake for, like, twenty-four hours in a car. For some reason, that made me really tired, so when I got back, I slept a lot."

"Sorry." Harper smoothed out a wrinkle in his blankets. "I mean, thank you for coming with. And all the stuff you've been doing to help me, and Gemma. You really have been so helpful lately, and it means a lot to me."

"That's so weird how you can do that," Daniel said, and she looked up at him. He was staring out the window, his lips pursed.

"What?"

He shook his head and smiled crookedly. "You can say something that's supposed to be nice, like you're trying to compliment me, and you make it sound so *bad*."

Harper bristled. "How was that bad? I was just thanking you!"

"Exactly!" He motioned to her, the sad, crooked smile still on his face. "You're thanking me, and I can just hear the 'but' coming." He changed his voice to a high falsetto, presumably meant to sound like Harper. "'Thank you so much for helping me, Daniel, but the thing is, you're a dick.'"

"I never said that!" Harper shot back, genuinely offended by his impersonation. "I would never say that! I don't think you're a dick!"

"Sure you do." He scratched the back of his neck and wouldn't look at her. "You think I'm some kind of a slob and a loser. You have ever since we met, and I am sorry about the way we were introduced, but I think I've spent enough time trying to prove to you that I'm not like that. It was just a *really* bad first impression."

When they'd met, Daniel had just woken up and decided to pee over the edge of the boat. Harper looked up at just the wrong time and got a full of view of his nether region.

"That was an awful first impression," Harper said. "I will agree to that. But I've never . . . Okay, I haven't thought you were a loser for a long time. You've been so great with me and Gemma and everything that's been happening. I know that you are not a dick at all. You are kind and patient and brave and funny and so nice . . ."

She trailed off and stared down at her lap, because that wasn't what she wanted to say at all. And it actually embarrassed her that she'd admitted so much.

"You did it again, you know," Daniel said. "You just made a whole string of compliments sound terrible."

"Well, I'm sorry!" She threw her hands up in exasperation. "I meant them, but I don't know how else to say it."

"I believe you meant them. But you didn't come here today

to tell me any of that." He paused, and Harper looked at him. He appeared to be in the middle of a very serious thought. "You came here to tell me to leave you alone."

Harper was silent for a moment, then lowered her eyes. "I wasn't going to tell you to leave me alone."

"So you'd say it differently. More gently, then, but the sentiment remains the same."

She didn't say anything to that, and Daniel sat down next to her. Not too close, but close enough, and neither of them said anything for a minute. The silence felt a little awkward, but Harper didn't know how to fill it.

"What's the deal with us?" Daniel asked finally.

"What do you mean?" Harper lifted her head cautiously. "There is no deal with us. There's nothing. We're just friends—"

"Harper," Daniel groaned. "Stop."

"No, Daniel, I won't stop. There's really dangerous stuff going on right now, and I really do need to focus on that. And I don't want you getting hurt. That's what's going on. That's the deal with us. I don't have time to like you, and I don't want you to get hurt."

He met her eyes evenly and simply said, "Bullshit."

"What?" She blinked. "Those are all perfectly valid reasons. Things are crazy and—"

"*Bullshit,*" Daniel repeated, more emphatically.

"You can't just keep saying that," Harper said. "That's not an argument."

"You want an argument?" Daniel asked. "You want me to present a valid argument?"

"I want you to say something more than *bullshit,*" Harper allowed.

She actually expected him to swear again, probably just to spite her, but instead he turned and pushed her back on the bed. She was too surprised to even try to stop him. He hovered inches above her, supporting himself with an arm on either side of her.

He hadn't pinned her back, so her arms were free, and she could push him off if she wanted to. But she didn't.

Instead, she just stared up into his eyes, breathing harder than she would've liked. She licked her lips, and tried to slow the frantic beating of her heart.

"This is your argument?" Harper said quietly when he didn't say anything.

"My argument is that if I kissed you right now, you'd kiss me back," Daniel said, his voice low and sure.

"You don't know that," she argued without conviction.

"I do." He nodded once, his eyes never leaving hers. "You'd do it because you like me, and it doesn't matter if you have time to or not. When you care about someone, you just do, and nothing changes that."

She swallowed hard. "If you're so sure, then why haven't you kissed me?"

Before he could answer, the phone in Harper's pocket started playing Silverchair's song "Mind Reader"—Gemma's ringtone. For a split second Harper considered not answering. She didn't want to spoil the moment with Daniel, because he was right, and she wanted very badly to kiss him.

But the moment was already broken, and Gemma might need her. She hadn't left her that long ago, but if Gemma was in trouble and Harper missed the call because she was busy making out with some guy, she'd never forgive herself.

"That's Gemma," Harper said. "I have to get it."

"I know," he said, his voice heavy with regret.

He didn't move, though. Harper reached into the pocket of her jeans and pulled out her phone, all while Daniel was above her.

"Hello?" Harper answered the phone, and that's when Daniel finally rolled back, allowing her to sit up. "Gemma? Is everything okay?"

"Yeah, everything's fine," Gemma said. "I just woke up, and you weren't here. Alex said you had an errand to do or something. When are you coming back?"

"Um, I'll be back in a few minutes." Harper stood up and walked away from the bed, away from Daniel. "I'm just leaving. Did you need anything?"

"No, I just . . ." Gemma paused. "I wanted to make sure you were okay. I'm just feeling a bit edgy, I guess."

"Yeah, I understand," Harper said. "I'll be home really quick, though, and we can talk more then. Okay?"

"Yeah, sounds good," Gemma said, and she did sound a little relieved. "I'll see you soon."

Harper hung up the phone and stood with her back to Daniel for a minute, thinking. She was right at the bottom of the steps leading out of his boat. When she turned back around to face him, he was still sitting on the bed, watching her.

"If I don't talk to you anymore, I want you to know that it's not because I don't like you," Harper said carefully. "Because it's pretty obvious that I do."

He lowered his eyes then, probably knowing that whatever was coming next wasn't good.

"I can't have you as a part of my life, because I need to take care of my sister," Harper said. "And I do like you, so I don't want you to end up getting your heart ripped out."

"When you say you don't want me to have my heart ripped out, do you mean that metaphorically or literally?" Daniel asked.

"Maybe both," she admitted. " 'Bye, Daniel. And thank you in advance for understanding."

He gave her a small wave before she turned and darted out of the boat. She had to climb over the rail to get back to the dock, and she practically fell in the water again, but there was no way she was asking for his help.

Once she was safely on the dock, she walked quickly back to her car, nearly jogging, and the entire time she had to fight not to cry.

TWENTY-FOUR

Today

Harper sat on her bed, watching intently as Gemma spoke. Gemma sat curled up at the other end of the bed, holding Harper's worn-out old teddy bear in her arms. If they hadn't been talking about monsters and murders, it would've reminded Gemma of the late-night girl talks that she and Harper used to have.

When Harper came home a few hours ago from whatever errand she'd done, she'd looked rather sad. Gemma had tried to talk to her about it, but Harper wouldn't have it. Harper sent Alex home and insisted that the two of them really talk about what was going on. Not just because Harper wanted to understand what Gemma had been through, but because she was hoping it might help them figure out a way to break the sirens' curse.

Gemma had been happy to tell Harper, even if it hadn't been necessary for giving her more information. It was such a relief to be able to talk to someone about the crazy stuff that had been going on. It was like a giant rock had been lifted from her chest, and Gemma could finally breathe again.

Gemma started from the beginning and told Harper everything she knew. About how the sirens had tricked her into drinking out of the flask, and how turning into the mermaid form felt amazing. When she told Harper exactly what was in the flask, Harper paled, but Gemma pressed on.

She explained the curse as best she could—about why Demeter had punished the girls, so now they were stuck together, shifting between mermaid form and bird-monster. She told Harper why she'd left, about what had happened at Bernie's Island, how she didn't know Bernie was dead then, but she knew she had to do whatever it took to protect Alex and Harper.

She told Harper about the way things had been at Sawyer's house, and how she'd been so sick at first that her hair had been falling out. She even told her about the weird hunger lust she'd felt, and how she'd lost control for a moment and kissed Sawyer.

There were only two things she left out of the story. Gemma just couldn't bring herself to tell Harper about feeding and that she'd killed someone. Nor could she tell her that the sirens needed to eat boys' hearts to survive. And thankfully, Harper didn't ask.

Gemma knew that Harper had to have suspicions. She'd seen the bodies, so Harper had to know the sirens killed boys and tore them open for a reason. But it must have been one of those things that Harper didn't really want to know, the way sometimes parents suspect their kids are having sex but never ask. Sometimes not knowing is better.

The other thing Gemma couldn't tell her was that she might die. Harper was hoping the sirens would wait as long as possible to find Gemma, but what she didn't know was that they couldn't wait too long. If they didn't find her within a couple weeks, Gemma would be dead.

The reason Gemma didn't tell Harper this wasn't so much that she didn't want to worry her, but that she didn't want Harper to prevent it. Gemma didn't want to die, but right now it was the only way she knew how to break the curse. It might be better if they didn't find her: if she died, so would the sirens.

"I'm sorry," Harper finally said. Her knees were pulled up to her chest, and she rested her chin on them.

"Why are you sorry?" Gemma asked, tilting her head to look at her sister.

"I'm sorry that you had to go through all this," Harper said. "And you had to go through it alone. So much of this happened when you were at home, and you didn't feel like you could tell me or Dad any of this."

"Harper." Gemma pushed herself up so she was sitting straighter. "You guys didn't do anything wrong. I couldn't tell you any of this because it's *insane*."

"No, I know, I'm not looking for reassurance," Harper said. "I understand why you did what you did, and I don't blame you. I just wish . . . I wish you didn't have to go through all this, and I wish I knew how to help you."

"You're, like, two years older than me, and you're my sister,"

Gemma said. "You're not supposed to have all the answers or be able to save me from anything."

Harper pursed her lips and stared down at her bedspread without saying anything. Gemma hadn't meant to make her sad, and now she almost wished she hadn't told her anything. It felt good getting everything off her chest, and for the first time Gemma felt like she wasn't completely alone in this. But she didn't know if it was worth upsetting Harper like this.

"You remember when we were kids, after Mom had her accident?" Harper asked at length.

"Yeah, of course I do," Gemma said.

"Mom was in a coma for, like, six months, and I was positive she was gonna die," Harper said. "But you never gave up hope. Every day, we'd visit her, and you'd say, 'Today will be the day she wakes up.' And we'd get there, and she'd still be in a coma, and you'd just say, 'Tomorrow, then. Tomorrow she'll wake up.' "

"In the beginning, you and Dad tried to tell me that I was wrong," Gemma said. "Dad would tell me, 'The hospital will call if Mom wakes up, and they didn't call. So she's not awake today.' And I would just insist that she would be."

"Yeah, so eventually we just gave up and told you not to be upset if she wasn't," Harper said. "Not that you ever did get upset. I mean, sometimes you would, and you'd cry because you missed Mom. But you never threw a fit or anything. You just said, 'Tomorrow.' "

"I guess I was a pretty optimistic kid." Gemma smiled sadly at the memory of herself.

"You were," Harper agreed. "But what you don't know is

that every day when we got to the hospital, even though I was certain Mom hadn't woken up, a little part of me believed she had. Because you had so much conviction. I thought one day you'd have to be right."

"And I was," Gemma said with pride. "One day, Mom woke up. Not exactly the way I had imagined or hoped for, but she woke up."

"But you knew everything would be okay," Harper said, looking at Gemma with tears in her eyes. "And I didn't."

"It's okay." Gemma didn't understand why Harper was so upset, so she slid closer to her. "Everything turned out the way it was supposed to."

"I know." Harper sniffled and looked over at her. "But this time, I feel like you don't know everything's going to be okay."

"Things are a lot more complicated than they were then," Gemma said. "And I understand what's happening. I was seven then, I didn't know what a coma even meant. But now I fully understand the seriousness of what we're up against."

"I don't know how everything is going to work out," Harper admitted. "I honestly haven't a clue about how we're going to stop the sirens and break the curse. But I do know that everything will be okay."

Gemma lowered her eyes and shook her head. "You don't have to say stuff just to reassure me. I appreciate you trying, but I know how impossible this all is."

"No, Gemma, listen to me." Harper put her hand on top of Gemma's and met her eyes. "Today, I don't know how to stop this and save you. So, tomorrow, then. Tomorrow we'll know how."

Gemma smiled at her sister with tears in her eyes. "What if we don't find it tomorrow?"

"There's always a tomorrow," Harper said. "And we'll keep looking every day until tomorrow finally comes. I never stopped believing in you when we were little, and I'll never stop fighting for you now."

Gemma wanted to believe her sister's words, but she knew something that Harper didn't—that there wouldn't always be a tomorrow. She only had a handful left if the sirens didn't come for her.

But she also knew that they would stop at nothing to find her. Penn cared too much for her own life to just let Gemma slip away, dooming them all to die.

Harper put her arm around her and squeezed her shoulders, hugging her closer. "Life would be so much easier if we got to have normal sister conversations again. Remember when we stayed up all night talking because you were upset that some guy didn't call you after a party?"

"Yeah." Gemma laughed. "And now Alex calls me all the time. But it could be worse. We could have the siren issues *and* Alex not calling me after a party."

"Yeah." Harper laughed. "That would be worse."

TWENTY-FIVE

Dinner

The house should've been tenser. Gemma was still in trouble, and Brian should've stayed angry with her. Not to mention that they hadn't figured out how to save Gemma from the sirens. Harper had stayed home from work again, refusing to leave Gemma unguarded, even for a few hours.

Both Harper and Gemma knew the sirens were coming after her—it was just a matter of time. They spent a long time discussing possible ways to break the curse and doing what research they could think of, but when they came up with nothing new or substantial, they prepared themselves to fight the sirens.

Harper put earplugs in her dresser drawer so the siren song couldn't enchant her, and she shoved a butcher knife under her pillow. She put a baseball bat under her bed, and they brought in the shovel from out back and put it in the front hall closet.

Their father had plenty of tools, like saws and even an ice pick, out in his work area in the garage. Harper considered bringing them in, but they felt too gruesome to fight with. She could still get to them if she needed to, but she hoped it wouldn't come to that.

In a way, all the prep work they'd done reminded Harper of *Home Alone*, like they were children setting up booby traps for burglars. Gemma went along with everything, but she seemed dubious.

The trouble was that neither of them knew what else to do. They hadn't found a way to break the curse, so they were only left with fighting back. Harper would do whatever it took to protect herself and her family, and if she had to kill the sirens, she would.

Once the preparation was done, and Harper had stashed weapons everywhere she could think of without Brian finding them, an odd peace settled over her. She'd done everything she could. Now they had to wait.

Brian came home from work that night in an astonishingly good mood. His daughter was home safe and sound. Because of the holiday on Sunday, he had Monday off, giving him a three-day weekend. That seemed to set the tone for the whole night.

Harper was making spaghetti and meatballs for supper, and Gemma offered to help. Brian cracked a beer in the living room to watch TV and relax after work for a bit, leaving the girls in the kitchen to handle supper.

"Harper," Gemma said, barely stifling a giggle as she held

up a misshapen meatball for Harper to inspect. "What do you think of my balls?"

"You're so immature." Harper rolled her eyes, but she couldn't help smirking at her sister.

They stood at the kitchen counter, making the meatballs. Harper seasoned the raw hamburger, and they rolled it into balls. She'd done it a hundred times before, sometimes with Gemma's help, but this was the first time that Gemma had been unable to stop giggling.

"Oh, come on, Harper," Gemma said, refusing to be deterred. "It's funny. Admit it's funny."

"It's really not." Harper laughed, but only because Gemma's laughter was contagious. She shook her head and motioned to the meatball Gemma was making. "That one's lumpy."

Gemma burst out laughing at that, and when Harper scowled at her, it only made her laugh harder.

"What has gotten into you?" Harper asked.

"I'm just glad to be home, I guess."

Gemma tossed a meatball at Harper, and it narrowly missed her, landing on the floor with an unpleasant splat.

"Hey," Harper said. "Don't waste food."

"Sorry." Gemma grabbed a paper towel to wipe the meatball off the floor. "When was the last time we had a food fight, though?"

"I don't know." Harper looked over her shoulder to watch her sister. "When I was, like, six or something."

"Exactly!" Gemma insisted, and leaned on the counter next to Harper. "We're really overdue for another one."

"I really don't think we are." Harper shook her head, but she smiled. "It's a waste of food, and it's a mess that I'll have to clean up."

"Harper!" Gemma threw her head back and groaned. "Let's say this is my last night here—"

"It's not." Harper cut her off and looked at Gemma severely. "We'll find a way—"

"No, Harper, listen to me." Gemma cut her off. "I'm not saying it *is*. I'm just saying, what if? Because there is a chance that we might not have that many nights together as a family. I mean, even if we fix this whole curse thing, you're leaving in a matter of weeks for college."

"That's your justification for wasting food?" Harper raised an eyebrow.

"No, I'm just . . ." Gemma sighed. She looked at Harper, smiling, and her honey-colored eyes were hopeful. "Let's just have fun tonight, and worry about the mess tomorrow."

"Okay," Harper relented. "But I am *not* having a food fight."

"Fine." Gemma turned and started making meatballs next to Harper. "But will you at least laugh at my jokes about the balls?"

"Probably not." Harper grinned. "Plus, we probably have enough meatballs by now."

"You can never have too many balls," Gemma said.

"That's what she said," Harper said, attempting to make a bad joke, and Gemma burst out laughing.

"It's not even that funny," Gemma said through her own laughter. "I just can't believe *you* said it."

"Hey, I'm trying," Harper said.

She might've even laughed along with her sister, but a loud knock at the front door interrupted her thoughts. Gemma didn't seem to notice, happy to continue giggling, but Harper went over to the sink to wash her hands. She wasn't sure if the sirens would knock at the front door, but they'd done it before when they came to get Gemma, so she wouldn't put it past them.

"Harper," Brian said as he came into the kitchen. "Someone's at the door for you."

"Who is it?" Harper asked as she hurried to dry her hands with a towel.

Gemma had finally gotten her giggling fit under control and turned around to see Brian standing in the kitchen doorway.

"Daniel," Brian said, and that explained the pained expression on his face. He clearly wasn't thrilled about boys coming around for his daughters.

"Oh, um . . ." Harper pushed her hair back behind her ear and shook her head. "I'm busy making supper."

"Nonsense," Gemma said. "You go talk to Daniel. Me and Dad can handle this, can't we?" Brian seemed reluctant to agree to this, so Gemma smiled at him. "Come on, Dad. If you don't help me make supper, I'll find a way to burn everything. Even the noodles."

"Go on." Brian nodded at Harper and offered her a small smile. "I'll help your sister."

"Okay, then." She smiled thinly at Brian and Gemma, trying to look grateful, when she really didn't feel that grateful.

She'd spent the day with her sister preparing for a siren

attack, so she probably looked horrible. Besides that, she'd told Daniel she didn't want to see him anymore just the day before. And that had been hard enough to do the first time. She didn't want to do it again.

In the living room, Daniel was standing with his back to her. He was bent forward slightly, admiring the pictures that lined the mantel.

Harper watched him for a moment, feeling a pang of regret at having to send him away, then she cleared her throat.

"Daniel?" Harper said, and he turned to face her.

"Are these your parents?" Daniel pointed to a wedding photo of her mom and dad.

She nodded. "Yeah, that's them."

"Your mom is very pretty," Daniel said.

"Yeah, she is," Harper agreed, and walked over to him. "Gemma really takes after her."

"Yeah, I can see that." Daniel glanced back at the picture as if to confirm the observation, then smiled back at Harper. "But you're prettier."

Harper looked down at her feet, blushing slightly. "You shouldn't say things like that."

"Why not?"

"You know why not," she said. Gemma and Brian laughed in the kitchen, and Harper looked back toward the other room. "I should really go back and help them."

"They're laughing, Harper, not screaming for help," Daniel pointed out. "And your dad is a grown man. I'm pretty sure he can handle making supper without you."

"What are you doing here, Daniel?" Harper asked, finally looking up at him. "Yesterday, I thought I made things perfectly clear."

"You did," Daniel agreed.

Harper stared up at him in disbelief. "So . . . why are you here?"

"After you left yesterday, I thought hard about what you said," Daniel explained. "What stood out the most is that you finally admitted that you like me."

"Ugh." She sighed. "You totally missed the point of everything I said."

"No, I didn't," Daniel insisted. "It came through loud and clear. You say you're busy with your sister. I say I can help you with that, the same way Alex and Marcy can help you. Only better, because I'm the one that actually found Gemma, remember?"

"I'm the one that knew which house it was," Harper said, avoiding his eyes. "I mean, I appreciate your help, but we could've . . . we probably would've found her. Eventually."

"Maybe, maybe not," Daniel allowed. "But I helped you find her this time, and I helped you fight the sirens on the island, and I helped you rescue her on the beach, and I scared the sirens away from her once. The point is, if you want to take care of your sister, you want me on your side.

"No, scratch that." Daniel waved his hand. "You *need* me. So you can't use that as an excuse to stay away from me anymore."

"It's not an excuse," Harper said. "I'm trying to do the right thing here. I really am. I'm trying to protect Gemma and you! You conveniently forgot about that part, Daniel." She lowered her voice, in case her dad might overhear. "These are monsters that kill boys, and you're a boy. I don't want them to hurt you."

"I didn't forget about that," Daniel said. "You just don't get to make decisions for me."

Harper was genuinely offended. "I'm not!"

"You're trying to," Daniel said. "If I choose to be in danger, that's my choice. If I want to be with you, even knowing how dangerous it's going to be, I can do that."

"But Daniel—" She started to protest, but he put his hands on her shoulders to reassure her, startling her into silence.

"So the only question that really matters is, do you like me?" Daniel asked.

"You know the answer to that."

"You're right." Daniel smirked. "I think I do know the answer, but I want to hear you say it anyway."

"Yes," Harper said, almost as if it pained her to do so. "I like you."

She lowered her eyes and opened her mouth to argue with him, so Daniel slid his hands from her shoulders to her waist.

He gently pulled her closer to him, and she looked up. His arms were loose around her waist, so he wasn't forcing her to stay in place, but she didn't move away. She put her hands on his chest and stared up into his eyes.

"I like you," Daniel said softly. "And I don't need you to

protect me. I can take care of myself. And I can take care of you, too."

"You don't need to."

"I know," he said, brushing her hair back from her forehead. "But I want to."

His hand was warm on her face, and Harper could've sworn she felt his heart hammering through his chest. His palm pressed harder on the small of her back, pulling her against him, and she slid her arms up around his neck. She stretched up, standing on her tiptoes . . . and then her dad said her name.

"Harper." Brian almost barked her name as he appeared in the living room. Harper jumped away from Daniel.

"Hi, Dad, sorry." Harper flushed and looked everywhere around the room except at her father or at Daniel. "We were just talking. We weren't doing anything. How's supper going? Do you need help with supper? I can help you. Do you want me to go in the kitchen?"

"No, supper is fine," Brian said. His voice was gruff, but it softened a bit. "It's cooking, and it won't be that long. Gemma was just setting the table, and so I thought I would ask if your boyfriend would be staying to eat with us."

"Oh, um, he's not my—" Harper tried to stammer out but Daniel interjected.

"That would be fantastic, Mr. Fisher," he said. "I would love to join you. I don't get a lot of home-cooked meals."

"So you're still living out on that boat, then?" Brian asked, crossing his arms over his chest. Harper stood off to the side, her eyes bouncing nervously between the two of them.

"For now." Daniel nodded.

"Why are you staying out there?" Brian asked. "Aren't you working?"

"Yeah, I'm working," Daniel said. "I mostly do odd jobs, but it keeps me busy."

"You make any money doing that?" Brian asked.

"I make enough to support myself," Daniel said. "But it's hard to save up enough to get my own place. I'm working on it, though."

"The boat must get pretty cold in the winter?" Brian asked.

"It can get cold," Daniel admitted. "But I make do."

"Yeah, I bet." Brian scratched his temple and shifted his weight. "You know about the island, don't you? You helped Harper clean it up last weekend?"

"You mean Bernie's Island?" Daniel asked. "Yeah, I was out there helping Harper."

"I don't have any use for it," Brian said. "If you wanted to stay out there, rent the place, that'd be fine by me. It wouldn't be free, of course, but I wouldn't charge you too much."

"Really?" Daniel asked, sounding surprised.

"Yeah, seriously?" Harper chimed in.

"If you're going to be seeing my daughter, I can't have you living on a boat," Brian attempted to explain. "So . . . it's there if you want it. Think about it, and . . . you can decide later."

"Supper's ready, guys!" Gemma called from the other room.

Harper let Daniel go into the kitchen first, so she could smile up at her dad. She mouthed the words *Thank you* at him, but he just brushed it off and ushered her into the next room.

Supper started off slightly awkward, but thanks to Gemma's almost unnatural cheer, the tension eased quickly. The four of them were soon talking and laughing, and it had been a very long time since Harper remembered a family dinner when they'd been happier.

TWENTY-SIX

Restraint

Harper had been missing so much work lately that she picked up a Saturday at the library. That meant she wasn't able to take Gemma for their usual visit out to Briar Ridge to see their mom. Harper had told Gemma how it had gone last week, so Gemma knew she couldn't miss this week, lest Nathalie have some kind of breakdown. Besides that, she wanted to see her mom.

After much discussion, Brian finally relented and agreed to let Alex take Gemma. Her car still wasn't working, and Brian thought Gemma would be less likely to run off again if she had a chaperone.

Ordinarily, Gemma would've been mad that Brian was still avoiding Nathalie. It'd been years since he'd last seen her, and that drove Gemma nuts. But today she was happy to be able to spend some time alone with Alex.

Since she'd been back in Capri, she'd hardly been able

to see him, except for when Harper let him come over. Brian had her on lockdown, and while she understood his reasons, it was still driving her crazy not to be able to see Alex.

On the car ride to Nathalie's group home, Alex and Gemma hardly spoke, but she was content just to hold his hand and be with him. Sometimes he'd just look at her and smile, and that was enough.

When they pulled in the driveway, Alex had barely turned off the car before Nathalie came running out of the house, waving her arms like a madwoman.

"Gemma?" Nathalie was yelling, and Gemma got out of the car as quickly as she could.

"Mom?" Gemma said. "Is everything okay?"

As soon as Nathalie saw Gemma, she froze. She put her hands to her face and let out a loud sob. Then she ran to her daughter and nearly knocked Gemma down when she threw her arms around her.

"I missed you so much," Nathalie said, crushing Gemma to her. "I was so worried about you."

"I'm okay, Mom," Gemma said, her voice coming out in small grunts since Nathalie was hugging her so forcefully. "I missed you, too."

"Nathalie?" Becky, one of Nathalie's staff, had come out of the group home and was waving her back in. "Why don't you and your guests come inside and visit?"

Nathalie finally released Gemma. "Do you want to go in the house? Should we go in?"

"Sure," Gemma said. "That sounds great, Mom. Do you remember Alex?"

"Alex?" Nathalie's face scrunched up in confusion. "Is that your father?"

"No, Mom, it's not. That's Alex." Gemma motioned to where Alex stood next to the car. He'd gotten out after they parked, but Nathalie had been so focused on Gemma that she hadn't even noticed him.

"No, I don't know him." Nathalie shook her head, then looked sadly at her daughter. "Should I?"

"Probably not," Gemma said. "It's been a really long time since you met him."

Alex had moved in next door to them about a year before Nathalie's accident. He'd been over to their house a number of times before she got hurt, and he'd even been over during her brief attempt at living at home after the accident.

But considering that Nathalie couldn't remember her own husband anymore, it wasn't surprising that she'd forgotten the boy next door.

"Hello, Mrs. Fisher." Alex walked over to her and shook her hand. "It's so nice to see you again."

"Call me Nathalie." She smiled at him and looped an arm around her daughter's shoulders. As they walked toward the house, she whispered loudly, "He's so cute, Gemma!"

"He sure is," Gemma agreed, and Alex laughed nervously as he followed them inside.

The visit went really well, as far as visits with Nathalie went. She was very hyper, but she was in a good mood. She seemed especially excited to see Gemma, hugging her many times. Once or twice she got a little overly affectionate with Alex, hanging on him or holding his hand. Alex handled it well, and when Gemma reminded Nathalie that Alex was her boyfriend, Nathalie stopped what she was doing.

Nathalie even took a run at braiding Gemma's hair. Unfortunately, Nathalie wasn't so great at fine motor skills anymore, so it turned into a knotty mess. It was incredibly painful to endure as Nathalie yanked on her hair, but Gemma smiled through it.

When Gemma and Alex left, her hair was still tied up in a messy "braid."

"How bad is it?" Gemma asked on the drive back home.

"It's really . . . it's really something." Alex smirked as he glanced over at her.

"Thanks." Gemma laughed and flipped down the visor mirror so she could admire it herself. "I think it's sweet that she tried to do it. She hasn't attempted to do my hair since I was about seven."

"And you can pull it off. Not many other girls could wear a rat's nest, but on you it works."

"Too bad it hurts like heck." Gemma flipped her visor back up and started pulling at the tangles and knots, trying to undo them. "I have to take this out before I get a migraine."

"So when we get back to Capri, you just want to go home?" Alex asked.

"Dad said I'm supposed to," Gemma said. "But he didn't tell me what time I had to be home. So maybe we could go out to the cliff?"

Alex grinned. "Sounds good to me."

In another age, the cliff might have been called "Makeout Point" or something silly like that. It had a wonderful view of Anthemusa Bay, and it was rather secluded, surrounded by cypress trees and loblolly pines.

Alex pulled up the gravel path that wound through the trees and parked as close to the edge of the cliff as he could. Gemma had finally gotten her hair free of the mess her mom had put it in, and she got out of the car, letting the wind blow through her hair.

"It's a beautiful day," Alex said, getting out of the car after her.

"It sure is." Gemma walked to the edge of the cliff and sat down, letting her legs dangle over it. "Come on." She patted the dirt next to her. "Sit by me."

When he sat down, he moved more carefully than Gemma and eyed the waves crashing against the face of the cliff warily. He slipped off his shoes before dangling his legs over the edge. Once he was settled, he took Gemma's hand, holding it gently in his.

From this vantage point, they could see the entire bay. Closest to them were the docks where her father worked, large barges pushed up to the pier. Farther out, there were rows and rows of personal boats, some of them huge yachts and some boats even smaller than Daniel's.

The public beach was full of people. It was a gorgeous day, and a holiday weekend, so it was packed. Red, white, and blue decorations were hung up anywhere there was room along the beach.

Where the soft sand along the coast started giving way to sharp rocks, the crowds disappeared. The rocks led up to a cypress forest, the same forest where Alex and Harper had found the bodies a few weeks ago. A thick belt of trees wound all the way to the cove, which sat almost directly across from the cliff where Gemma and Alex were.

Then, a few miles away from the cove, sitting by itself in the ocean, was Bernie's Island.

"My dad's renting out the island to Daniel," Gemma said.

"Really?" Alex said. "That's cool. Right?"

Gemma nodded. "Yeah, I think so." She paused. "I guess Daniel is Harper's boyfriend now."

"Wow," Alex said.

"I know, right?" She smiled. "I think they're cute together, but I kinda never thought Harper would ever date. You know what I mean?"

"Yeah, I do," Alex agreed.

"But I'm glad she is," Gemma said. "It makes me feel better about all of this. Now I know that no matter what happens, she won't be alone."

"Gemma." Alex squeezed her hand. "Don't talk like that. We'll find a way to keep you safe."

"But what if we can't?" Gemma turned to face him, pulling one knee up to her chest. "Or . . . what if we shouldn't?"

"What do you mean?" Alex asked. His dark eyes were full of concern and confusion, and Gemma didn't know how to answer him.

Seeing the trees where Alex and Harper had found Luke

and the other boys reminded her of how horrible Alex had looked afterward. And Gemma didn't need any reminders about how she'd killed Jason. She was waking up from nightmares about it every night.

She'd been trying so hard to pretend that everything was fine, to forget the horrible things she'd done, the creature she'd become, and just enjoy the moment she was in. With the full moon approaching in a matter of weeks, there was a very real chance that Gemma might not live to see it.

Sitting here with Alex, Gemma found it hard to swallow back her current thoughts. They needed to find a way to kill the sirens, definitely, but only if the sirens came for her. And maybe they never would. Maybe they would just replace her instead, letting her die alone and away from them.

Either the sirens would come for her and they would probably all die in the fight, or she would die before they did. With options like that, Gemma had begun to accept her own death, which was feeling more and more inevitable. She was attempting to make peace with it, and wanted to relish what time she had left with the people she loved.

"Gemma?" Alex put his hand on her knee and leaned toward her. "What's wrong? What are you thinking?"

There was no way she could look into his eyes. She couldn't tell him what was really bothering her—that she was a murderer, and the best-case scenario was that she would be dead soon.

Gemma lowered her eyes. "There's something I should tell you."

"You can tell me anything," Alex said.

"I know, and I . . ." She swallowed hard, and she accidentally looked up at him. That's what did it. As soon as she looked in his eyes, she lost all her nerve, and she blurted out, "I kissed someone else."

"What?" Alex's face twisted in confusion, and his eyes flashed darkly, so Gemma hurried to explain. She didn't know why she thought confessing that she'd kissed Sawyer would be the way to go. Clearly she'd panicked.

"It was an accident. No, I mean . . ." She closed her eyes and shook her head. "It wasn't an accident. I didn't like him, though. I didn't want to kiss him. It was . . . a siren compulsion thing. But almost as soon as I kissed him, I stopped. I didn't want to hurt you. And I'll never do it again."

"It was a siren thing?" Alex asked.

"Yeah," Gemma said sheepishly. "That sounds like a cop-out. But for, like, five seconds, I wasn't in control of my body. This weird . . . urge took over me, and I kissed this guy. But then I took back control of myself, and that was it. It meant nothing. I never would've done it if I wasn't a siren. But I thought I should tell you. And I'll understand if you hate me."

"Hate you?" Alex actually laughed at that. "Gemma, I could never hate you."

"Oh, I'm sure you could." She forced a smile at him and was surprised to find tears brimming in her eyes. "There are things I could do that would make anyone hate me."

"No, Gemma, listen to me." He moved to face her completely, so he had to kneel in front of her, and he took both her hands in his. "There's nothing you can ever do that would make me stop caring about you."

"Alex, you don't know . . ." She trailed off, because if she kept talking, she would cry, and she didn't want to cry.

"I have known you for years," Alex said. "You've always been kind, considerate, smart, determined, and stubborn. You have a good heart, and you'd never let anybody change you. That's part of why I fell in love with you."

"What if I can't stop it, though?" Gemma asked, wiping at her eyes. "What if the sirens are making me evil, and I can't control it?"

"*You* can," Alex insisted. "You're too strong and too stubborn. You can fight this. We will beat them. Together. I promise you that, Gemma."

"You really think so?"

He nodded. "Yes, of course I do."

"And you've really fallen in love with me?" Gemma asked, and Alex smiled at that.

"You think I would've spent a week searching for you if I didn't?" he asked.

She laughed a little. "No, I don't suppose you would."

"I love you, Gemma," he said softly.

"I love you, too."

She leaned forward, kissing him fully on the mouth, and wondered how much longer she'd be able to do that.

TWENTY-SEVEN

Logic

Harper hadn't wanted to go to work, but as Gemma pointed out, it would probably be good if she still had a job when this was all over. Just because her sister was a siren didn't mean that Harper's car insurance payment wasn't due or that she didn't need to save up money for college.

She'd gotten scholarships for school, but it didn't cover everything. Besides that, she didn't have a job lined up yet for when she left. Not that she was even sure she was still leaving. If she didn't go, she'd lose her scholarship, but it wasn't like she could just abandon Gemma with all this supernatural danger going on.

Harper winced when she thought about leaving for school. She hoped everything with Gemma would be solved by then. But now Harper would have to leave behind Daniel, who was apparently her boyfriend now.

Even if the new title made her smile, it would only make it

harder to leave him behind. Maybe she should've corrected him before he left after supper last night. They were obviously dating, but the "boyfriend" label might be too heavy of a commitment.

"Okay, what the hell is going on with you?" Marcy asked, snapping Harper out of her thoughts. "You look like you're having a stroke over there. You wince, and then smile, then scowl. Are you schizophrenic?"

"No." Harper shot her a look. "I just have a lot on my mind."

"You didn't need to come in today," Marcy said. "I usually handle Saturdays by myself, and thanks to it being the Fourth of July tomorrow, the library isn't its usual happening self."

Marcy gestured to the empty expanse of the library. Harper had been there for nearly two hours and had yet to see a single patron.

"Thanks, but I need the hours," Harper said. "You can go if you want, though."

"I know. But then I'd have to be out there." Marcy shuddered as she pointed to the front window of the library.

The big glass pane that served as the storefront was partially blocked thanks to a massive poster explaining all the festivities going on over the weekend. But around that, Harper could see all the people walking by. Even Pearl's across the street looked packed.

"It's not so bad. You could watch the parade," Harper teased. "Or I think there's an ice-cream social this afternoon."

"Gag me with a spoon," Marcy muttered. "But that's the

kind of stuff you get a kick out of. You should be doing that. You and your sister should be eating ice cream socially."

"I don't actually know what an ice-cream social is," Harper said. "And Gemma is grounded, so that's a no."

"You have other friends," Marcy said. "Ask Alex or that Daniel fella."

"Are you trying to get rid of me?" Harper asked.

"You are cutting into my nap time, yes," Marcy said. "But I'm just saying that if you want to go out and have a good time, you should. You've been stressing too much lately, and it'd be good for you to have some fun."

"Maybe." Harper chewed her lip, debating whether or not to tell Marcy about Daniel, before deciding just to go for it. "Daniel did ask me to go with him to the fireworks tomorrow night."

"Oooooo," Marcy said. "Fireworks, eh? That sounds serious."

"Marcy." Harper groaned, but she was smiling and blushing.

"Oh, my god, look at you," Marcy said. "It is serious. Are you and Mr. Tall Dark and Tattooed finally an item? Did you kiss each other with tongue?"

"*Marcy!*" Harper's cheeks turned so red, she nearly matched Marcy's sunburn. "It's not . . . We haven't kissed yet, but . . . You can't ask me things like that. It's weird when you say it."

"Should I toss my hair and chew bubble gum?" Marcy asked. "Would that make you feel more comfortable?"

"I don't know." Harper waved her hands. "Maybe we shouldn't talk about it at all."

"Fine." Marcy leaned back in her chair. "So are you going with him tomorrow?"

"I don't know." Harper shook her head. "I don't think I should. With everything going on with Gemma, I don't feel like I should leave her alone."

"Do you want me to go babysit her tomorrow so you can have a night on the town?" Marcy offered.

"No. My dad will be home, and Alex will be next door."

"So what's the problem?" Marcy asked. "It sounds like she's all set for babysitters."

"She is, but . . ." Harper trailed off and fiddled with a pencil on the desk. "I just don't know how to stop the sirens, and they're coming for her."

"Stab them through the heart and cut off their heads," Marcy said. "I don't know anything that can survive that."

Harper thought about it for a minute, then shook her head. "They turn into freaky giant bird-monsters. Who the hell knows what they're capable of?"

"Well, stab them through the heart, and you'll find out."

"That's your advice?" Harper arched her eyebrow. "Stab them through the heart and see if it kills them?"

"No, my actual advice would be, stab them through the heart, run like hell, and *hope* it kills them," Marcy corrected her.

"But what if it doesn't kill them?"

"Then you have one really pissed-off freaky giant bird-monster after you," Marcy said matter-of-factly.

"That's not very comforting," Harper replied.

"It wasn't supposed to be. You want comforting, talk to your boyfriend or your dad or Gemma. You want the truth, talk to me."

"What if they're unstoppable?" Harper asked.

"For thousands of years, the *T. rex* thought it was unstoppable. Then a giant rock came, and boom!" Marcy snapped her fingers. "He's not the king of the world anymore."

"I don't have a meteor, and if I did, that would kill more than just the sirens," Harper said.

"My point is that nothing is unstoppable, and the *T. rex* wasn't as great as he thought he was. I mean, what were those little arms for?" Marcy pulled her arms back into her sleeves, so her hands made short imitation *T. rex* arms, and she wiggled them back and forth. "What an idiot."

"The dinosaurs weren't as smart as they thought they were." Harper leaned forward on the desk. "Maybe that's it."

"If he fell over, how did he get back up?" Marcy continued to wiggle her hands. "Those little arms weren't doing anything."

"Maybe we can't kill them," Harper said, ignoring Marcy's dinosaur impersonation. "But maybe we can outsmart them."

"How?" Marcy asked, and finally pushed her arms all the way out of her sleeves.

"I don't know. But they're still partially human." She turned to face Marcy. "Maybe we can reason with them and work something out."

"Hey, anything's possible." Marcy shrugged. "Except for a *T. rex* doing push-ups. That just isn't happening."

"Oh, my gosh, Marcy, you have a one-track mind," Harper said, and got up from the desk to find some actual work to do.

"I have a one-track mind?" Marcy scoffed. "We spend every day talking about sirens, but I want to spend an afternoon talking about the *T. rex* and his ridiculous appendages, and I have a one-track mind?"

"You're right." Harper paused, unable to tell if Marcy was actually annoyed or just pretending. "I'm sorry. We can go back to talking about the *T. rex*."

"Good. Because yesterday I read *1001 Exciting Facts About Dinosaurs* while you were gone," Marcy said. "And today I plan on sharing all of them with you."

TWENTY-EIGHT

Fireworks

It still didn't feel right. Gemma had reassured Harper a hundred times that she'd be fine, and Harper had talked to Alex, who told her he'd be right next door keeping watch on the house. Plus, Brian was in the living room, watching an Indiana Jones marathon on TV.

So it wasn't like Harper was leaving Gemma unguarded. Still, when Daniel knocked on the door, Harper almost told him that she couldn't go. But Gemma all but pushed her out of the house, insisting that Harper have a nice time on her date.

Most of the Fourth of July festivities were being held in the park in the center of town, but the fireworks were shot off over the bay. So as the day drew to a close, most of the activity moved over to the beach. The grassy area that ran along next to it was filled with concession stands that sold alcohol, food, and glow sticks and bracelets.

Parking anywhere near the beach would be impossible, so

Daniel and Harper had decided to walk from her house down toward Anthemusa Bay. The sun was setting when Daniel arrived to retrieve her, and the fireworks were set to go off at twilight.

"So," Daniel said as they walked down the street.

Neither of them had said much since they'd left her house. In fact, Harper hadn't really said anything to him, other than "Hello" and "Yes" when he asked if she was ready to go.

"Yep." Harper smiled up at him, then quickly looked away.

"You wore your hair down today."

"Yeah." She self-consciously ran her hand through her long dark hair. "I wanted to do something different."

"It looks nice," Daniel assured her. "*You* look nice."

"Thank you." She smiled.

"How did you wanna do this?" he asked.

"What?" Harper lifted her head, instantly afraid she'd misunderstood something.

"Watching the fireworks," Daniel said. "I thought maybe we could take my boat out and watch them from there."

"Like out in the water?" Harper asked.

"That's generally where I take my boat," Daniel said. "In fact, my boat spends most of the time in water. But I was thinking we'd take it a bit farther out in the bay."

"Won't that be all crowded with other boats doing the same thing?" she asked.

"Probably," he allowed. "But not quite as crowded as the beach."

They were still a couple blocks from the bay, and they could already hear the noise of the crowd. Every year, while the fireworks went off, a small orchestra played instrumental music. They'd apparently started, and the works of John Williams were echoing through the town. Even still, Harper could hear people laughing and talking over the music. The crowd was going to be intense.

"I don't know." Harper stared down at her flip-flops as she and Daniel continued toward the bay. "I think I'd rather stay on land."

"Are you afraid to be alone on my boat with me?" Daniel asked. "Because I promise to be on my best behavior. Scout's honor."

"No, that's not it," she said with a laugh, but that was part of it.

The larger part, however, was that she wanted to be closer to her sister if something happened. Being way out on the water, in a boat that had stalled out on her once before, didn't sound ideal.

"Well, this is your date," Daniel said. "So if you want to watch fireworks from the beach, then the beach it is."

"This is *my* date?" Harper asked. "Not ours? Just mine?"

"Yep." He grinned down at her. "I'm all yours for the night."

As they got nearer to the bay, the conversation got easier between the two of them. The awkward date jitters began to wear off, thanks in large part to Daniel. He had a way of making her feel at ease. Or at least he had a way of teasing her until she forgot to be uptight.

The beach was packed, but not unbearably so. They checked

out the booths that were set up on the grass first. Most of them sold food or beer, and Daniel offered to buy both for Harper, but she declined. He did buy her a glow-in-the-dark bracelet, even though she insisted it was silly, though she secretly wanted one.

They stopped to watch a juggler. He wore a black-and-white harlequin getup, and he juggled color-changing light-up balls. In the fading light, this became more impressive, especially when he kept tossing more up into the air.

Harper clapped along with the crowd when the juggler threw the flashing lights even farther up into the sky, but she caught a glimpse of something else when she looked up. Three birds were circling above them.

In the dim light, it was hard to make them out precisely, but their wingspan appeared much larger than that of an ordinary bird. She couldn't tell exactly how high they were in the sky, but as Harper squinted at them, she was certain they were too big to be regular birds.

"What's the matter?" Daniel asked. He leaned down, almost speaking in her ear, so she'd hear him over the crowd and the nearby band.

"Those birds." She pointed up at the sky, and glanced back at him. "Do they seem too big to you?"

"Are they ravens?" Daniel asked.

When Harper looked back, the sky had filled with a small flock of black birds. The three birds that she thought she'd seen before had either flown away or gotten lost in the flock. Either way, she couldn't see them anymore.

"Never mind." She shook her head. "I'm probably just being paranoid."

"That does sound like you." He smiled at her, then took her hand in his. "Come on. Let's go find a place to sit before there aren't any more places."

As Daniel led her away, weaving through the crowd toward the beach, Harper tried to still the butterflies in her stomach. She'd held hands with guys before, and this wasn't even the first time Daniel had taken her hand.

But something about this felt different. It was knowing that this meant something more. He linked his fingers through hers, and her heart nearly skipped a beat. She felt like a silly little girl again, but she couldn't help it.

She was too busy thinking about how rough his skin felt against hers to pay attention to where she was going, and she nearly tripped over someone sitting on a blanket. To squeeze by the people, she had to walk among a few cypress trees, letting her free hand run along the bark of a tree as she walked by.

"Be careful," Daniel said, apparently assuming that she was using the trees to steady herself. "That's why I got you the glow bracelet. So you can see where you're going."

"Glow bracelets don't give off as much light as you'd think. They're more decorative than functional."

"Ah, I understand now," Daniel said, taking her wrist in his hand. "That makes so much sense."

She turned to smile up at him, leaning back against the tree behind her, and he let go of her wrist. She thought they'd start walking away, but he moved closer to her. One of his hands was on the tree trunk next to her, the other rested warmly on her waist.

A strange smile played on his lips, and he shook his head.

"What?" Harper asked.

"I just wish you weren't so beautiful," he replied simply.

She laughed. "That's a strange thing to wish."

"Well, it's true."

"And why is that?" she asked. She could feel him leaning down to her, his body pressing against her.

"Because I didn't want it to happen like this. Or at least not here, like this, with people swarming around us, against a tree," Daniel said. "But you look so, so beautiful, and I just can't resist."

"You didn't want what to happen like this?" Harper asked softly, but she already knew.

His lips were nearly touching hers when he said, "The first time I kissed you."

Then he was kissing her, and everything else went silent. Harper put her arms around his neck, pulling him to her, and he kissed her deeply, pushing her against the tree behind her. Daniel had a bit of stubble, and it scraped against her skin as he kissed, but she loved the way it felt.

It ended far too quickly, with Daniel pulling away, while Harper leaned against the tree, struggling to catch her breath. It was probably for the best, since there were people everywhere, and she didn't want to make out in front of everybody.

But she was still sad when it was over. Nobody had ever

kissed her like that before, and she actually felt weak in the knees. She'd always just assumed that was a figure of speech, but Daniel made her feel that way.

"Should we head down to the beach?" Daniel asked.

"Uh, yeah." She smiled and nodded.

He took her hand again. She stayed close to him, but this time it was because she was afraid she might fall. She hung on to his arm, and he made a joke that she couldn't really hear over the music, but she laughed anyway.

"Is here good?" Daniel asked.

They were at the top of the beach, right where the grass turned into sand. It appeared to be one of the few places where they could sit without being right on top of someone else.

"Yeah." She smiled. "Here's great."

She glanced around, just to make sure they weren't stealing the spot from anybody else, and that was when Harper saw her.

It was almost as if the crowd had parted around Penn just so Harper could see her. She stood at the edge of the grass, her black eyes blazing, and smiled widely at Harper, revealing her abnormally sharp teeth.

TWENTY-NINE

Instincts

Gemma had thought about hanging downstairs with her dad. She liked Indiana Jones well enough, and she was trying to spend time with Brian while she could. Unlike Harper and Alex, she wasn't convinced there was a way out for her.

It wasn't that she wasn't committed to trying. She just didn't have high hopes for it.

Just the same, she wanted to spend some time by herself. Between living with the sirens, then being babysat constantly since she got home, Gemma felt like she'd hardly had any time to be alone to collect her thoughts.

Gemma hadn't been sleeping well, either, and not just because of the nightmares about Jason or the watersong nagging her for being so far away from the other sirens.

Yesterday, Alex had told her that he loved her, and while that [illegible] endlessly, it also raised a new question. How was [illegible]? The sirens had repeatedly told Gemma that it wasn't possible, that nobody could ever truly a love a siren, but Alex did love her.

There wasn't a doubt in her mind that he did. Alex couldn't lie that convincingly, and when they were together, he acted like a normal person. She'd spent enough time around Sawyer to understand what a guy acted like when he was under the spell of a siren.

Alex wasn't acting that way at all. He was clearheaded, and when he told Gemma he loved her, he meant it.

She'd actually woken up this morning hoping the curse would be broken. But of course it wasn't that simple. She was still a siren, no matter how Alex felt about her.

So that meant one of two things: either the sirens had lied to her, or they were wrong about humans being able to love sirens.

They could be lying to her. That sounded like something Penn would do. But Thea had seemed convinced it was impossible for sirens to be truly loved, too, and Gemma had come to trust Thea. She doubted that Thea would lie to her for the hell of it.

So Gemma was inclined to believe that they were wrong. And if they were wrong about this, about something they considered to be a major part of the curse, what else were they wrong about?

Gemma'd wanted to discuss this with Harper, but she hadn't gotten the time. Once Gemma was back from visiting Nathalie, Brian had spent the rest of the day with her, so she couldn't talk to Harper about it.

And today Harper had been so busy getting ready for her

date that Gemma didn't want to spoil it. She could talk to her about it tomorrow. And besides, it would probably do Gemma some good to relax and not worry about curses or sirens for a while.

She stole Harper's e-reader and decided to crash out on her bed. Harper and Gemma's reading tastes were vastly different, so Gemma spent most of the time just scanning through the reader and rejecting the choices.

Harper did have a subscription to *Spin* magazine, though, and Gemma read through that. She lay on her back with one leg crossed over her knee, humming to herself and reading about Florence + the Machine.

Then suddenly it hit her. It was like somebody had punched her in the gut and knocked all the air from her lungs.

She sat up in bed, and with absolute certainty she said, "They're here."

She jumped off of her bed and her mind raced, trying to figure out what to do. The sirens weren't *here*, as in at her house, but she knew they were back in Capri. And it wasn't because of her connection with the sirens, although that strengthened her conviction and knowledge.

It was because Harper knew. There wasn't any other way she could explain it. When Harper was in serious trouble, she would just feel it. The same way Harper knew when Gemma was in real trouble. That was probably how Harper had been able to figure out that Gemma had been staying in Sawyer's beach house.

There was some kind of bond between the two of them, and it had been there as long as Gemma could remember. Whether it was an intense intuition or some kind of psychic link, Gemma didn't know or care. But she felt it stronger than she ever had before, maybe because she was a siren now and it heightened any supernatural connection she already had. She just knew that she trusted this feeling, and right now it was telling her that Harper had discovered the sirens. If she wasn't in danger right now, she would be very shortly.

When Gemma ran away from home, she'd left her cell phone here, and Brian had threatened to shut it off when she got back. Fortunately, he hadn't yet, and Gemma grabbed it. She called Harper, but the phone went straight to voice mail.

That didn't necessarily mean anything. It was getting dark, and the fireworks were about to start. It was probably so loud down at the beach that Harper wouldn't be able to hear her phone.

But Gemma had to do something. She had to sneak out of the house without Brian stopping her.

That ended up being easier than she thought. He'd had a couple of beers today, and he was nodding off in his chair in the living room in front of the TV. He'd probably wake up once the fireworks started going off, and then he'd notice that Gemma wasn't there.

But really, that wasn't her concern right now. She just had to get out of here.

She walked quietly down the stairs, then hurried through the kitchen and out the back door. She'd barely made it outside when Alex came rushing out the back door of his house, and Gemma swore under her breath.

"What are you doing?" Alex asked. "Where are you going?"

"The sirens are here," Gemma told him.

"Where?" He turned around in a circle, as if he expected them to be lurking behind him.

"I don't know. I think maybe down at the bay," Gemma said. "Harper's there with Daniel watching the fireworks, and I have to go get her."

"Wait. What?" Alex asked. "Shouldn't we be running away from the sirens, not getting closer to them? It's dangerous for you to be around them."

"No, I need to face them," Gemma said. "But first I have to find Harper."

"So what's going to happen when you do run into the sirens?" Alex asked.

"I have to stop them," Gemma said. "I can't let them hurt anyone anymore. I'll find Harper, then I'll find a way to chase them off."

Gemma wasn't completely certain that she could pull that off, but she'd do everything she could. She was going to fight the sirens and get them to leave her and her family alone, or she would die trying.

"Okay," Alex said. "But I'm going with you."

"Alex." Gemma groaned. "You can't—"

"Look, I'm not letting you go off and get hurt," Alex insisted. "I have my earplugs, and I'm going with you. Now, do you want to stand around and argue with me about it, or do you want to go find your sister?"

Gemma didn't want to waste any more time discussing it, so

she started jogging down toward the bay. She was much faster than Alex, and he worked hard to keep up with her. She slowed down a bit because she didn't want to lose sight of him, but she also wanted to get to the beach as quickly as she could.

Unfortunately, she'd grossly underestimated how crowded it would be at the bay.

Gemma figured that the sirens would be closer to the water, or at least in a more secluded area. She doubted they would do anything in public, not when there were so many witnesses, so they'd be drawn to places where there were fewer people.

She ran to the edge of the beach, the closest to the docks, where the crowd was the thinnest. She looked around, but she didn't see Harper, Daniel, or any of the sirens.

Then Gemma realized she didn't see Alex, either. He'd been right behind her a few seconds ago, but when she darted through the crowd, she must've lost him.

"Dammit." Gemma rubbed her forehead and regretted bringing him. Getting Alex killed in an attempt to protect her sister wasn't exactly a winning situation.

She turned back around toward the docks, trying to figure out where to look, and Sawyer was standing right behind her. So close, she nearly bumped into him when she turned around.

"Sawyer!" Gemma gasped. "You scared me."

"Good." He smiled, and before she could react, he grabbed her, clamping one hand over her mouth to keep her from calling out for help or singing.

THIRTY

Lyrical

"They're here," Harper said, doing her best to keep the panic from her voice, as she locked eyes with Penn.

"What?" Daniel leaned down to hear her better.

"They're here!" Harper repeated, shouting this time.

Daniel looked up, and then he saw Penn, too. "Oh, shit."

A person walked in front of Penn, and then she was gone, disappearing into the crowd.

"What do you wanna do?" Daniel asked. "We can try to follow Penn, maybe stop her before she finds Gemma, or we go try to protect Gemma."

"We go get Gemma," Harper said. "Penn knows where we live, so she'll go there eventually. If she isn't already on her way, or the other sirens aren't already there."

"All right. Let's go."

Daniel took her hand, but all the earlier flutterings had dissolved. The only thing Harper felt was panic.

And all the people didn't make it easier. They were all going toward the beach, since the fireworks were about to start, and Harper and Daniel were pushing against them. It felt a bit like they were salmon swimming upstream, and it made it hard for them to hurry.

"Go towards the trees!" Harper advised.

"What? Why?" Daniel asked, pushing past a guy who wouldn't get out of his way.

"Nobody's going to be there because they block the view of the fireworks," Harper said. "We'll be able to get to my house quicker!"

Daniel did as he was told, leading the way and pushing through the crowd. Harper was dimly aware that she'd just told Daniel to go to the forest where she'd found Luke's body. That was where the sirens disposed of their kills, so they were familiar with it.

But it was the quickest way home. And that was all that mattered to Harper. Getting home and making sure that Gemma was safe.

They'd just started on the path through the trees when Penn appeared in front of them. She hadn't materialized, exactly, but she stepped out from behind a tree and blocked their path. Her eyes glowed yellow in the dim light.

"Where are you off to in such a hurry?" Penn asked, her voice a soft purr that nearly made Harper forget how much she hated and feared her. "The fireworks are the other direction. And you don't want to miss the show, do you?"

"No, I don't want to . . ." Harper's brow furrowed, because

for a second she couldn't remember exactly what she wanted to do. "I'm leaving, and you can't stop me."

Still hanging on to Daniel's hand, Harper walked forward, but Penn moved to block her path.

"Let me get by," Harper said as firmly as she could.

"Or what?" Penn smirked. "What are you going to do?"

"Harper, let's just go back the way we came," Daniel suggested.

Penn's eyes flashed when she heard Daniel speak, and she tilted her head toward him. Harper let go of his hand and moved in front of him, standing between him and Penn.

"I don't know what I'll do," Harper admitted. "But we won't let you go after my sister."

She glanced back at him, checking to make sure it was okay she'd said "we." Daniel had repeatedly told her he wanted to help her, and he had in the past. So Harper had decided to include him, instead of sending him away the way she normally would. If he was going to be her boyfriend, then they should be equals standing up against the enemy together.

"No, we won't," Daniel agreed, and stepped forward so he stood next to Harper, both of them staring Penn down. "We're not going anywhere."

"Look at the two of you." Penn laughed. "You really think you have a say in anything that's going to happen?" She stepped closer to them, smiling wider. "You'll let me do whatever I want."

Penn began to sing, low and soft, so as not to enchant all the people crowded around the bay. But the song was just as tempting as the last time Harper had heard the sirens sing.

Her panic melted away, and her whole body relaxed. A haze filled her mind, and she couldn't remember why she'd been so worried. She knew she had been, but Penn was so beautiful, and the song was so wonderful. Harper wanted nothing more than to stand there and listen to Penn sing for all eternity.

"Harper, you're going to do whatever I say," Penn said in her lyrical way.

Harper nodded dazedly and said, "Okay."

"Harper?" Daniel said, but she didn't respond. She just stared dreamily at Penn.

"As for you . . ." Penn turned her attention to Daniel.

"She might do whatever you say," Daniel allowed. "But I sure as hell won't."

Penn's eyes widened when Daniel talked back to her; her eyes were like those of an animal surprised to be caught in a snare. She opened her mouth to command Daniel to do something, but then he punched her.

THIRTY-ONE

Defiance

Sawyer had one arm around Gemma's waist as he pulled her away from the crowd and toward the docks. Her legs flailed wildly, and she knocked off one of her flip-flops. His hand was pressed so tightly against her mouth that she could hardly breathe, and she clawed viciously at his arm.

As strong as she was, Gemma felt powerless against him. His arms were like granite around her, and he dragged her away with the singular determination of a man on a mission. The sirens had told him to get Gemma, and he wouldn't be able to stop until he fulfilled their orders.

That explained his insane strength. When under the spell of a siren, Sawyer could tap into every ounce of strength to carry out their bidding. He could act like an uncontrollable speed freak if he needed to.

He was pulling Gemma down an embankment, toward the

docks where her father worked. The docks would be deserted right now, and there Sawyer and the sirens could do whatever they wanted with Gemma. Or Alex, if they found him.

As a new panic took over, Gemma felt a change slowly wash over her. It reminded her of the familiar transformation when her legs shifted into a tail, but this was different. Her vision changed first. At first it blurred, then the night became clearer than it ever had before.

Her mouth trembled and tingled, like her teeth were beginning to itch. Her hands felt like they were stretching out, and the fingernails she'd been scratching Sawyer's arms with were turning into full-on talons.

She was turning into a bird-monster, and she couldn't let it happen. The last time she had, she hadn't been able to control it. She couldn't even remember what she'd done, but somebody had ended up dead. She couldn't risk it this time.

And even though Sawyer was basically kidnapping her, she didn't want to hurt him. Not really. He couldn't control what he was doing, and in the few moments of clarity he'd had around her, he'd been a nice guy. He didn't deserve to get hurt, and she didn't want to tear him apart.

Gemma closed her eyes, concentrating as hard as she could to stop the change. She'd never tried to prevent herself from shifting into a mermaid before, or vice versa, so she didn't completely understand how it worked.

One thing she knew for sure was that she had to get away from Sawyer. He'd gotten her down to an isolated dock, and her fear of being trapped was triggering the transformation. The siren part of her was instinctively trying to protect her by turning into a monster.

Using her talons, she clawed more forcefully at his arm, and finally his grip slipped and Gemma pulled away from him. They were on the docks, and she only ran a few steps down from him. She was in mid-transformation and had no idea what she looked like, but she knew she couldn't be seen by the public.

She crouched down, putting her hands over her head, and concentrated as hard as she could. Her back had begun to itch, and she was afraid wings might unfurl from it. But then the itching stopped, and slowly the tingling began to fade as her body went back to normal.

"What are you doing?" Sawyer asked, and Gemma lifted her head to see him standing beside her, looking down at her. His arms were scratched up from her fighting him off, but none of his wounds looked particularly awful.

"I'm trying not to kill you," Gemma admitted, and stood up. "So I suggest you let me go."

"I can't let you go," Sawyer said, like it hadn't even occurred to him. "We have to wait at the docks until the sirens come."

"Listen to me, Sawyer," Gemma said. "If you try to stop me from leaving, I will hurt you. I don't want to, but I will. Just let me go, and everything will be okay."

"No, Gemma, you can't go." His eyes were glassy, but his voice was firm. He grabbed Gemma's wrist with the same iron grip he'd had before. "You must wait here until Penn tells me otherwise. I can't let you go."

"Sawyer, please," Gemma begged him. "You're enchanted right now, but you just need to clear your head and remember that you don't have to do everything the sirens say. You don't even like them that much."

She started pulling her wrist, trying to get away from him, but Sawyer wouldn't let go. The damn sirens had him trained too well, and her only hope of escape might be turning into a monster.

"Gemma!" Alex shouted from behind her, and she turned to see him running down the embankment toward the docks. He must've seen her struggling with Sawyer, so he was charging at them.

The sky above them suddenly exploded in bright red and blue lights as the fireworks began. The booming sound of them seemed to startle Sawyer for a second, but his grip on her never wavered.

"Please, Sawyer, you need to let me go!" Gemma shouted at him, but he ignored her.

"Let her go!" Alex yelled, appearing at her side.

"I can't," Sawyer insisted, his words barely audible over the crackle of fireworks.

That was all Alex needed to hear. He hauled off and punched Sawyer, hitting him so hard in the face that Sawyer let go of Gemma and fell backward to the dock.

"Thank you," Gemma said, unsure how else to respond as she watched Sawyer hold his bleeding lip.

"What?" Alex turned toward her. Between his earplugs and the fireworks, he must not have been able to hear anything.

She kissed him once quickly on the mouth, since she knew he could understand that. But she didn't have any time for more, even though, honestly, she thought it was pretty hot the way Alex had just come over and hit Sawyer.

But she did feel bad for Sawyer. She wanted to run off with Alex and find Harper, but she paused and turned back to Sawyer.

"Go," Sawyer said. He sat up and wiped the blood off his lip with his arm. "Get out of here before the sirens find you."

"What?" Gemma stepped back, surprised to hear him thinking for himself.

"The sirens will be here soon," Sawyer said. "They knew I had you."

"Wait. Are you *you*?" Gemma asked. "Can you think for yourself?"

"I think so." He stood up slowly and rubbed his head.

"What's going on?" Alex asked, but Gemma held up her hand to silence him. She couldn't explain now, when he couldn't hear.

Besides, Gemma didn't know how to explain this anyway. Something about Alex hitting Sawyer must've cleared his head, but Gemma wasn't sure if it was temporary or not. But his eyes had lost their glassy quality, looking a clear, brilliant blue.

"I can't remember the last few days very well, but I know . . ." Sawyer furrowed his brow. "I don't want to listen to the sirens anymore."

"Then come with us." Gemma beckoned him. "You don't need to stay with them. You can escape with me."

"No, if I leave . . ." Sawyer shook his head, his smooth features looking pained. "Penn will kill me. I can't ever get away from her."

"She'll kill you if you stay," Gemma warned him. "You need to leave with us, right now. We're going to find my sister, and we'll find a way to break free from the sirens. But you have to come with us."

Gemma held out her hand to his, meaning to grab it so she could drag him along with her. She didn't really have time to stand here and argue with him anymore, but she wanted to help him. Taking him with her would really piss off Penn, but he knew Penn better than Gemma. He might know some of her weaknesses and could help fight against her.

Sawyer reached out and just about took her hand, when Lexi surfaced in the water nearby. Her golden hair shimmered under the sparkling lights of the fireworks above them, and she pulled herself out of the water in one graceful move.

"That can't be good," Alex said.

Her sundress clung to her body as she walked up behind Sawyer, and he dropped his outstretched arm back to his side.

"You weren't thinking about leaving us, were you, Sawyer?" Lexi asked, her voice flirty and playful.

"No, of course not," Sawyer said. She was still behind him, rubbing up against his back, and he turned to Gemma, mouthing the word *Go*.

"Lexi, where's Penn?" Gemma asked, trying to distract her. Gemma still hoped to get Sawyer away from the sirens, but she had to do it before Lexi put a spell on him again.

"Around," Lexi replied absently. She rested her chin on his shoulder and whispered in Sawyer's ear, "You'd never leave us, would you?"

"No, I'd never leave you," Sawyer said, but he stammered a bit. He was still thinking for himself. Even though Lexi was whispering to him, she wasn't enchanting him.

"I know you wouldn't." Lexi smiled. "Do you know how I know?"

Sawyer shook his head. "No. I don't."

"Because your heart belongs to us." Lexi smiled wider at that.

Then her hand burst through his chest.

She was standing behind him, and her human hand had shifted into the awful monster hand, the long, powerful fingers with curved talons at the end. It had torn through Sawyer's chest easily, spraying a bit of blood as it did, and she now cradled his heart in her hand.

THIRTY-TWO

Immune

Penn lay on the ground, a small stream of blood running from her nose, and blinked up at the trees above her. The fireworks had just begun, and the light glimmered through the leaves.

"I normally don't justify hitting girls, but if you're going to try and kill me and my girlfriend, then I'm gonna hit you," Daniel said as he stood over her. "I'll do whatever it takes."

Harper stood behind Daniel, and she couldn't shake the confusion from her mind. She wanted to go up and touch him, but she felt frozen in place, and had no idea what she should be doing.

"*Daniel,*" Penn tried singing, her silky voice causing a warm euphoria to spread out over Harper, and she smiled to herself. "*Daniel, you will help me.*"

"Why are you singing?" Daniel asked. "You're just lying in the dirt and singing. That's weird. I thought you were supposed to be some kind of scary monster."

"Why aren't you doing what I say?" Penn sat up, propping herself on her elbows. "Are the fireworks drowning out the song?" Then she glanced over at Harper. "No, she's over there smiling like an idiot, so it's working. What's wrong with you?"

"There's nothing wrong with me, but I don't have time to argue about this." Daniel grabbed Harper's arm and attempted to drag her back the way they had come, but she wouldn't move. "Harper, let's go."

"No, I can't go." She shook her head. "I have to stay here for . . . for . . ." She stared up at the lights flashing through the trees. "Fireworks."

"What did you do to her?" Daniel turned back to face Penn, who'd gotten to her feet. "Undo it."

Her eyes were no longer glowing and had gone back to their usual black. She crossed her arms over her chest and pursed her lips as she watched Daniel and Harper.

"You've never listened to me, have you?" Penn asked. "You're the guy with the boat that intervened when we were talking to Gemma before, and you ignored us. Nobody ever ignores us."

"I'm ignoring you right now," Daniel shot back, and he put his arms around Harper to pick her up.

"Daniel," Harper complained, pushing wanly against him. "I don't think I should go."

"That's right, *Harper*," Penn said, using her singsong voice. "You can't go!"

"Daniel!" Harper screeched when he tried to carry her away. "Put me down!"

"Dammit." Daniel sighed and set her down carefully, then

he walked over to Penn and got right in her face. "I don't know what the hell your problem is, but you don't want Harper. You don't need her. Let us go."

"Why can't I enchant you?" Penn asked, narrowing her eyes at him.

"You're not that enchanting," Daniel said. "What do you want? Why are you doing this?"

"I want you," Penn decided. "I want to experiment on you and find out how you can resist me. Then I want to eat your heart. But first I'm going to kill your girlfriend."

"That isn't going to happen," Daniel assured her. "I'll kill you first."

"Hmm." Penn smiled. "Maybe I won't kill you. It's been so long since a man has stood up to me. I've forgotten how much fun it can be."

"Let's have some fun, then," Daniel said, and he punched her again.

Or at least he tried to. He swung, but Penn grabbed his fist. She squeezed it hard, beginning to crush it with her hand. He grimaced, and started to crouch down. Then he kicked out with one foot, swiping Penn's legs out from underneath her. She let go of his hand and fell back.

"Daniel?" Harper said, flinching when one of the fireworks exploded loudly in the sky.

She was watching Daniel and Penn, and she wanted to do something. In her heart, it felt like she should, but it was as if her feet were locked in place, and her mind was still so foggy.

Daniel kicked Penn in the side, but she grabbed his leg and

pulled him down. Once he was on the ground, she jumped on top of him, straddling him between her legs. Her eyes had shifted back to bird-yellow, and her teeth were razor-sharp and couldn't seem to fit inside her mouth anymore.

He punched her again, and she laughed, an odd cackling that sounded as if it belonged more to a raven than to a person. She grabbed his wrist and pinned it to the dirt so he couldn't hit her again, and with her other hand she gripped his throat, her fingers elongating around his neck.

"You would be a lot of fun," Penn said, cocking her head at him. "But you're probably not worth the trouble. I think I'll just kill you now."

"Harper!" Daniel managed to yell as Penn tightened her grip around his throat. He was pulling at her arm with his free hand, but she wasn't moving. "*Harper!*"

Something about the panic in his voice broke through the fog in her mind, and when she blinked, it was as if she were seeing the scene for the first time. She remembered watching it all, but that had been like a dream. This was real, and Daniel was in trouble.

Acting quickly, Harper grabbed a huge stick from the side of the path. Penn was too focused on Daniel, opening her mouth wider as if she meant to swallow him, so she didn't notice Harper coming up behind her.

Using all her might, Harper swung, and the stick cracked hard against the back of Penn's skull. She howled in rage and pain, the monster roar mixing with her voice and sounding totally inhuman.

Daniel arched his back and threw Penn off, and she landed in the brush nearby. Before Harper could ask Daniel if he was all right, he'd sprung back to his feet. Penn was back up, too, seething as she stepped toward Daniel and Harper.

"Penn!" Thea snapped, and Penn jerked her head back to look at her sister. "What are you doing? Why are you messing with those two?"

"I was looking for Gemma, and things got out of hand." Slowly, Penn's face shifted back, looking more human again.

"We don't have time for that. Sawyer's down at the docks with Gemma, and who knows how long he'll be able to hold her there," Thea said. Penn looked reluctantly back at Daniel and Harper, like she still really wanted to kill them both. "Penn! Let's go!"

"Fine," Penn relented, and stepped back from them. "I have some business to attend to, but I'll be back for both of you."

Penn turned around, hurrying after Thea, and Harper took a second to catch her breath before turning back to Daniel.

"Are you okay?" she asked.

"Yeah, I'm fine." He nodded. "Let's go get your sister."

Harper swallowed hard, wishing she had more time to inspect Daniel and make sure he really was okay. But she didn't have time, so she took Daniel's hand, and the two of them started running toward the docks. They had to go all the way across the beach to the other side, while everyone stared up at the light show above them.

THIRTY-THREE

Iniquity

Lexi pushed Sawyer off her arm, his body, sliding over it, making a sickening slippery sound before he fell face-first on the dock. Almost casually, she kicked his body, and it rolled off the dock and splashed into the water.

Gemma had wanted to scream, to do something, but she merely watched in shock and horror. Some of his blood had splattered on her, and it still felt warm on her skin. She'd been trying to save him, and Lexi had ripped out his heart.

"That bitch means business," Alex said, sounding almost as dazed and horrified as Gemma felt. "We need to get out of here. Like *now*."

"Right," Gemma agreed.

Lexi was busy licking the blood off her hand, so Gemma thought this would be the perfect time to make her escape. She grabbed Alex's hand, and they turned to make a run for it.

But Lexi rushed around them, moving at a speed so fast it

would've been impossible for Gemma to match. She ran so quickly, it was like a blur of color, and then she was standing in front of them.

"I'm really fast," Lexi told them, smiling brightly. "That's what happens when you eat a lot, Gemma. You get faster and stronger and just plain better. Too bad you didn't take my advice when I told you to eat, huh?"

"It doesn't make you smarter, though, does it, Lexi?" Gemma asked. "Or if it does, you must've been *really* stupid before you became a siren."

"Those are big words coming from someone who's about to die," Lexi said. "Here. Let's make it fair. You eat this." She held out Sawyer's heart toward Gemma, who struggled not to gag.

"I'm not going to," Gemma said. "I'm not going to be one of you."

"I don't really have time to eat it, either." Lexi stared down at the heart and sighed. "Oh, well." She tossed it over her shoulder and it landed on the dock, bouncing once before splashing into the water. "It's probably time for you to die anyway."

Alex charged at Lexi first. Gemma wasn't sure if he'd heard what she'd said, or if he'd just had enough. He swung at her, but Lexi knocked him down, and he fell back on the dock.

"You know what would be so fun?" Lexi sounded excited as Gemma ran over to help Alex. "Since you two like each other so much, it'd be way fun if he killed you. Or at least tried to. I doubt he'd be able to finish the job, but it'd be fun to see him try."

"You are so messed up, Lexi," Gemma said. "Like, seriously. You are one sick bitch."

"Aw, thanks." Lexi winked at her, and when she spoke again, her voice came out as a song: *"Alex, my weary wanderer, my voice is the way. Alex, my young love, do as I say."*

Alex, in an apparent daze, let go of Gemma's hand and walked toward Lexi. Gemma called his name, but he ignored Gemma, following the song into Lexi's arms.

She smiled at Gemma as she embraced Alex. One of her arms was around his shoulder, and the other was stroking his hair back. She leaned in to him, like she meant to kiss him, and when Alex leaned closer, she pulled away and laughed.

"Oh, this is almost too easy to be fun," Lexi said, watching Gemma from the corner of her eye.

"No, Alex, don't listen to her," Gemma said. He'd wrapped one arm around Lexi's waist, and she saw him reaching into his back pocket for something. "Alex. Don't listen to her. I love you."

"Alex, my love," Lexi said as seductively as she could. "I want you to kill Gemma."

Just before Lexi's lips touched his, he reached up, pulling his pocketknife out and stabbing it right into Lexi's heart. He pressed her close to him, so he could stab the knife in deeper.

"What the hell?" Lexi asked, her eyes wide with shock.

"Earplugs," Alex said simply, and walked back to where Gemma was standing.

Lexi stepped back, holding her hands in front of her, and she still looked dazed and shocked. She started coughing, and Gemma grabbed Alex's hand, squeezing it hopefully.

"You stupid *bitch*." Lexi spat blood, and then ripped the knife out.

"Okay, so I guess that doesn't kill them, then," Gemma said.

"Of course it doesn't kill me!" Lexi shouted, and her voice started changing, losing its silky quality and sounding more like a demon's. "It only pisses me off!"

Her eyes changed, shifting from their usual bright blue to an eerie green, and they grew larger, almost too large for her face. Her teeth became more pointed. Several rows sprang out from behind the others and protruded jaggedly from her still-human lips. The last thing to change was her arms, growing longer and sprouting taloned fingers.

Lexi had begun shifting into the bird form, but she stopped changing mid-shift. The whole beast was probably a bit cumbersome for being in public, but even this smaller shift would make her stronger. Gemma had felt it when she'd been fighting with Sawyer. Just the little change had enabled her to break away from him.

Alex charged at Lexi while Gemma ran over and grabbed a heavy rope that had been left on the dock. When Alex ran at Lexi, she knocked him back, but that was what Gemma had wanted. He lay on the dock, and while Lexi hunched over him, Gemma ran and jumped on her back. She wrapped the rope around Lexi's neck, choking her, and wrapped her legs around the siren's waist to get a better grip.

Lexi squawked and tried to buck Gemma off, but that only made her hang on tighter. Alex kicked Lexi in the stomach, and she fell to her knees. She reached back behind her head and grabbed Gemma's hair.

She yanked on it hard enough to make Gemma scream, but Gemma refused to let go of the rope. Alex kicked Lexi in the face, probably afraid that if he punched her, he might accidentally rip his hand off on her incisors.

"Will you stop screwing around?" Penn snapped, and all three of them turned to see her standing on the dock with her hands on her hips. Thea was right beside her.

Lexi squawked again, trying to speak but unable to, since Gemma had the rope so tight around her neck.

"Gemma, let go of her," Penn said wearily. "If you don't, I'll come over there and rip your boyfriend's head off. It's as simple as that. I'm sick of fighting, so do as I say, or I'll kill you all."

Reluctantly, Gemma let go of the rope and got off Lexi. As soon as she did, Lexi turned to her like she meant to attack in some way, but Penn hissed at her.

"Lexi," Penn commanded. "I said I was sick of all this fighting, and I meant it. Clean yourself up and get off the ground."

"Sorry," Lexi said awkwardly through her mouthful of teeth.

The fireworks were finishing up, and they ended on a noisy, rapid-fire note, with lights exploding every second in the sky. Lexi shifted back to her normal self and stood up. Gemma and Alex had gotten to their feet, and they stood together, holding on to each other.

"That's so obnoxious," Penn said as the display finally finished and the crowd on the beach erupted in applause. "Humans are so stupid."

"They are," Lexi agreed, and took her spot on the other side of Penn.

"So what was going on here?" Penn motioned to the blood all over the dock. "Whose is that?"

"That's Sawyer's," Lexi said, then she made a pouty face. "He was going to leave us, so I killed him."

"Lexi." Penn sounded genuinely irritated, then shook her head. "Fine. Whatever. Great. I'm sick of all of this."

"If you just let me go, you can be rid of all of this," Gemma said.

"I can't let you go," Penn snapped. "Why won't you get that through your thick skull? If you want to be free of this curse, I'll be more than happy to set you free, but I'll have to kill you. Is that what you want? Do you want to die?"

"Penn," Thea said, gently interjecting. "It was so hard to find a replacement for Aggie. It'll be just as hard to replace Gemma. Don't do anything hasty."

"I'm not being hasty!" Penn shouted.

"Wait," Gemma said. "You guys were wrong."

"Seriously?" Penn raised an eyebrow. "This is how you plan to plead for your life? Telling me I'm the one that's wrong?"

"No, I'm saying that you were wrong about something, so you might be wrong about other things," Gemma said. "There might be a way to break the curse."

"Do you know what that is?" Thea asked.

"No, but . . ." She took a deep breath. "Alex loves me."

"Boys lie, you're an idiot, blah blah blah," Penn said, waving her hand.

"No, he's really in love with me! Ask him!" Gemma motioned to Alex, and he took out his earplugs. "Alex, tell them how you feel about me."

"That I love you?" Alex asked, confused.

Penn rolled her eyes. "Oh, my god. Just for that, I'm going to kill you both. I was only going to kill you, Gemma, but because you wasted my time, I'm taking him out, too."

"No, Penn, wait!" Thea held up her hand to silence Penn.

"What now?" Penn groaned.

"Alex," Thea said, and walked over to him.

"Don't hurt him," Gemma said, making her voice as firm as she could.

"I'm not going to hurt him," Thea told Gemma, but her eyes were on him. She stared at him directly in his eyes, then sang, *"Alex, tell me the truth. Do you love her?"*

His pupils dilated and mouth slacked, and for a second Alex didn't say anything. Gemma waited with bated breath until finally he spoke.

"Yes," he said, his voice sounding dreamy. "I'm in love with Gemma."

"That doesn't prove anything," Lexi said.

"Yes, it does!" Gemma insisted. "He loves me, and you said that wasn't possible."

Thea swallowed hard and lowered her eyes. Her expression had become pained, but Gemma couldn't read it exactly.

"Thea, this doesn't change anything," Penn said, trying too hard to sound calm and reassuring.

"This changes everything," Thea said, then turned back to

face Penn. "We've believed something for thousands of years, and it's not true. What else are we wrong about?"

"Maybe it's a fluke." Penn shrugged. "But we can figure it out later. I still think we should kill Gemma. She's more trouble than she's worth."

"No, I don't think so." Thea shook her head. "We should keep her alive."

"She'll just keep running away!" Penn gestured to Alex. "Her being in love is all the more reason that we should kill them!"

"Then we stay," Thea said.

"What?" Lexi asked, appalled. "We can't stay here. This town sucks."

"Just for a while," Thea said. "Until we figure out what's going on."

Penn sighed and seemed to think it over.

"We can't!" Lexi insisted. "We wouldn't be able to feed whenever we wanted. We'd have to use discretion so the humans wouldn't chase us out of town with pitchforks and torches. That means we might have to go, like, weeks without eating."

"That's true," Penn agreed. "But there's something really weird going on with the boys in this town."

"What do you mean?" Thea asked.

Penn just shook her head in response. "Fine. We'll stay. And Gemma can live. *For now.*"

Lexi groaned loudly, and Gemma tried not to let out a sigh of relief.

"But you will do as I say." Penn stepped around Thea and walked right up to Gemma. "None of this running off shit or doing what you want. I'll let you stay here, live with that hideous sister of yours, and run around with this idiot boy. But if you disobey me, if you act out against me or the other sirens, I will not hesitate to kill you all. Do you understand me?"

"I do." Gemma nodded.

"Do you?" Penn asked. "Because I don't think you do. We made a similar deal before, and you broke it. In fact, I should be tearing out lover boy's heart right now just to punish you."

"Penn, please, I'll do what you say," Gemma insisted in a hurried breath. "I'm sorry. I won't do it again."

"I know you won't do it again," Penn said. "Because I've given you more chances than I've given anyone else. And you screw up one more time, *one more time,* and I will destroy everyone you care about. I'll kill everyone in this entire bullshit town if I have to."

Gemma swallowed hard. "I understand."

"Gemma!" Harper shouted as she raced down the embankment toward the docks. "Gemma!"

"I really don't want to deal with them again," Penn said, and turned back to Lexi and Thea. "Let's get out of here."

"Gladly," Lexi said, and dove into the water.

"Wait," Gemma said, stopping Penn before she followed Lexi. "What do you want me to do?"

"Go home, play house with your little friends," Penn said. "I'll find somewhere to live, and when I want you, I'll come get you."

Before Harper and Daniel reached them on the dock, Penn and Thea dove into the water, disappearing in the waves. They swam out as far and as fast as they could, and Gemma knew they had to be careful to avoid being spotted by people who were in all the boats in the bay.

"So we're just gonna stay here and let Gemma do what she wants?" Lexi asked Penn, once they'd gotten far enough away from the docks that they could speak. Thea was swimming on ahead of them, but Lexi had slowed to talk to Penn.

"No, of course not," Penn said. "We find a replacement first, then we kill her. And we need to find out what the hell is going on with the boys in this town. There's something strange about this place, and I want to find out what it is, so I can rub it in Demeter's face."

THIRTY-FOUR

Tomorrow

Gemma knew what she had to do. After everything that had happened tonight, she had no other option. While Gemma had told Harper what she planned to do, she couldn't tell if Harper approved or not. In the end, it didn't matter. Gemma had made up her mind.

Once the sirens had gone, Gemma had explained to Harper why the sirens had spared her and let her stay in Capri. That had actually been relatively easy compared to explaining to Brian what she'd been up to when they got back home. She lied and told her dad that she'd just snuck out to watch the fireworks with Alex, but that still left him pretty pissed off.

Brian stayed up really late that night, maybe because he was so angry, but the second Gemma was certain he was asleep, she snuck outside. She'd made sure to tell Harper what she was doing before she left, so Harper wouldn't freak out when she saw Gemma's bedroom empty.

As she crept across the yard and climbed up the trellis to Alex's window, Gemma could almost feel Harper watching her from her bedroom window. That was the condition. Harper would let Gemma sneak out to talk to Alex without telling their dad as long as Harper could see her the entire time.

Crouching on the roof outside his darkened bedroom window, Gemma knocked sharply on the glass. After the night they'd had, he was probably sound asleep, and she wanted to be sure she woke him.

The light in the room flipped on, casting a glow through the curtains. She knocked on the glass again, and a few seconds later, Alex pushed back the curtains. As soon as he saw her, he hurried and opened the window.

"What are you doing here?" Alex asked. His hair was standing up all over from sleep, and he wore only his boxers, revealing his well-muscled chest. "Do you want to come in?"

"No, I can't." She shook her head and tried to fight back the tears that were already brimming in her eyes. "I just stopped by for a sec."

"What's wrong?" Alex leaned out the window and put his hand on her arm. "What's going on? Did something happen?"

"No. I just . . . I needed to see you."

"How come?"

"I love you," she whispered, and before he could respond, she leaned forward and kissed him.

She wrapped her arms around him and held him tightly to her. When she finished kissing him, he kept hugging her, and she rested her head on his shoulder, sniffing back tears.

"Gemma, what's going on?" Alex asked.

"Alex," Gemma sang softly into his ear. *"Alex. You will do as I say."* She took a deep breath, letting her song take effect on him. "You're breaking up with me. You don't want to go out with me anymore. You don't want to be around me. You don't care about my safety. You don't . . ." She paused. "You don't love me anymore."

"Gemma?" He sounded confused. His arms had felt strong and firm around her, but they loosened now, letting her go.

"Do you understand me? *Alex?"* She pulled away from him and looked him in the eyes. "Are you my boyfriend?"

His face scrunched up, and his dark eyes looked pained underneath the haze of the spell. Then finally he shook his head. "No. We broke up."

"That's right." She nodded.

"What are you doing here?" Alex asked. "Why did you come over?"

"I didn't." She wiped her eyes. "This is all a dream, and when you wake up, you'll only remember that you don't want to be with me."

Gemma couldn't handle it anymore, so she turned and climbed down his roof. Alex was still standing at his open window, staring out at her, and she told him to shut it and go back to bed. Before she could see if he'd really done it, she raced back to her house and to her own room.

Convincing Alex that he didn't love her anymore might not play out well with the sirens. Even though Thea had seen it and believed it was true, they might be pissed that they couldn't experiment with him. And if Penn was pissed, she might take it out on him or Gemma or Harper.

But she didn't know what else to do. They'd almost killed him tonight—*again*. And after seeing what Lexi had done to Sawyer, Gemma knew it was only a matter of time before the same fate befell Alex if he stayed involved with a siren. Especially considering what she'd done to Jason.

Penn might punish her or Alex over this, that was true. But if he didn't break up with her and get away from her, then he would definitely end up dead.

Besides, there were still plenty of puzzles for the sirens to obsess over. Harper had told Gemma that Daniel wouldn't fall under their spell. Penn thought there was something strange going on in Capri in general. They didn't need Alex in order to figure out what was happening.

Gemma had considered doing the same thing to Harper that she'd just done to Alex, convincing her that she didn't care about Gemma anymore, and then Gemma could leave with the sirens.

But it would be better if the sirens stayed here. Penn had agreed to behave. They would slow down their feedings, so their staying in Capri would help save lives.

Not only that, but it sounded like Thea would be looking into the curse more. Since a human had fallen in love with Gemma, the sirens obviously had been misled about the curse's terms. Maybe Thea could find a way to break the curse. Or, at the very least, free Gemma.

She had to stay here. She had to leave Harper, their dad, and Daniel in danger. For now.

But Gemma had been able to spare Alex. Even if that meant he'd never be able to love her again. She knew it was the right thing to do. She had to keep Alex safe—from the other sirens, and from herself.

The Watersong Series continues with

Tidal

Coming soon